ONE DEADLY PREMIERE

AN AGATHA ROYALE MYSTERY
BOOK 6

ELLA ANDREW

This is a work of fiction. Names, characters, places, and incidents either are the product of the author's imagination or are used fictitiously. Any resemblance to actual persons, living or dead, events, or locales is entirely coincidental.

www.ellaandrew.com

First paperback edition April 2026

Backspace Press

Houston, Texas

Cover design by BACKSPACE PRESS

ISBN 979-8-9945482-4-0 (paperback)

Printed in the United States of America

1

BACK ON CENTRAL AVENUE

Agatha Royale pulled her 1962 baby blue Ford Falcon to a gentle stop in front of One Deadly Chapter Books & Brew, the worn tires crunching against the snow-dusted cobblestones of Bristol Lake's Central Avenue. Her miniature schnauzer, Mike, who had been dozing in the passenger seat, perked up instantly, his bushy eyebrows twitching with recognition.

"We're home, boy," she whispered, reaching over to scratch behind his ears. The January cold nipped at her nose as she opened the door, but the sight of her bookshop, its windows glowing warmly against the gray winter sky, felt like wrapping herself in her favorite blanket.

Stepping out of the car, Agatha's hazel eyes scanned the familiar façade of her bookstore. She tucked a strand of tousled light brown hair behind her ear and pulled her wool coat tighter, the slight crow's feet around her eyes crinkling as she smiled. A couple of years ago, this place had been nothing more than a dusty, forgotten storefront, an inheritance from her late stepmother. Back then, Agatha had just lost everything. Her husband to a younger woman and her librarian job to budget cuts, all in the same week. With nowhere else to turn, she'd packed what she could into her Falcon, clipped Mike's leash into the passenger seat, and pointed the car north.

She reopened the bookstore as One Deadly Chapter Books & Brew, a mystery-themed shop where paperbacks filled cozy corners and the café area served fresh pastries alongside coffee and specialty teas. Mismatched chairs invited readers to stay awhile, and the comforting clink of cups created the perfect backdrop for getting lost in a good whodunit. Somewhere between shelving murder mysteries and hosting book club nights, Agatha had built a new life, quiet, steady, and exactly hers.

The sight of her bookshop, with its bay windows displaying mystery novels and a few lingering evergreen garlands from the holidays, filled her with a contentment that even her recent adventures couldn't match. Agatha had spent the past two weeks visiting her friend Shannon in Boston, extending her post-Christmas break after the whirlwind of the holiday season at the bookshop. Emma had been in Connecticut with family, and Lorraine had embarked on what she called a "spiritual and culinary pilgrimage" to New Orleans. Now they were all trickling back to Bristol Lake, ready to settle into the quiet rhythm of January.

Agatha breathed in deeply, savoring the mingled scents of wood smoke from nearby chimneys, Mrs. Henderson's pine wreaths still hanging on doors, and Eliza's cinnamon rolls wafting from the bakery across the street.

Bristol Lake had that effect on people. The small lakeside town with its cobblestone side streets and Victorian lamp-posts seemed plucked from another era, one where neighbors still borrowed cups of sugar and everyone knew whose sidewalks would be shoveled first after a snowstorm. Central Avenue curved gently around the town square, lined with maple trees standing bare against the winter sky, their branches occasionally weighted with fresh snow.

"Still standing," Emma said brightly, appearing beside her with two steaming paper cups from Eliza's bakery, her breath forming small clouds in the cold air. She handed one to Agatha and adjusted her library tote bag emblazoned with the words 'So Many Books, So Little Time.' Her green eyes sparkled behind tortoiseshell glasses as she surveyed their beloved Central Avenue. "Though I must admit, between the Christmas rush and now, I worried about Celeste handling the Thursday night book club alone. Mrs. Finch can be quite insistent about proper tea steeping times."

"Three minutes and forty-five seconds exactly," Agatha quoted with a perfect imitation of Mrs. Finch's pinched tone, "and not a moment more, unless one wishes to poison the entire gathering." She accepted the cup gratefully, breathing in the comforting scent of her usual order, Earl Grey with a splash of milk, no sugar. The warmth seeped into her cold fingers.

Emma laughed, the sound as familiar and welcome as the bell above the bookshop door. They'd been friends since Agatha's first week in town, when she'd just moved in next door and Mike had discovered a skeleton buried in her flower bed. Emma, hearing the commotion from her own yard, had hurried over and instead of shying away from the macabre discovery, she'd offered both her neighborly support and her librarian's research skills to help Agatha solve her very first Bristol Lake mystery.

Agatha gestured toward the far end of Central Avenue,

where the Acadia Theater stood with its newly restored marquee gleaming even in the pale winter light. "Speaking of changes..."

The Acadia had been the crown jewel of their downtown for decades until financial troubles shuttered it several years ago. Now, shrouded in whispers and speculation, the theater was coming back to life under new ownership. "I see they settled the color debate," Agatha noted, nodding toward the theater's freshly painted facade.

Emma followed her gaze. "Gold won, thankfully. Celeste filled me in on all the drama. At least three town-wide debates about whether the Acadia should be painted blue or restored to the original gold."

"Let me guess, Martha Peck led the blue faction?"

"Naturally. She claimed blue would better reflect contemporary aesthetics while respecting our town's moral fiber. Whatever that means."

Mike tugged at his leash, his paws leaving small prints in the light dusting of snow as he led Agatha toward Eliza's bakery across the street. The delicious aroma of fresh sourdough, apple tarts, and Eliza's famous lavender-lemon scones drifted through the cold air, even more inviting against the winter chill. The scones, buttery, flaky, and just sweet enough, had won the county fair's blue ribbon three years running.

Agnes and Pearl, sisters in their eighties who attended every book club meeting with matching teacups, waved from a bench outside the post office, bundled in their matching wool coats. Their knitting needles clicked in rhythm as they offered cheerful hellos.

"Look who's back from her travels," called Mr. Porter from his hardware store doorway, his breath visible in the cold air. His weathered hands, perpetually stained with paint or varnish, waved a friendly hello. "Gladys is waiting for you at the diner. Says she's got news that can't wait."

"I bet she does," Agatha replied with a knowing smile. Gladys, with her silver hair always perfectly arranged in a bun, was Bristol Lake's unofficial historian and expert gossip collector. If something happened within town limits, Gladys not only knew about it but had probably already formed three theories on the matter.

"Do we dare delay?" Emma asked, arching an eyebrow.

"Not if we value our standing in town. Last time I kept Gladys waiting, she spread a rumor that I was secretly writing a tell-all about the town's 'scandalous underbelly.' I had three people ask me if their affairs would be featured."

"Were they having affairs?"

"That's beside the point," Agatha laughed, then stopped as Mike suddenly tensed, his nose working overtime despite the cold. "What is it, boy?"

As if summoned by some cosmic cue, Lorraine Dubois appeared, having paused to admire a display in the window of Vintage Treasures. Her oversized hat and clunky jewelry announced her presence before her voice did, though today she'd added a dramatic faux-fur collar to her ensemble.

"Mes chéries! At last, we're all back together," she cried, arms outstretched dramatically. "After the holidays and everything, I thought we'd never have a proper catch-up. Though I must say, Eliza's gingerbread during Christmas week nearly made up for the separation." She looked wistful for a moment. "But nothing beats January for settling back into routines with good coffee that actually stays hot in this weather."

"You seemed to enjoy that peppermint mocha phase well enough," Emma teased.

Lorraine waved that away, her bracelets creating a musical accompaniment to her dismissal. "The point is, we are all back to normal. And the Acadia is nearly ready. The scaffolding's down, and rumor says the Monroe sisters are planning something extravagant." She lowered her voice to a stage whisper that could probably be heard three shops away. "Vivian personally selected the velvet for the new seats. Imported. From Italy."

"How do you know that?" Agatha asked, her investigative instincts perking up.

"Because," Lorraine said with a triumphant smile, "I happened to be having my nails done next to the delivery man's wife yesterday. He unloaded the fabric himself. Said it was the finest he'd ever seen." She leaned in closer, her French perfume cutting through the cold air. "And he said that Vivian inspected every inch of it personally, wearing white gloves like she was handling the Queen's jewels."

Mike circled at Agatha's feet, then sat attentively as a group of schoolchildren passed by, their backpacks bouncing as they trudged through the snow toward the corner shop that served hot chocolate after school.

Agatha gave a small smile. "They're not really sisters, you know."

"No, but everyone's pretending they are," Lorraine whispered, leaning in as if revealing state secrets. "Vivian Monroe gives me witness protection vibes, and Bianca looks like she's hiding a secret soufflé recipe. Something is off, I tell you."

"They're not exactly mingling, are they?" Emma added, tucking a strand of her red hair behind her ear. "Celeste said Vivian came in for a coffee right before Christmas, said nothing beyond 'espresso, no syrup.' No smile. No tip. Didn't even look at the local author display she set up, which took her hours."

Lorraine gasped, pressing a hand to her heart. "No tip? Scandal."

"Apparently they avoid questions about their Hollywood days," Emma continued. "Celeste mentioned that Vivian was in that thriller, 'Midnight Alibi'? But when she mentioned it, Vivian just stared at her like she'd committed some terrible faux pas."

"I heard she walked out mid-interview with the Bristol Gazette when they asked about her co-star from that film," Lorraine added. "Just stood up and left poor Tabitha Elms sitting there with her tape recorder running."

"To be fair," Agatha pointed out, "Tabitha's interviewing style is somewhere between a Spanish Inquisition and a police interrogation."

Agatha laughed, the sound visible in the cold air. "This is what I missed. Scandal over coffee orders and Hollywood gossip." The warmth of friendship and familiar streets wrapped around her like a favorite sweater. After all the adventures of recent months, the mundane drama of Bristol Lake felt like coming home to a crackling fireplace.

2

VIVIAN MONROE

The winter morning light caught the windows of the shops lining Central Avenue, turning them into mirrors that reflected the snow-dusted awnings and the warm glow from within each storefront. Evergreen wreaths still hung from many doorways, a Bristol Lake tradition where residents kept their holiday decorations up through January to brighten the gray winter days. Agatha's own shop had a handsome wreath with pinecones and red berries that Mrs. Henderson had crafted, now sporting a light dusting of frost.

Outside the diner, Sheriff Salinger tipped his hat to Agatha, his gray-specked mustache twitching in what might have been a smile, his breath forming small clouds in the cold air. "Noticed you all were back," he said gruffly. "Town's been quiet. Almost too quiet."

"Don't jinx it, Sheriff," Agatha replied, but there was an understanding between them. They'd worked together, reluctantly on his part, on previous cases, and something in his tone suggested he'd missed her methodical approach to trouble.

The sheriff lifted his chin toward the Acadia. "New folks keeping to themselves mostly. Can't figure if that's good or bad yet."

"Hollywood types," Lorraine stage-whispered. "They're always either hiding something dreadful or planning something spectacular."

"Or both," the sheriff said dryly, adjusting his belt. "Just so long as neither involves my office working overtime."

Before Agatha could respond, Celeste Parker burst out of the bookshop's door, her brown braid swinging and her tortoiseshell glasses crooked. At twenty one, she was the bookstore's assistant and though not officially part of Agatha's investigations, her enthusiasm and technological know-how had proven invaluable on more than one occasion.

"I'm so happy you're back!" she exclaimed, practically bouncing with excitement. "The shop's been fine... Well, mostly fine. We had a plumbing issue on Tuesday, but Mr. Porter fixed it. And business is booming! I set up a new display of classic whodunits and three people asked if we could order more Agatha Christie first editions. And..." she paused to catch her breath, "I think that's Vivian Monroe's car pulling up down the street."

"Coincidence?" Emma raised an eyebrow.

"In Bristol Lake? Never." Lorraine's eyes sparkled with anticipation.

Mike barked once, low and deliberate. His eyes were fixed on the far end of the street where a sleek black car had just parked in front of the Acadia Theater.

The passenger door opened, and out stepped Vivian

Monroe, shoulder-length dark hair, a pearl earring glinting in the pale sunlight, and not a single smile in sight. She wore a tailored pantsuit that looked like it came straight from a fashion runway, the material shifting like liquid silver in the morning light. No winter coat, as if she were impervious to the January cold.

Even from a distance, Agatha could sense the command in Vivian's posture, the kind of confidence that came from years in the spotlight, or perhaps from harboring secrets too dangerous to share.

"Well," Lorraine said, dropping her voice theatrically, "brace yourselves, ladies. Curtain's going up."

As if feeling their gaze, Vivian turned sharply in their direction. For a moment, her icy blue eyes locked with Agatha's hazel ones across the expanse of Central Avenue. Something passed between them, a recognition, perhaps, or a challenge. Then Vivian's lips curved into what might have been a smile but looked more like a warning. She reached into her purse, retrieved an envelope, and began walking directly toward One Deadly Chapter Books & Brew.

"Is she coming here?" Celeste whispered, fingers nervously adjusting her glasses.

"She most certainly is," Agatha replied, feeling a familiar tingle at the base of her neck. The one that always seemed to show up right before trouble found her. "And something tells me she's not looking for the latest bestseller."

Mike growled softly at Agatha's side, his ears pricked forward in alert. In Bristol Lake, even the dogs could sense when trouble was brewing.

The entire group pressed closer to the shop's display window, transfixed, as Vivian Monroe crossed the street with the deliberate grace of a jaguar. Through the glass, they watched her heels click against the snow-dusted cobblestones in perfect rhythm, her gaze never wavering from the bookshop's door. A delivery truck rumbled past, momentarily blocking their view, and when it cleared, Vivian was already at the shop's entrance.

The women hurried away from the window, taking their positions like actors preparing for an unexpected performance. Agatha moved behind the counter, Emma pretended to arrange a display of new releases, and Lorraine settled into a reading chair with a book she held upside down.

Vivian stepped inside like a woman walking onto a stage she owned. Up close, she was even more striking, flawless skin, sharp cheekbones, and eyes that seemed to catalog everything at once. The subtle scent of her perfume, something expensive and vaguely citrusy, filled the small entry. A blast of cold air followed her inside before the door closed.

The few morning customers browsing the shelves glanced up, then quickly back down, as if afraid to be caught staring. Mr. Wilson, who came every Thursday to peruse the true crime section, nearly dropped the forensic investigation handbook he'd been examining.

"Ms. Royale," Vivian said smoothly, offering a slim cream-colored envelope. "For you."

Agatha took it, the heavy cardstock warm from Vivian's hand. Up close, she could see the fine lines around Vivian's eyes that makeup couldn't quite conceal. Evidence of either age or worry, perhaps both.

"What is it?" Agatha asked, her voice steady despite the sudden tension in the room.

"An invitation," Vivian replied. "To a private reception for local business owners at the Acadia. We believe in supporting community partners."

"Why me specifically?" Agatha asked, her fingers tracing the gold embossed lettering on the envelope.

Vivian's gaze swept the shelves of One Deadly Chapter with the faintest flicker of something, amusement? Contempt? Nostalgia? "We're especially interested in connecting with... Literary voices."

She held Agatha's gaze for one deliberate moment, as if measuring her worth.

Without waiting for a response, Vivian turned and left as swiftly as she had arrived, the door swinging shut behind her.

Through the window, Agatha watched her slide back into the black car, which pulled away from the curb with hardly a sound. She stared at the envelope in her hand.

Mike let out another low growl, his eyes still fixed on the door as if expecting Vivian to return.

"Well," she muttered, turning the heavy envelope over in her hands. "That's going to be interesting."

"Aren't you going to open it?" Celeste asked, practically vibrating with curiosity.

Agatha broke the seal and pulled out a card of thick cream-colored stock. The text was embossed in gold leaf:

The Monroe Sisters request the pleasure of your company at a private reception celebrating the revival of The Acadia Theater. Friday evening, seven o'clock. Cocktail attire. RSVP appreciated.

"Friday," Emma noted. "That's only two days away."

"Short notice," Agatha agreed.

"But we're going, yes?" Lorraine's eyes gleamed with excitement. "I'll finally have a reason to wear my new Parisian scarf. It's peacock blue with actual golden threads. Cost a fortune, but as my mother always said, 'Lorraine, darling, you can't put a price on making an entrance.'"

Agatha smiled despite herself. "I suppose we have to go. Professional courtesy and all that."

But as she tucked the invitation into her pocket, the weight of it felt heavier than mere cardstock. Vivian Monroe's calculating eyes and practiced smile were not the look of a woman with nothing to hide.

In her experience, people who worked that hard to appear perfect were usually hiding something far from it.

Mike seemed to agree. He sat at Agatha's feet, his body alert, eyes still trained on the door.

Bristol Lake had been quiet lately, almost too quiet, as the Sheriff had said.

But Agatha had a feeling that was about to change.

3

BIANCA MONROE ARRIVES

Rosa Fielding pushed through the door, letting in a gust of cold air. She was a slight woman in her mid-sixties with silver hair pinned beneath a knitted cloche hat and hazel eyes that missed nothing. Dressed in a perfectly pressed blouse and skirt that might have been fashionable two decades ago, she carried herself with the air of someone who had once wielded authority and hadn't quite accepted its passing.

"So this is what you've done with the old Royale place," she announced, surveying the bookshop with a critical eye. Her gaze lingered on the cozy reading nook, the coffee station, the carefully arranged displays. "Hmm."

Agatha recognized that particular "hmm." It was the sound of judgment being withheld only because its expression would be impolite. "Good morning, Mrs. Fielding. Can I help you find something?"

"Rosa, please. Mrs. Fielding makes me sound like I'm as old as I am." She chuckled at her own joke, though her eyes remained sharp. "I hear the Monroe sisters have been in town. Quite the splash they're making with the Acadia renovation."

"They seem committed to restoring it properly," Agatha offered, watching as Rosa picked up a new mystery release, checked its price, and set it down with a small tsk.

"Properly?" Rosa's eyebrows shot up. "What would Hollywood types know about 'properly'? I was an usher there for fifteen years. Head usher for ten of those. If anyone knows what that theater should look like, it's me." She patted the large leather handbag hanging from her arm. "I have the records to prove it."

Emma appeared from between the shelves, carrying a stack of Agatha Christie novels. "Records?"

Rosa turned, assessing Emma with a quick up-and-down glance. "Photographs. Newspaper clippings. Programs. I document everything. Old habit. You'd be surprised what becomes important years later." She paused, her eyes drifting briefly toward the window. "Or who."

Agatha's interest piqued. "Have you met the Monroe sisters yet?"

"Vivian, yes. Very... Polished." Rosa's tone suggested this wasn't entirely a compliment. "The younger one, Bianca, I only glimpsed from a distance, but..." She frowned, her forehead creasing with the effort of recollection. "Something about her seemed familiar. Can't quite place it."

"Maybe you saw her in a movie?" Emma suggested.

Rosa waved the idea away. "No, no. It wasn't that. More like..." She trailed off, then shook her head decisively. "Well, it'll come to me. My memory isn't what it used to be, but it's still sharper than most people half my age."

She moved to a display of true crime books, her nose wrinkling. "I see you favor these... Cozier mysteries. Not much blood and guts." She picked up a Jessica Fletcher novel and examined its back cover. "In real life, murder isn't so tidy. Learned that during my courthouse days."

"We stock a variety of mystery subgenres," Agatha replied diplomatically. "Everyone has different tastes."

"Indeed they do," Rosa said, the slight arch of her eyebrow making it clear which taste she considered superior. "Though I must say, real mysteries, the ones that happen right under our noses. Are rarely solved by amateur sleuths and their pets." She glanced pointedly at Mike, who was dozing in his basket near the counter.

"I should dig through my archives," Rosa mused, more to herself than to them. "If I'm right about the younger Monroe... Well." She straightened her shoulders. "Information has value, especially in this town. Always has."

The calculating look that flickered across her face made Agatha reassess the older woman. Rosa Fielding wasn't just a nostalgic former usher with a sharp memory for faces and details. She was a collector of secrets, and she knew exactly how valuable those secrets could be.

Rosa left, leaving her perfume lingering faintly in the air. Agatha exhaled, the shop suddenly feeling too quiet after the weight of their conversation.

That quiet didn't last long. The door swung open again, this time with a dramatic sweep.

Lorraine flung her cashmere cardigan over one shoulder like a cape, the emerald fabric catching the afternoon light. "Well, I never," she declared, hand fluttering to her throat. "Not even a whiff of an invitation? The cultural cornerstone of Bristol Lake?"

Agatha blinked, startled by the outburst. "Invitation?"

Lorraine pointed to the counter, where the heavy cream-colored envelope still sat. "That invitation, from the Monroes! You've already received one, and yet I, Lorraine Dubois, pillar of taste and culture, have been cruelly overlooked."

Agatha bit back a smile. "It was probably an oversight."

"An oversight?" Lorraine gasped, pressing a bejeweled hand to her chest. "I've lived here for twelve years! I hosted a foreign film night in my living room. I once got a standing ovation for my interpretive reading of Rebecca!"

Emma, who'd just arrived, settled into one of the leather armchairs by the window, her library tote still slung over her shoulder. "Maybe she's inviting people in stages. Building anticipation."

"Like a theatrical release," Celeste added, offering a sheepish smile as she restocked the new releases display.

The morning rush had died down, leaving the bookshop quiet except for the occasional turning of pages from Mrs. Hudson, who had been reading Sherlock Holmes in the corner for the past two hours. Mike had strategically positioned himself in a warm patch of sunlight on the hardwood floor.

Lorraine raised a hand, silencing them both. "No, no. The message is clear. Vivian Monroe doesn't think I'm red carpet material." She sniffed dramatically. "After my portrayal of Lady Macbeth last year, one would think I'd merit at least a courtesy invitation. The Bristol Lake Gazette called my performance 'unforgettable.'"

"I believe the exact quote was 'an unforgettable interpretation that will haunt audiences for months to come,'" Emma murmured to Agatha with a barely suppressed smile.

"Well, she did hand-deliver this one," Agatha said. "Maybe she's doing them all personally."

"Perhaps she's bringing yours to your house," Celeste suggested brightly. "Saving the best for last."

Lorraine seemed to consider this possibility. "Well, that would be appropriate. Though showing up unannounced sounds like something a villain in a Hitchcock film would do."

Before Agatha could respond, the front door opened with a cheerful jingle. Gladys stepped inside, cheeks flushed from the cold winter air, her silver hair perfectly arranged despite the January wind.

"Did you hear?" she called, not even waiting for a greeting. "Martha Peck's already started a petition against the theater."

Agatha raised a brow, guiding Gladys toward the book club corner. "That was fast, even for Martha."

"She claims the Monroes are corrupting the moral fabric of Bristol Lake." Gladys settled into one of the reading chairs and accepted the cup of tea Agatha offered. "Already has seventeen signatures, including poor Stanley's."

"What moral fabric is she worried about, exactly?" Emma asked.

"It's not the theater," Gladys said with a knowing smile. "It's Vivian herself. Martha's still sore about the time Stanley drooled over Vivian Monroe's swimsuit spread in Life magazine back in '95. Kept it folded up in his tackle box for years."

Celeste's eyes sparkled. "Vivian was in Life?"

"Twice," Gladys said with a knowing nod, setting her teacup down with a satisfied clink. "Once for a beach fashion feature and once for a rising star spread. And if you believe the whispers at the salon, once on the cover of Photoplay, though no one's ever found the issue." She leaned forward conspiratorially, lowering her voice even though the shop was nearly empty except for their small group. "But that's not even the juiciest bit. You'll never guess what I found out this morning over blueberry pancakes at the diner."

"What?" Emma and Celeste asked in unison.

Even Lorraine perked up visibly.

Gladys paused, taking a sip of tea, clearly savoring her moment. "Seems our mysterious Vivian Monroe didn't choose Bristol Lake at random. Apparently, she heard about our little town from none other than your aunt Edna, Agatha."

Agatha nearly spilled her tea. "My Aunt Edna? I had no idea she knew Vivian."

"Edna and Beatrice Belafonte," Gladys confirmed. "Apparently, they're quite the social butterflies in certain Hollywood circles? Your aunt had connections you never mentioned to us, Agatha."

Agatha blinked, genuinely taken aback. The Edna she knew knitted tea cozies shaped like vegetables and sent birthday cards with pressed flowers inside. "She rubbed elbows with Vivian Monroe? She's told me stories from her Hollywood days, but never once mentioned Vivian."

Mike suddenly lifted his head, ears perked as if he, too, found this revelation suspicious.

Gladys's eyes twinkled. "According to Marjorie at the diner, someone spotted a comment from Edna on the Green Acres Assisted Living Facebook group, then it vanished five minutes later. Apparently, she's quite keen on keeping that connection quiet. Something about 'the less said about those days, the better.'"

She leaned in, lowering her voice conspiratorially. "Marjorie says she tried to screenshot it, but her phone froze right as her hash browns arrived. Divine intervention, if you ask me."

"And this Hollywood connection somehow led Vivian to our doorstep?" Agatha asked, her brow furrowed.

"Seems that way," Gladys confirmed. "Marjorie said she saw another post pop up on the Green Acres Facebook group, apparently from Beatrice this time. She was going on about this 'charming little town with the lovely old theater.' Said it was the perfect place to 'bury the past and start fresh.'" She raised her eyebrows meaningfully. "Interesting choice of words, don't you think?"

Agatha tilted her head, a faint smile playing at her lips. "In Bristol Lake, the past never stays buried for long." She gave a soft laugh and shook her head. "If Aunt Edna ever ran in the same circles as someone like Vivian Monroe, she sure never said a word about it."

"You never know," Emma said thoughtfully. "People have layers. I once discovered my grandmother had been a roller derby champion in the 1950s."

Lorraine sank into the armchair opposite Gladys, momentarily forgetting her invitation grievance. "I knew it! I told you all there was something mysterious about those women." She leaned forward dramatically. "What if they're running from something?"

"Running in those heels?" Gladys quipped. "Unlikely."

"People do not just abandon Hollywood for sleepy little towns like Bristol Lake without a very important reason," Lorraine insisted. "No offense."

"Some taken," Emma muttered.

Mike gave a single bark as if in agreement. He trotted toward the door, his nose working furiously, eyes fixed on something outside the window.

Agatha stood, feeling the energy in the shop shift. "Something about Vivian's visit didn't sit right. It was too deliberate. Like she was making sure I saw her."

"And you think she's hiding something?" Gladys asked.

"I don't know yet," Agatha said, watching Mike settle by the window, his ears still alert. "But I plan to find out. First, I should talk to Aunt Edna." She paused, tapping her fingers lightly against the counter. "Though that's not happening anytime soon. She and Beatrice are still on that Mediterranean cruise they've been planning forever. Won't be back for another two weeks."

"Convenient timing," Lorraine muttered. "Very convenient indeed."

Outside, Central Avenue buzzed with talk. Eliza had stepped out to sweep her storefront, but was spending more time listening to the knot of townsfolk clustered near the post office than actually sweeping. Their voices carried through the open door:

"Vivian is here for a reason..."

"...never trusted Hollywood types..."

"...seems odd they'd come all the way to Bristol Lake, doesn't it?"

The rumor mill had started spinning, and in Bristol Lake, once it gained momentum, it was nearly impossible to stop.

Agatha tapped her fingers against the envelope. "Maybe we're getting ahead of ourselves here. Maybe Aunt Edna just mentioned the theater to Vivian, told her what a charming place Bristol Lake is. It's not that strange for someone like her to want a quiet place away from the paparazzi."

"In Bristol Lake?" Lorraine asked skeptically. "Where the coffee comes in exactly two varieties, regular and decaf, and the closest thing to paparazzi is Tabitha Elms with her ancient Polaroid camera? "No, ma chérie. People like Vivian Monroe go to private islands when they want peace. They come to places like Bristol Lake when they're hiding something."

"Or maybe we've read one too many of our own mystery titles," Agatha said.

Mike let out a soft sneeze, which Agatha took as agreement. She smiled, but her fingers still lingered on the edge of the envelope. "That said... I'll keep my eyes open. Just in case."

As if sensing her thoughts, Mike let out another low growl by the window. His tail stiffened, and his hackles rose.

Outside, the sleek black car that had brought Vivian was now parked directly in front of Eliza's Bakery. Stepping out of the passenger side was another woman, this one softer, with a gentler demeanor, but with eyes that scanned Central Avenue like someone memorizing escape routes.

She wore a wrap dress in muted sage green, her brown hair twisted into a simple chignon. Where Vivian had been all angles and sharpness, this woman moved with careful grace, like someone trying not to disturb the air around her.

"That's her," Gladys whispered. "Bianca Monroe."

"The sister who isn't really a sister," Emma added.

Bianca said something to the driver and then made her way toward the bakery door. She moved with precision, her steps measured, her gaze sweeping the street in what might have appeared to be casual interest but struck Agatha as something more calculated.

"Look at how she walks," Lorraine murmured. "Like a ballet dancer, always aware of exactly where her body is in space."

"Or like someone who doesn't want to be noticed," Agatha added.

They watched as Eliza greeted Bianca warmly at the bakery door. Bianca smiled, a perfectly pleasant expression that somehow didn't quite reach her eyes and followed Eliza inside.

"Interesting," Agatha said, more to herself than to the others.

Gladys gathered her purse, preparing to leave. "Well, I'd better get going. Bridge club at noon." She paused at the door, fixing Agatha with a knowing look. "You'll be at the theater opening, I assume?"

"Of course," Agatha stated. "Professional courtesy."

"Well, do keep your eyes open, dear. And your ears. People say the most interesting things when they think no one's listening."

With that pearl of wisdom, she swept out, the bell jingling merrily in her wake.

"You know," Celeste said after a moment, "maybe we should do some research on Vivian and Bianca. Just basic background stuff."

"For welcoming purposes only, of course," Emma added with a small smile.

"Of course," Agatha agreed. "Purely in the interest of being good neighbors."

Lorraine snorted. "Please. We're all thinking the same thing. Those women are hiding something, and it's bound to be delicious." She stood, smoothing her cardigan. "I'm going to see if I can wrangle an invitation out of Vivian myself. Direct approach."

"Good luck with that," Emma said.

"I don't need luck, ma chérie. I have charm." Lorraine

blew them a kiss and sashayed toward the door. “And if that fails, I have the ability to show up anyway and pretend the invitation was lost in the mail.”

THE WOMAN who came in just after ten was a stranger, which wasn't unusual for January. Bristol Lake picked up the occasional tourist even in the dead of winter, drawn by the lake views or the promise of a quiet weekend away from the city.

She was somewhere in her mid-fifties, well-dressed in a charcoal wool coat, her dark hair cut close around her jaw. She moved through the mystery section with the focused deliberateness of someone who actually read the books rather than displayed them.

"Can I help you find something?" Agatha asked.

"Just browsing." The woman smiled, pulling a title from the shelf and turning it over. "Actually — do you have anything set in California? Old Hollywood, that sort of thing?"

Agatha pointed her toward the back wall. They exchanged a few words about the selection, easy and unhurried.

"I'm Agatha, by the way. I don't think I've seen you in Bristol Lake before."

The woman glanced up. Something flickered across her face — there and gone in an instant. "Beth—" She stopped. "Brittany. Brittany Adams. Just passing through."

"Well, welcome to Bristol Lake, Brittany." Agatha smiled and left her to it.

But as she moved back toward the counter, the small hesitation stayed with her, light as a thread caught on a coat button. Probably nothing. People misspoke their own names all the time.

Didn't they?

After she left, a comfortable silence settled over the bookshop. Celeste returned to her display, Emma pulled out a novel from her tote bag, and Agatha absently stroked Mike's head, lost in thought.

From the outside, Bristol Lake appeared unchanged. Same storefronts, same cobblestones, same lazy curl of smoke from the diner's chimney. The town had weathered countless seasons and stories, absorbing each new arrival into its tapestry of local lore.

As Agatha watched a young couple pause to admire the newly painted Acadia marquee across the street, their breath forming small clouds in the cold air, she wondered what stories the old theater could tell if its walls could speak. Every building in Bristol Lake had its secrets. Some charming, some bittersweet, and the Acadia was no exception.

Whatever brought the Monroes to their quiet corner of the world, one thing was certain: Bristol Lake would be talking about it for quite some time.

4

ENTER HENRY MADDOX

The morning sun climbed high over Bristol Lake as the Monroe sisters stepped onto the sidewalk together, a picture of contrast and curiosity.

Vivian led the way. Poised, polished, and unbothered by the growing cluster of onlookers. Beside her, Bianca moved with a hesitation that didn't match her expensive cashmere coat or perfectly knotted silk scarf. Everything about her outfit screamed wealth and careful curation, but her body language told a different story. Shoulders hunched, eyes darting, fingers nervously adjusting her cream-colored gloves.

Vivian's gaze swept Central Avenue like someone expecting trouble.

"They're not what I expected," Celeste murmured, leaning against the bookshop's front window. "Kind of reminds me of teachers on opposite ends of the report card. Vivian's the one who assigns the extra homework, and Bianca's the one who sneaks you an extra cookie."

"Mm-hmm," Agatha murmured, absently wiping a coffee ring from the counter.

"Eliza's headed out to greet them," Gladys reported from her post near the window, her silver bun bobbing as she craned her neck for a better view. "Look at her, toting a tray of scones like a diplomatic offering."

"She's smart," Lorraine said, pulling her purple cardigan tighter. "If you can't beat the drama, feed it baked goods."

Mike trotted to the window, ears perked forward as he watched the scene unfold outside.

Eliza offered a smile and a sample from her tray. Vivian declined with a tight shake of her head and a frosty smile. Bianca, however, accepted with both hands and a polite thank-you that seemed genuine. From where Agatha stood, it looked like Bianca said something. Agatha noticed the way she tilted her head toward the theater as she spoke, then toward the bakery sign, taking in every detail.

"She's the nice one," Celeste said softly. "Or at least she wants us to think she is."

"Nice doesn't always mean harmless," Agatha replied, remembering how the sweetest smiles sometimes hid the sharpest secrets.

Before Emma could elaborate, the bookstore bell jingled with enough force to make everyone jump. The door swung open, admitting a man who seemed to fill more space than his physical body should allow.

He wore a blazer two sizes too tight, had styled dark hair with just enough gel to look deliberate, and carried a wireless microphone like a badge of honor. His cologne arrived a full second before he did, sharp and assertive.

"Well, he looks like he walked straight out of a second-rate true crime show," Lorraine whispered, eyeing his microphone with distaste. "Self-important type, I'd bet my Parisian scarf collection on it."

"Let's not judge before we meet him," Agatha murmured, though she couldn't help but share Lorraine's instinctive wariness. "Though I could do without another drama in town right now." She nudged Lorraine gently as the man approached. "Shh, he's coming over."

Henry Maddox grinned like he'd just stepped onto a soundstage. His teeth were unnaturally white, his tan too perfect for January

in New England. His gaze swept over the women until it landed on Agatha.

"Afternoon, ladies," he said, drawing out the words like a game show host. "Which of you is the famous Agatha Royale?"

Agatha raised a brow, crossing her arms. "That would be me. And you are?"

"Henry Maddox. Maddox Unfiltered Podcast," he said, tossing a glossy business card onto the counter. "True crime, Hollywood scandal, the occasional alien sighting. Three million downloads last quarter." He winked. "I've got ears everywhere."

"I bet," Agatha said dryly, not picking up the card. "What brings you to Bristol Lake? We're usually short on aliens."

Mike let out a growl from beside her, not a warning exactly, but more of a disgruntled protest.

Henry seemed unfazed. He turned the mic on and gave it a dramatic tap, the sound echoing through the shop. Several customers winced.

"And this little town is buzzing." His voice dropped to what was clearly his 'broadcast voice,' deeper, with artificial intensity. "Theater reopens after decades, mysterious women from California show up, and a former A-lister who vanished from the spotlight without so much as a press release? Color me intrigued."

"Color me nauseated," Lorraine whispered.

Henry continued, strolling through the shop, trailing his fingers along book spines. "Thought I'd swing by and get the locals' take before everything gets sanitized for opening night." He paused at the true crime display. "Though I hear you've got some experience with the unsanitized version of events, Ms. Royale."

Agatha felt a chill. Her involvement in previous investigations wasn't exactly a secret, but something about Henry's tone was predatory.

"We prefer our scandals with a side of cinnamon roll," Agatha replied coolly. "Can I interest you in today's special? It pairs nicely with minding one's own business."

Several customers snickered. Gladys raised her teacup in a small salute.

Henry chuckled, but annoyance flashed across his face. "Oh, you're good. No wonder they say you're the town's own Jessica Fletcher."

"Who says that?" Agatha asked.

"I do. Now." He tapped something into his phone. "Though honestly, I'm more interested in Vivian Monroe's story. You know she was on track to be the next big thing? Then poof... vanished after that screenwriter's suspicious death." He looked up, suddenly serious. "People like that don't just open theaters in sleepy towns for the aesthetic."

The shop went quiet.

Agatha straightened. "Wait, what death?"

Henry glanced around, clearly savoring the attention. "A screenwriter she was close to... Vincent Cleary. Back in the early 2000s. Found dead in his Hollywood Hills apartment. Overdose, officially, but there were rumors. Loose ends."

He moved closer to the counter, voice dropping confidentially. "And the interesting part? After the inquest, Vivian wasn't the only one who disappeared. Cleary's assistant vanished too. Young woman named Bethany Marks. Poof. Gone."

"And Vivian was involved?" Agatha asked, keeping her voice neutral.

Henry shrugged. "No one ever proved anything. But she disappeared not long after. Some say it was a breakdown. Others think she was pressured into silence."

"You think she's running from something?" Lorraine asked, unable to contain herself.

"Or toward something," Agatha murmured. A theater in a small town would be the perfect cover for someone looking to reinvent themselves.

Henry smiled. "Now you're asking the right questions."

Celeste suddenly touched Agatha's arm. "They're leaving," she whispered.

Outside, Bianca and Vivian were walking briskly toward the Acadia Theater, Vivian's hand on Bianca's elbow, guiding her with what looked like urgency rather than affection.

"They're not exactly hiding," Emma pointed out. "Opening a theater seems like a very public way to keep secrets."

Henry turned to her. "The best place to hide is in plain sight, Red."

She crossed her arms, unamused by the nickname. "My name is Emma."

"Of course it is," he replied dismissively. He swiveled back to Agatha. "Tell me, what do you really think brought them here? Because my sources say Vivian's running from something. And her so-called sister? The family resemblance is questionable at best."

"Your sources?" Agatha repeated. "You've been here less than twenty-four hours."

"I do my homework. Though the local paper here is a goldmine of gossip poorly disguised as news."

Agatha's gaze drifted to the window overlooking Central Avenue. "Speculation makes for poor coffee conversation."

"But excellent podcast material," Henry countered, finally turning off the mic. "I'll see you at the gala. Try not to do anything too interesting before then. Save the drama for my microphone."

With that, he pushed through the door, heading directly toward the Acadia with confident strides.

Once he left, Lorraine threw her hands in the air. "He's going to be insufferable. I can feel it in my follicles."

"Did you catch what he said about the screenwriter's death?" Emma asked. "I wonder if that has something to do with why they're presenting themselves as sisters when they clearly aren't."

"And the missing assistant," Celeste added. "Bethany Marks. Do you think she's still missing?"

Gladys, who had been suspiciously quiet, finally spoke up. "I might be able to find out more. My niece works at the library in Concord. They have digital archives going back decades."

"You know what troubles me?" Gladys said suddenly. "That man knew about you, Agatha. About your involvement in those previous cases. That suggests he's been researching you specifically."

A chill settled in Agatha's chest. Henry hadn't just stumbled into town chasing a story about Vivian Monroe. He'd come prepared with information about her, too.

"He's building a narrative," Emma said. "And he's already decided who the characters are."

"Well," Lorraine said, squaring her shoulders, "I refuse to be cast as the comic relief. If he wants a story, I say we give him one, just not the one he's expecting."

Agatha smiled despite herself. "What did you have in mind?"

Lorraine's eyes gleamed with mischief. "Information control, ma chérie. We find out what he knows before he realizes we're looking."

"That's actually not a bad idea," Emma admitted. "Keep him talking about himself instead of asking questions."

"Exactly," Lorraine said. "Men like Henry Maddox love nothing more than the sound of their own voice. All we have to do is listen."

THE NEXT MORNING, Agatha found herself at Eliza Martin's bakery, hoping a strong cup of coffee might clear the fog of questions circling her head. She'd slept poorly, dreams filled with shadowy figures and half-heard conversations. Even Mike had been restless.

The warm scent of vanilla and cinnamon washed over her as she stepped inside. Mike trotted beside her, sniffing for crumbs, his tail wagging.

"Look who's back!" Eliza called from behind the counter, cheeks flushed from the oven's heat. "I saved you one of the strawberry scones. Had to hide it from Sheriff Salinger."

"Bless you," Agatha said. "You're an angel in an apron."

"An angel who heard you had an interesting visitor yesterday," Eliza replied, lowering her voice. "Tall, thinks he's God's gift to broadcasting?"

"News travels fast," Agatha said.

"Martha Peck was in first thing this morning. Said he cornered her outside the post office and asked if she knew anything 'suspicious' about the Monroe women."

Emma was already seated at a corner table with a notebook open. She looked up and smiled. "You're just in time. Eliza and I were wondering how long it'll take Vivian Monroe to redecorate the entire town."

"You, too?" Agatha asked, sliding into the opposite chair.

Emma grinned. "Gladys came in twice this morning to mention that Bianca was spotted doing tai chi in six-inch heels outside the Acadia."

Eliza joined them briefly. "And she ordered three lemon tarts without blinking. Who does that?"

"Someone trying too hard to blend in," Emma offered.

"Or maybe someone who just likes lemon," Agatha pointed out, though privately she wondered.

Lorraine swept through the door, a dramatic scarf fluttering behind her. "I may have been doing a little reconnaissance at the theater," she announced, clearly pleased with herself. "And I caught Vivian wearing gloves in the heated lobby. Refused to take them off even when adjusting the thermostat. What kind of woman wears gloves in a seventy-degree room?"

"Isn't it a little early to be spinning spy theories?" Agatha asked. "She came from California. A Maine winter probably feels Arctic to her."

"It's never too early for espionage. Besides, you should've

seen the way she looked at Martha Peck. Like she knew exactly where the bodies were buried."

"Maybe keep the volume down on the murder speculation?" Agatha suggested.

"I also saw our mysterious Vivian at the drugstore this morning," Lorraine continued. Buying hair dye. Dark brown. And she spent ten minutes staring at burner phones before deciding not to buy one."

"So what is she now? Actress, heiress, or undercover agent?" Emma asked.

"Nobody that polished is that normal," Lorraine said. "Did you see how she studied the bookstore window? As if she was calculating how many copies of her life story she could shelve there."

Agatha smiled into her teacup. "Or maybe she and Bianca just wanted a quieter life. A small-town reset."

But even as they laughed, Agatha found herself glancing toward the Acadia's marquee. Workers adjusted the gold-trimmed lettering. GRAND REOPENING, it proclaimed. FRIDAY, 7PM. INVITATION ONLY.

Just below: A NEW ERA BEGINS.

Something about Vivian and Bianca's sudden appearance in Bristol Lake didn't quite sit right. Their mysterious connection to her Aunt Edna combined with what Henry had revealed yesterday about the screenwriter's death made the whole situation feel increasingly suspicious. "Penny for your thoughts?" Emma asked.

"Just wondering who Bethany Marks was," Agatha replied. "And why she disappeared."

Emma was already reaching for her notebook. "I can do some research at the library. Old newspaper archives might have something."

"And I'll keep my ears open at the salon," Lorraine offered. "Thursday is senior discount day. They know everything."

"Thanks. It's probably nothing, but..."

"But your instincts are rarely wrong," Emma finished. "And if they are this time, we'll have wasted a few hours of research. No harm done."

As they finished their pastries, Agatha couldn't shake the feeling that they were standing on the edge of something much bigger than they realized.

Outside, Henry Maddox strolled past the window, microphone in hand, heading purposefully toward the Acadia Theater.

The clock was ticking.

5

OPENING NIGHT

The Acadia Theater had never looked so polished. Gone were the cracked tiles and dusty windows that had marred its façade for several years. In their place: gold-trimmed posters of vintage films nestled in ornate frames, warm amber lights that cast a nostalgic glow across the restored marble floor, and a velvet rope that made the entrance feel like something out of a 1940s premiere. The marquee gleamed against the darkening sky, its gold letters spelling out: "GRAND REOPENING. JANUARY 27TH" with the kind of elegance Bristol Lake hadn't seen in decades.

Agatha stepped out of her car and tugged her coat tighter, the cold nipping at her cheeks. A thin crust of snow edged the sidewalk, and the air smelled faintly of salt and woodsmoke. She smoothed down her navy A-line dress. Careful not to snag the hem on the wind, and reminded herself she could shiver later. Tonight was opening night.

Mike hopped out behind her, a miniature gentleman in his finest attire - collar freshly polished and a jaunty bow tie fastened at his neck. The bow tie tilted to one side despite

Agatha's best efforts, but his tail wagged with unearned confidence, as if he were the evening's guest of honor rather than an unauthorized plus-one.

"I still say he should've had a little cape," Emma said, adjusting her tortoiseshell glasses for the third time in as many minutes. She looked lovely in an emerald dress that brought out the copper highlights in her hair, though her nervousness showed in the way she kept fiddling with her necklace. "Would've given him that Sherlock Holmes edge."

Lorraine groaned, tossing her scarf over her shoulder with the flourish of a Broadway diva concluding her final number. The scarf, shimmering silver with delicate beadwork at the edges, drifted dramatically through the evening air before settling across her shoulders. "Mon dieu. No red carpet? Not even a proper velvet rope? This is the least glamorous premiere I've ever attended. And I once saw a student production of *Cats* in a gymnasium."

Agatha gave Mike's leash a gentle tug and smiled. "You didn't complain about that one when the cast served wine coolers at intermission."

"That's because I drank three and forgot I was watching *Cats*." Lorraine shot back, adjusting her elaborate updo where no fewer than six jeweled hairpins glinted in the marquee lights.

Mike barked once, whether in agreement or protest, no one could say.

"I could've brought my feather boa," Lorraine sighed dramatically, gesturing with flair toward the modest theater entrance where a small crowd had already gathered. "This was a missed opportunity, *mon amie*. In Paris, they never forget the red carpet."

"You've never been to Paris," Emma reminded her gently,

linking her arm through Lorraine's as they approached the theater.

"My soul has," Lorraine insisted, patting her perfectly arranged curls. "And my soul is *très* disappointed." She adjusted her scarf with a sniff. "It's hardly a real premiere, is it? Any woman who truly understood the arts would know the difference." She shook her head. "Grand opening. As if they were unveiling a new hardware store."

A small queue had formed at the entrance, Bristol Lake's residents dressed in their finest. A charming mix of decades-old formal wear, department store cocktail dresses, and the occasional bold fashion statement. Mr. Dunkirk, the florist, had added a fresh boutonniere to his tweed jacket that looked like it had last been fashionable when Nixon was president. Mrs. Finch wore a powder blue ensemble complete with pillbox hat that Eleanor Roosevelt might have admired.

Agatha smiled despite herself. It felt good to settle back into Bristol Lake's rhythms after the whirlwind of the holidays. Even with Lorraine's theatrics and Emma's constant adjusting of her glasses when she was nervous, which she was doing now. There was comfort in their familiar presence, in the predictable quirks of the town she'd come to love.

Inside, the lobby buzzed with townsfolk in their Sunday best, exclaiming over every restored detail of the once-beloved theater. The ornate crown molding had been repainted in its original gold leaf, the art deco sconces polished to a high shine, and the terrazzo floor restored to its former glory, each colorful chip gleaming beneath their feet.

Popcorn popped cheerfully behind the concession counter, filling the air with a buttery aroma that mingled with the scent of fresh paint and the subtle notes of a distinctive perfume. Vivian's, Agatha guessed. Eliza passed around mini cherry tarts on a silver tray, chatting with Martha Peck, who looked far from pleased despite the festive atmosphere.

"She thinks Vivian's devil spawn in heels," Emma whispered, nodding toward Martha, whose pinched expression soured further when Stanley, her husband, openly admired Vivian from across the room. Stanley's gaze lingered a beat too long on Vivian's silver gown, and Martha's elbow found his ribs with practiced precision. "I swear she's been practicing that scowl all day."

"Sounds about right," Agatha replied, eyes scanning the crowd. The usual suspects were all present. Mayor Crawford glad-handing his way through the crowd, Gladys and her book club friends clustered near the refreshments, Sheriff Salinger looking uncomfortable in a suit that clearly hadn't seen daylight in years. "Martha hasn't stopped glaring since we walked in."

"She cornered me at the store yesterday," Emma said, accepting a flute of champagne from a passing server. "Spent twenty minutes explaining why 'Hollywood types' would ruin our town's moral fabric. But I think she's just never forgiven Stanley for keeping that Vivian Monroe poster in his workshop thirty years ago."

Agatha chuckled. "Some grudges only improve with age, like fine wine or Lorraine's French accent."

The crowd parted momentarily, offering Agatha a clear view of their hostess. Vivian stood near the grand staircase, a vision in icy silver. Her dress, a sleek column of fabric that might have been liquid mercury, caught the light with each subtle movement, making her seem to shimmer like a mirage. Her dark hair was swept into an elegant updo, showcasing diamond earrings that sparkled with cold brilliance against her pale skin.

But it was her eyes that held Agatha's attention, cool, calculating, sweeping the room like she was mentally cataloging the guests, or perhaps identifying escape routes.

Beside her, Bianca smiled politely, offering programs to the early arrivals. Her sage green dress was beautifully tailored but far more subdued than Vivian's showstopper, and her movements were contained, modest, almost meek. Every gesture she made was deliberate, controlled, as though she'd rehearsed the role of "friendly business partner" and was determined to play it perfectly.

"Doesn't Bianca seem a little... I don't know, artificial?" Agatha murmured, accepting a program with a smile that Bianca returned with mechanical precision.

"She's trying too hard," Emma agreed, observing the woman over the rim of her glass. "Like she's auditioning for a part she's afraid of losing."

Mike let out a small whine from his position at Agatha's feet, his eyes fixed on Bianca. He'd been strangely agitated since they'd arrived, his usual relaxed demeanor replaced by something more vigilant.

"Even Mike senses something's off," Agatha said, patting his head reassuringly. "He's usually the first to beg for attention from anyone who might slip him treats."

Across the lobby, Henry Maddox worked the room with his portable microphone, inserting himself into conversations and speaking just a touch too loudly. His tuxedo was clearly expensive but a little too tight across the shoulders, as if he'd chosen image over comfort. His laugh, when it erupted, was jarring against the sophisticated atmosphere Vivian had cultivated, too brash, too forced.

"Recording live from this quaint little backwater's attempt at culture," he announced into his microphone, though nobody had asked him to narrate. Several people nearby winced at his volume. "Will the Acadia Theater bring Bristol Lake into the modern age, or will it be another small-town flop? Stay tuned to find out."

Sheriff Salinger, standing near the refreshment table with Detective Dawson, rolled his eyes. "That man makes me consider early retirement," he muttered, tugging at his too-tight collar. "Or at least investing in earplugs."

Detective Dawson, younger, sharper, with the kind of jawline that belonged on a movie poster, smiled sympathetically. "Just be glad he's only here for the weekend. My cousin in Portland had him lurking around for two weeks when they reopened that old brewery."

The tribute film was set to begin shortly: a restored black-and-white short from the theater's golden era. Celeste had found a write-up in an old newspaper clipping and declared it "the perfect tone-setter." She now hurried through the crowd, a vision in navy blue with her thick braid bouncing against her back as she distributed the last of the programs.

"It's from 1947," she told Agatha excitedly as she hurried past with a stack of glossy papers. "A lost gem about second chances and redemption. Very on-theme for the theater's revival."

Agatha smiled at her enthusiasm. "You should be running this place, not just our bookshop."

Celeste blushed. "Oh, I just like old things. Speaking of which, did you notice that Henry seems particularly interested in Vivian? He's been watching her all night." She glanced discreetly toward Henry, who had positioned himself near a large floral arrangement where he had an unobstructed view of Vivian.

Agatha followed her gaze. Indeed, Henry's attention kept

returning to Vivian, his expression a mix of calculation and anticipation, like a cat watching a mouse hole. When he caught Agatha looking, he smirked and tapped his microphone meaningfully.

"Big story brewing," he mouthed across the room, his smile smug and knowing.

Goosebumps prickled along Agatha's arms despite the warmth of the crowded lobby. Something predatory lurked in his gaze, something that went beyond journalistic interest.

The house lights flickered, once, twice, signaling it was time to find their seats. The murmuring crowd began to drift toward the double doors leading to the main theater.

Agatha took her seat with Emma on one side and Lorraine on the other, Mike nestled beneath her chair as the theater rules technically forbade dogs. The velvet seats, newly reupholstered but still with the original frames creaked pleasantly as people settled in. The scent of popcorn mingled with perfume and the faint musty sweetness of the old building.

The theater itself was breathtaking - a perfect restoration of 1940s splendor. Gilded moldings traced the walls and ceiling, where a mural of clouds and classical figures looked down from above. Heavy red curtains framed the screen, and ornate sconces cast a warm, inviting glow that dimmed gradually as the last few attendees found their places.

Vivian glided to the front of the theater, commanding attention without asking for it. She seemed distracted for a moment, her gaze drifting upward toward the projection booth before she caught herself. In the soft lighting, she was luminous, almost otherworldly. When she stepped into the single spotlight, a hush fell over the crowd.

"Welcome." The single word cut cleanly through the

murmur of the crowd, reaching the back row without effort. There was a slight musical quality to it, the legacy of proper stage training. "Tonight marks the rebirth of the Acadia Theater. A space that has meant so much to Bristol Lake for generations. We begin with a short film that once graced these very screens in 1947."

She paused, and Agatha noticed something flicker across her face. Was it nostalgia? Fear? But it vanished so quickly she couldn't be sure. Vivian's perfect composure returned like a mask sliding back into place.

"Please enjoy 'Shadows of Yesterday,'" Vivian concluded, stepping aside as the lights dimmed completely.

The projector hummed to life, a beam of light shooting across the darkened theater. The reel caught, stuttered, then found its rhythm, and the screen filled with grainy black and white images of a bygone era.

On screen, an actress in a wide-brimmed hat stood at a train station, her face capturing that particular melancholy of golden age cinema. She recited lines about lost dreams and second chances, her voice tinny through the restored sound system. The quality was remarkable for something so old, crisp blacks and whites, only occasional scratches marring the film.

Agatha found herself drawn into the story despite its simplicity. A woman fleeing her past, seeking refuge somewhere no one knew her name. The similarity to Vivian's own arrival in Bristol Lake was almost eerie.

That's when the flicker started.

At first, it was subtle, just a soft stutter in the picture, a momentary distortion that might have been part of the aged film. But then came the buzz, a low electrical drone that grew in intensity until it was impossible to ignore.

A sharp *snap* echoed through the theater.

The screen went black.

Gasps rippled through the audience, followed by confused murmurs. In the sudden darkness, someone laughed nervously.

A second later, the house lights blinked twice and then steadied, returning the theater to a dim half-light. People shifted in their seats, looking around with confusion.

Agatha leaned toward Emma. "That didn't seem planned."

"Definitely not," Emma whispered back, her eyes wide behind her glasses. "Look at Vivian's face."

Indeed, Vivian's icy composure had cracked. For the first time since arriving in Bristol Lake, she looked genuinely alarmed. A flash of something... panic? Recognition? crossed her features before she smoothed them back into professional concern. She was already striding toward the back of the theater with Bianca close behind, her heels clacking on the vintage tile, the sound unnaturally loud in the confused hush.

Celeste appeared in the aisle beside them, breathless, her cheeks flushed. "I think something happened in the projection booth," she whispered urgently. "Quentin just ran up there, and he looked worried."

"Maybe it's just technical difficulties," Emma suggested, but her voice lacked conviction. "First night jitters, old equipment..."

"Did you see how quickly Vivian reacted?" Agatha asked, already rising from her seat. "That wasn't surprise, that was fear."

"I'm staying right here," Lorraine declared, clutching her purse like a shield. But curiosity won out over caution, and she was soon trailing behind them, muttering under her breath. "I knew this night was cursed the moment I had to walk past that garbage bin in these heels. Never a good omen, *jamais*!"

Mike followed at Agatha's heels, ears perked forward and body tense. As they approached the stairs leading to the projection booth, he began to growl softly, a sound Agatha recognized from their previous adventures. It was his danger signal, a warning that something wasn't right.

The narrow back staircase leading to the projection booth was poorly lit, the walls close on either side. The steps creaked beneath their feet as they climbed, the sound too loud in the tense silence. At the top, a door stood ajar, a sliver of light spilling out onto the landing.

And that's where the smell hit them first. Acrid. Burned. Not just electrical, but something far worse. Something that made Agatha turn away, her hand covering her nose, her mind refusing to name what she already knew.

Quentin stood frozen in the doorway, his face drained of color. The contractor's usual easy confidence was gone, replaced by shock. "Don't come in here," he said, his voice tight. "Please. Just... someone call Sheriff Salinger."

But Agatha had seen too many crime scenes to heed warnings now. She stepped beside him anyway, heart in her throat, already knowing what she would find.

6

THE PROJECTION BOOTH

There, slumped over the equipment, was Henry Maddox. His wireless microphone lay beside him, and a heavy electrical cord snaked across the floor near his hand. His headset crackled with faint static, the only sound in the hushed booth. One of his shoes had come off, revealing a sock with tiny microphones printed on it... an incongruously whimsical detail in the grim tableau. His hand rested near the reel controls, still reaching for something he'd never touch again. The air carried a sharp, acrid scent that didn't belong in an old theater.

Emma gasped behind her, her hand flying to her mouth. “Oh my God.”

Lorraine crossed herself, murmuring what might have been a prayer or a French curse. “Oh no... Oh, Henry.”

Bianca stood frozen on the landing, her face unnaturally pale, one hand gripping the railing so tightly her knuckles had gone white. Vivian's face was unreadable, though she clasped her hands in front of her as if trying to hold herself together.

"I told him to leave the equipment alone," Quentin said, his voice hollow with shock. "He kept asking about the old wiring, the original projection setup... Said it was for his podcast. Wanted to know if we'd kept any of the vintage components."

Agatha crouched just inside the projection booth, her gaze sweeping slowly across the cramped space. The scent of scorched wiring bit at the air, sharp and unnatural, clinging to the back of her throat like burnt toast left too long in the oven.

The projector itself had clearly shorted, charred black around the power port, thin tendrils of soot crawling outward across the metal casing like spiderwebs spun in panic.

But it wasn't just the damage that caught her attention.

It was the order.

Her eyes narrowed on the small red toolkit at Henry's feet. The lid had been flipped open, every screwdriver and wire cutter nestled perfectly in its slot. Not a single tool out of place. Not even a smudge on the handles.

That was the first nudge of wrongness. The second came when she glanced up at the old console panel, the projector's dusty side rails, the narrow ledge beneath the control switches. Places no one had touched in years.

Except someone had touched them. Because now... They were clean. No handprints. No swipes. No smears. Just oddly smooth surfaces surrounded by untouched grime.

Agatha reached out instinctively and ran her finger along the edge of the nearest vent. Dust came away in a thick gray streak. She turned to the adjacent panel, clean. Her gut tensed with the certainty of experience. This wasn't right.

If Henry had been in the booth examining the equipment for his podcast, why weren't his prints all over the place? He wasn't the kind to observe without touching. Based on what Agatha had seen of him, he would've smudged, scattered, poked at buttons, maybe left fingerprints in the dust. He was tactile, intrusive. Not someone who would stand back and simply look. This wasn't a mess. This was staged. Someone wiped this down.

She glanced back at Henry, slumped over the equipment in a way that didn't look natural. His wireless microphone lay on the floor beside him, positioned too neatly for a man who'd collapsed suddenly.

Mike's growl deepened as he stared at the doorway, his hackles raised. Not at the body, but at someone on the landing. Agatha turned to follow his gaze but saw only the stunned faces of their small group.

"Did anyone see him come up here?" Agatha asked, her voice steady.

"He said he wanted to record the sound of the old projector for his podcast," Bianca offered, her voice barely above a whisper. "For atmosphere." She twisted her hands together, the gesture oddly childlike against her sophisticated appearance. "I saw him heading toward the stairs about twenty minutes ago."

The sound of heavy footsteps on the stairs interrupted any further questions. Sheriff Salinger pushed through the small crowd that had gathered at the bottom of the stairs, his face grim beneath the brim of his hat. "What's going on up there?" His question died as he took in the scene, his expression hardening. "Everyone back. Now. This is a potential crime scene."

As people began to shuffle backward, Detective Dawson appeared behind him, already pulling out his phone. "I need the paramedics and the medical examiner," he said, his voice low and efficient. "And get Johnson over here with the camera and evidence kit." He glanced at Henry's body and added quietly, "No rush on the paramedics."

Quentin turned toward them slowly, as if moving through water. "The projector shorted. But this wasn't an accident." He gestured vaguely toward the panel. "I double-checked all the wiring myself last week. Everything was grounded, up to code. This shouldn't have happened."

Agatha didn't respond right away. Instead, she took one last look at the booth. The placement of the tools. The way Henry's body was positioned. His phone sitting face-down on the console beside him — wouldn't it have fallen to the floor if he'd collapsed suddenly? And that wireless microphone, too neatly placed beside his body.

She looked at Emma, who gave a small nod. She'd noticed something too.

"Are you thinking what I'm thinking?" Emma whispered, adjusting her glasses.

"That someone wanted it to look like an accident?" Agatha responded softly, careful that her voice didn't carry beyond Emma's ears.

Mike sniffed at something on the floor, his tail wagging despite the grim scene. Agatha glanced down—cookie crumbs scattered near the equipment. Someone had been eating up here.

She glanced back at the stunned crowd behind them. Vivian's face had composed itself again, remote and unreadable as a statue. Bianca was staring at her shoes, one hand still gripping the railing. Martha Peck was whispering furiously to her husband, her expression a bizarre mix of horror and vindication. And somewhere in the back, Tabitha Elms, the local reporter, was already taking notes, her eyes gleaming with the prospect of a headline bigger than Bristol Lake had seen in decades.

"Your assessment, Ms. Royale?" The question was casual, or at least Salinger wanted it to seem that way.

Dawson caught her eye and gave a small nod. Every now and then he'd find a way to let something useful slip her way — never officially, of course.

"No," Agatha said softly, meeting his gaze with certainty. "This wasn't an accident."

The sheriff sighed heavily. "I was afraid you'd say that." He turned to address the murmuring crowd, raising his voice to be heard over the growing whispers. "Ladies and gentlemen, I'm afraid the opening night celebration is over. I'll need statements from everyone before you leave."

The crowd found its voice all at once, shock giving way to noise. Agatha barely heard it. She was already turning the details over in her mind, the way she always did, whether she meant to or not.

The Acadia Theater's grand reopening had indeed been memorable, just not in the way anyone had planned.

Agatha's gaze drifted across the faces below, friends, neighbors, strangers. One of them had just committed murder and was standing right here, waiting to see if they'd get away with it.

7

SOMETHING FEELS OFF

The next morning didn't get the memo. The sky was a perfect robin's egg blue, the kind of day that had no business being so cheerful.

The Acadia Theater was cordoned off with yellow tape that fluttered in the breeze like cautionary streamers, the bright plastic a jarring contrast to the elegant gold façade. A handwritten sign in the ticket window read: Tonight's events postponed due to unforeseen circumstances, a masterpiece of understatement.

Agatha stood just beyond the tape, coffee in hand, watching as two uniformed officers entered through the side door. The steam from her cup curled upward in the crisp morning air, mingling with her breath. Mike sat beside her, unusually still, his ears pricked forward as if he sensed something the humans couldn't.

The street was quiet for a Thursday morning. Most of Bristol Lake's residents were giving the theater a wide berth, treating it with the same respectful distance usually reserved for funeral homes and fresh graves. But Agatha could see curtains twitching in the windows above Merriweather's Antique across the street, faces appearing briefly before vanishing again. News of Henry's death had spread through town faster than Lorraine's pastry reviews, which was saying something.

"I heard they're calling it an accident now," Emma said, approaching with a frown and two scones wrapped in napkins. Her red ponytail caught the morning light as she handed one of the pastries to Agatha. "A tragic electrical mishap. Poor Henry."

"Poor Henry?" Lorraine scoffed as she joined them, her hat, the sort of thing worn to a winter ball in a Tolstoy novel, sitting askew over her wild curls. "That man was a menace with a microphone. Still, electrocution feels a bit... theatrical, doesn't it?" She pronounced 'theatrical' with extra emphasis on each syllable, as if the word itself deserved special treatment.

Agatha didn't answer immediately. She turned her coffee cup in her hands, staring down at it. "Last night Sheriff Salinger was treating it like a crime scene," she said. "Detective Dawson even had his notebook out."

"I overheard him telling one of the deputies to secure the perimeter," Emma said, breaking off a piece of her scone. Crumbs scattered on her blue cardigan, and she brushed them away absently. "He was using all the proper police jargon. 'maintain chain of custody,' 'document everything exactly as found.' Sounded like he was quoting from a procedural manual."

"He said it to everyone," Lorraine said. "Right there in front of the whole room. 'This is a potential crime scene.' Every single person in that theater heard him."

"Then this morning the official story changes to 'accident'?" Agatha broke off a piece of her own scone but didn't eat it, rolling it between her fingers instead. "That doesn't make sense."

"Maybe the mayor got involved," Lorraine whispered dramatically, leaning in so close that the wide brim of her hat tilted precariously, nearly taking out Emma's eye. "Can't have a murder scaring away tourists from our quaint little town's newest attraction, can we? The Ice Carnival is only three weeks away!" She flung out an arm toward the town square, where workers were already hanging strings of white lights from snow-dusted tree branches and assembling the frame for an ice sculpture display.

Agatha took another sip of her coffee. "As much as I hate to say it, she has a point."

Emma looked up from her scone. "I wish Raymond Aguilar had stayed mayor. He would've known how to handle this."

"It's too bad he moved back to the big city," Agatha said. "Bristol Lake felt different with him in charge. Safer, somehow." She stared out toward the theater.

"Hmph," Lorraine sniffed. "This never would've happened on Raymond's watch. That man had backbone. And a fabulous collection of cravats."

She watched as Detective Dawson emerged from the side entrance of the theater, his normally crisp appearance noticeably rumpled. His blue shirt was wrinkled, his tie loosened, dark circles shadowed his eyes. He rubbed his face with one hand, checked his phone, then frowned deeply at whatever he saw there.

"He doesn't look like a man who thinks he's dealing with an accident," Emma observed quietly.

"Quentin said the tools were moved," Agatha continued,

almost to herself. "He'd just finished rewiring the booth last week. Said everything was grounded. And he's meticulous. It's not like him to miss something."

"Could someone have tampered with it after he left?" Lorraine tilted her head, one of the flowers on her hat drooping comically.

Emma blinked. "Wouldn't the police have caught that?"

Agatha shook her head. "Only if they were looking for it."

That was the problem with investigations led by small-town police departments, limited resources, limited expertise, and sometimes, limited willingness to dig too deeply. Especially when influential people preferred a neat resolution.

She took a slow sip of her coffee, scanning the theater's second-story windows. Sheriff Salinger had been calm at the scene, but almost too quick to change his assessment. "No signs of struggle," he'd announced this morning on the local radio. "Looks like an unfortunate accident."

But Agatha had learned long ago that appearances were often curated, especially in a town like Bristol Lake where image was everything. The Acadia's reopening had been featured in three regional papers; an unsolved murder would certainly dampen enthusiasm.

Mike gave a quiet whine, drawing her gaze downward.

"What is it, boy?" she asked gently, reaching down to scratch behind his ears. His fur was soft beneath her fingers, but his muscles were tense.

He was staring at the side alley beside the theater, ears alert, body rigid, his usual friendly demeanor replaced by something more vigilant. A low growl rumbled in his chest, too quiet for anyone but Agatha to hear.

She followed his gaze just in time to see a shadow slip

around the corner. A tall figure in a dark coat, walking briskly away from the theater's service entrance. Whoever it was moved like someone who didn't want to be seen.

"Did you guys see that?" Agatha asked, pointing toward the alley. "Did anyone see who that was?"

Lorraine leaned forward dramatically, one gloved hand pressed to her chest as if bracing for scandal. Then her eyes widened. "It was Gordon Lane. I'm sure of it."

"Who is Gordon Lane?" Agatha asked, still watching the spot where the figure had disappeared. The name wasn't familiar, though she prided herself on knowing most of Bristol Lake's residents.

"I haven't officially met him," Lorraine tilted her hat and dropped her voice to a conspiratorial hush. "But I *may* have been snooping around the theater before the grand opening. Just a little light trespassing. Nothing criminal."

She waved a hand like she was brushing away the very idea of boundaries. "Anyway, I saw this tall man from behind, broad shoulders, long coat, very *mysterious benefactor* chic. I asked one employee who he was, and she told me he was Gordon Lane... The investor"

Lorraine paused for effect, then added with a smirk, "I told her I'd never seen him before, and she said he prefers to stay behind the scenes. Makes him sound like the Phantom of the Opera, doesn't it?"

Agatha raised an eyebrow. "Which employee told you this?"

"That's just it," Lorraine said, leaning in closer, her perfume enveloping them like an expensive fog. "Young woman, sharp bob, bit of a snark to her. Haven't seen her since that day. Maybe she got fired for talking too much, or maybe she was never real to begin with," she added with a playful wink. "But mystery plus designer outerwear? Definitely gives off secret millionaire vibes."

"I didn't realize there was an investor," Emma said, brushing more crumbs from her cardigan. "I thought the Monroe sisters were financing everything themselves."

"Well, ma chérie, even glamorous Hollywood types need money," Lorraine said, tossing her head so that the cardinal on her hat bobbed in agreement. "And from what I hear, this Gordon fellow has plenty to spare. Some sort of entertainment executive from California who 'believes in preserving historic venues.' At least that's what Gladys told me, and she knows everyone's business."

Agatha filed the name away in her mental notebook. "Interesting timing for a silent investor to be sneaking around a potential crime scene."

"Maybe he's worried about his investment," Emma suggested.

"Or maybe he knows something we don't," Agatha replied, her eyes drifting back to the alley where the figure had disappeared.

They crossed the street and entered the bookstore. The scent of fresh coffee from the small café corner mingled with the papery perfume of books, a combination that always made Agatha feel grounded, no matter what chaos swirled around her.

Agatha ran her fingers along a shelf as she passed, the familiar texture comforting her racing thoughts. The shop was quiet this morning. Most of the town was either avoiding public places or gathering at the diner to exchange theories.

Celeste was already there, a stack of mystery novels in her arms. She'd spent the morning arranging the new release display, complete with a hand-lettered sign that read

MURDER MOST CLEVER. A section packed with Agatha's favorite authors. The irony wasn't lost on either of them.

She looked up from the counter as Agatha walked in, her tortoiseshell glasses slipping down her nose. "It's really nice having you back," she said, offering a warm smile. "The store wasn't the same without you."

Agatha slipped off her coat and hung it on the hook by the door. "You did such a great job while I was gone. Everything looks wonderful."

Celeste beamed at the compliment, then set the books down on the front table and gave the display one last nudge, squaring the edges. She reached for the feather duster that leaned against the window shelf, clearly mid-task, and started dusting the spines with practiced ease.

Then she paused, the duster hovering midair. Her expression shifted from focused to thoughtful. "Oh..." She turned back toward Agatha. "I just remembered. I saw something this morning that might interest you."

Lorraine leaned forward instantly, both hands flat on the table. "Do tell."

"I was grabbing a scone and coffee at Eliza's this morning," Celeste said, lowering her voice as she leaned her elbows on the counter, glancing toward the door as if expecting eavesdroppers. "I was tucked behind the specials board near the window when Detective Dawson came in. He didn't see me. He looked exhausted, his tie was loosened, his hair a mess. Definitely hadn't slept."

"The case keeping him up?" Emma asked, settling into one of the plush reading chairs near the window. She pulled her legs up beneath her, getting comfortable for what promised to be an interesting conversation.

"More than that," Celeste said, her thick braid swinging.

"He was on the phone, pacing by the condiment station. Said something like, 'I understand the optics, sir, but we haven't finished processing the scene.' Then he got really tense and said, 'With all due respect, evidence doesn't care about the tourism board.'"

Agatha raised an eyebrow. "So someone's pushing for a quick resolution."

"That's not all," Celeste continued, her voice barely above a whisper though the store was empty save for their small group. "After he hung up, he called someone else. I think it was Sheriff Salinger. Said the mayor called him personally about 'keeping things calm' and that there was 'pressure from above' to wrap this up quickly."

"Political pressure," Emma said with a frown, pulling her cardigan tighter around herself as if suddenly cold.

"That explains the sudden accident ruling," Agatha said, tapping her fingers against her coffee cup. "But it doesn't explain why."

"Maybe they really believe it was an accident," Emma suggested, though she didn't sound convinced.

"Or maybe someone very powerful wants it to be an accident," Lorraine countered, perching on the edge of a display table despite Agatha's pointed look. "In my experience, when someone insists on a particular truth this quickly, it's usually covering up a more inconvenient one."

Celeste set down the books, arranging them in a neat stack. "That's not even the interesting part. After my coffee, I saw Vivian Monroe at the courthouse steps. She looked completely untouched by the drama, perfect hair, heels clicking, like she'd just stepped out of a catalog shoot."

"The show must go on," Lorraine murmured. "Even when someone dies in your theater."

Celeste leaned in, her eyes wide behind her glasses. “But maybe fifteen minutes later? I spotted her again at the coffee cart near the square. This time, she was on her phone, pacing, tight little steps, like a caged panther. Totally different vibe.”

Lorraine leaned so far forward she nearly toppled off her perch on the table. “Could you hear what she was saying?”

“She kept her voice low, but I caught bits and pieces,” Celeste explained, gesturing with her hands as she spoke. “She said something like, 'We discussed this possibility,' and 'It's unfortunate but hardly catastrophic.' Then she said the whole thing was bad timing and that they 'couldn't afford to lose momentum.'“

Emma's frown deepened, creating a small crease between her brows. “That's not how you talk about someone dying.”

“It's how you talk about a business launch,” Agatha said, her jaw tightening. “Or a PR crisis.”

“And that's not even the strangest part,” Celeste added, wrapping her hands around her mug. “After she ended the call, she looked around, both shoulders, like she was checking if anyone had heard. Then she spotted me standing near the bench. Her whole demeanor changed, like flipping a switch. Suddenly she was all smiles and said, 'Lovely morning, isn't it?' like nothing had happened.”

She took a sip of her tea before continuing. “But her eyes... They didn't match the smile. They stayed cold. Like... like glass. It was creepy.”

A silence fell over the group as they processed this information. Outside, a mail truck rumbled past, its familiar sound somehow comforting in its normalcy.

“Did you see Bianca?” Agatha asked, remembering how the quieter Monroe sister had kept to herself at the screening.

There had been something in her demeanor, a nervousness that went beyond opening night jitters.

"No," Celeste replied, shaking her head. "But I heard Vivian mention her on the call. She said something about Bianca being 'too sensitive about these things.'"

"Too sensitive about what... electrocution?" Emma asked dryly.

"Or murder," Agatha added quietly.

Lorraine leaned dramatically against the counter, her bracelets jingling. "Vivian has ice water in her veins. But Bianca... She looked genuinely shaken last night."

Mike gave a soft chuff in agreement from where he'd settled under the nearest reading table. His eyes remained alert, tracking every movement in the shop.

"That's the thing," Agatha said, crossing to where Mike lay and crouching beside him. She ran her hand along his back, feeling the slight tension in his muscles. "Mike didn't bark at Bianca. Not even once."

Lorraine blinked, clearly not following. "So?"

"So he usually barks when something feels off," Agatha explained, watching her dog's intelligent brown eyes. "He barked at Henry, barked at the booth. But not at Bianca. Not even when she walked right by him."

Emma crossed her arms, considering this. "You think that means something?"

"Dogs sense things we don't," Agatha said, standing again. "And Mike has good instincts about people."

"That's true," Emma conceded. "You told me he growled at your ex a full month before you found out about the affair."

Lorraine gasped, delighted by the reminder of gossip. "He knew!"

"He knew," Agatha agreed with a hint of a smile. "And now he's telling us something about Vivian. I'm just not sure what yet."

The words hung in the air between them. Agatha felt a familiar tightening in her chest, that same mix of dread and determination she'd felt when Mike uncovered the skeleton buried in the flower bed behind her house, when Eliza was arrested for the poisoning at the French boulangerie, when Green Acres turned into a crime scene, and when she stood accused of murder at a writer's retreat in Botswana. Each time, the mystery hadn't just shown up. It had found her. And each time, she'd followed the trail, because walking away simply wasn't in her nature.

The morning sun climbed higher, casting long rectangles of light across the hardwood floor.

Emma pulled out a chair at the small reading table. "So what do we do now?"

"We?" Agatha asked, though she couldn't suppress a small smile. Her friends knew her too well.

"Don't even try to tell me you're not going to look into this," Emma said with a knowing look. "I know that expression. It's your 'something's fishy and I'm going to find out what' face."

"You get a little crease right here," Celeste added, pointing between her own eyebrows. "And you tap your fingers like you're already taking notes."

Agatha stopped her fingers mid-tap against her thigh, not having realized she was doing it.

Lorraine draped herself dramatically across a nearby armchair, one leg hooked over the armrest in defiance of proper furniture etiquette. "Oh, here we go again. Another mystery for our little detective club. Should I start working on my disguise? Perhaps a theater critic this time? Or a wealthy widow interested in supporting the arts?"

Despite herself, Agatha smiled. The thought of Lorraine attempting subterfuge was about as convincing as Mike trying to pass himself off as a Great Dane. "Let's start simple. We need to know more about Henry Maddox. His podcast, his research..."

"Why he was poking around the projection booth in the first place," Celeste added, already reaching for a notepad.

"And who might have wanted him silenced," Emma finished, her expression serious beneath her light tone.

Mike settled at Agatha's feet, resting his chin on his paws with a contented sigh, as if to say he was ready for the adventure ahead. His entire posture had changed. From alert sentinel to patient partner. He knew the routine.

Agatha crossed to her desk and pulled out a leather-bound notebook, her investigation journal. She'd started a new one after each case, partly as a record and partly as a promise to herself that life would eventually return to normal. This would be the sixth volume.

She opened it to a fresh page. "Let's make a list of what we know for sure, and what we need to find out."

"I still don't understand why the police are so quick to call it an accident," Emma said, tapping her pen against the table. "It's like they don't want to investigate."

"Or someone doesn't want them to," Agatha murmured. She drew a line down the center of her notebook page, labeling one side "Facts" and the other "Questions."

Under 'Facts,' she wrote in her neat, precise handwriting:

- Henry died in projection booth
- Electrical "accident"

- Tools moved from where Quentin left them
- Clean panels surrounded by dust
- Police changed story overnight
- Pressure from mayor/tourism board
- Vivian unconcerned
- Bianca upset
- Gordon Lane (investor) possibly at scene.

Under 'Questions,' she wrote:

- Why was Henry in the booth?
- What was he investigating?
- Who benefits from his death?
- Who had access to the booth?
- Who could tamper with wiring?
- Connection to Vivian's past?
- Who is Gordon Lane really?

"I'm going to check Henry's podcast," Emma offered. "See what he was working on, what stories he was chasing. Might give us a clue about what he discovered."

"Good idea." Agatha turned to Celeste. "Can you look into Gordon Lane? See what you can find about his connection to the theater, his business history?"

"On it," Celeste agreed eagerly. "I'll check business registrations, property records, the usual."

"What about me?" Lorraine asked, examining her manicure with feigned nonchalance.

"You," Agatha said with a small smile, "are our secret weapon. Nobody gossips better than Bristol Lake's most theatrical resident. See what you can find out about the Monroes, personal details, little things people have noticed."

Lorraine beamed. “Finally, my true calling is recognized. Consider it done.”

“I don't know yet,” Agatha said, staring at her list, feeling the weight of what they were undertaking. “But my gut says Henry's death wasn't an accident. And if I'm right, then someone in this town just got away with murder.”

The bookstore's warm glow belied the chill Agatha felt. Outside, Bristol Lake continued its peaceful Thursday routine. The mail carrier making rounds, Eliza opening her bakery, tourists window shopping along Central Avenue.

All normal, all ordinary.

Except for the yellow tape around the Acadia Theater, and the secrets Agatha suspected were hidden behind its ornate facade.

She glanced at Mike, who had settled into a patch of sunlight, his eyes half-closed but his ears still alert. He sensed it too. The wrongness beneath the surface, the danger lurking behind polite smiles and convenient explanations.

Someone had staged an accident. Someone thought they'd gotten away with it. Someone thought no one would notice. But they hadn't counted on Agatha Royale. And they certainly hadn't counted on Mike.”

8

UNEASY SUSPICIONS

The scent of cinnamon rolls and almond glaze wrapped around Agatha like a silk shawl as she stepped into Eliza's Bakery, Mike at her heels and a chill in the January air that seemed determined to linger. The morning's gentle drizzle had left everything damp, creating that peculiar freshness that came after rain, earth and stone and winter air mingling together.

Friday mornings in Bristol Lake were typically slow and sugar-sweet, with the kind of friendly familiarity that allowed gossip to rise faster than the bread in Eliza's oven. Today was no exception, though the usual cheerful buzz was tinged with whispers about the Acadia, about Henry Maddox, and about accident versus intent.

Eliza's bakery hummed with its usual Friday morning rhythm, a few retirees sharing the crossword puzzle at their regular table, Mrs. Finnegan gently rocking her grandson's stroller by the window, and the mail carrier waiting for his daily coffee refill. The familiar faces and quiet conversations created a sense of normalcy that Bristol Lake desperately needed after the events at the Acadia.

"Blueberry scone and a black tea?" Eliza called from behind the counter before Agatha could even reach the register. Her cheeks were flushed from the ovens, flour dusting her apron and a smudge of something sugary on her sleeve.

"You read my mind," Agatha replied, setting her umbrella near the door. It dripped quietly onto the mat, adding to the small puddle already forming there.

She was just sliding into a corner booth, her usual spot with the view of both the street and the bakery door, when Lorraine swept in, wrapped in a paisley shawl so vibrant it seemed to have its own weather system. Her oversized sunglasses perched like exclamation points atop her head despite the cloudy day, and at least three necklaces competed for attention around her neck.

"Mes chéries," Lorraine called, loud enough that Mrs. Finch, quietly enjoying her Danish at the window table, looked up with a start. "The beauty salon is absolutely *buzzing* this morning."

Emma looked up from her notebook and smirked. "With what? Hairdryers or gossip?"

"Both, ma chérie," Lorraine replied, sliding into the booth with dramatic flair. The paisley shawl billowed dramatically before settling around her like exotic plumage. "Though the gossip is far more electrifying than the hairdryers, if you take my meaning."

She looked around to make sure they had an audience. They did; three women at nearby tables had abandoned any pretense of conversation in favor of eavesdropping, before leaning in conspiratorially.

"Rosa Fielding told Alma, you know, the Tuesday perm

specialist with the lazy eye and that marvelous way with curling irons, that there's something familiar about those Monroe women. Said she can't quite place where she's seen them before, but something about them keeps nagging at her memory."

Agatha raised an eyebrow, accepting her tea from Eliza with a nod of thanks. "That's interesting." Rosa had said the same thing at the bookstore — which meant either it was true, or they'd gotten their stories straight.

"Interesting? It's practically a headline!" Lorraine leaned in further, her necklaces pooling on the table. "Rosa said she's been racking her brain trying to remember. Said it's like seeing someone from an old photograph but not being able to recall where the photograph was taken or who else was in it."

"Rosa's not one to exaggerate," Emma added, closing her notebook. Her glasses slipped down her nose, and she pushed them back up with an absent gesture. "She's usually pretty measured in her observations."

"Exactly," Lorraine said, accepting a cup of coffee from Eliza without taking her eyes off Agatha. "And... Don't shoot the messenger, but one of the ladies at the salon said Rosa's been hoping it's something significant she can use to squeeze a little money out of the Monroe women. Blackmail might be a strong word, but you know how some people get when strangers show up with deep pockets and secrets written all over them."

Agatha frowned. "That doesn't sound like Rosa. "She seemed pretty straightforward to me. Not the type."

"Well," Lorraine said, stirring sugar into her coffee, "desperate times, desperate measures. You know she's been struggling since her arthritis got worse. Can't work at the library anymore, pension barely covers her medications. A little financial assistance from someone with deep pockets might be tempting."

Just then, the bakery door opened, sending a flurry of snowflakes swirling onto the welcome mat. Rosa Fielding stepped inside, bundled in a wool coat that had seen better days and clutching a paper bag that seemed to be protecting something inside from the damp. She looked thinner than the last time Agatha had seen her, the fatigue etched deeper into the lines of her face, and her usually sharp hazel eyes carried a restless edge that didn't suit her.

"Rosa!" Agatha called, waving her over. "Join us?"

Rosa hesitated only a moment, her eyes scanning the bakery as if checking who might be listening, before nodding and crossing the room. She lowered herself into the booth beside Emma, wincing as her joints protested. Her mouth was pinched as if deciding how much to say. Her gaze swept the table before settling on Agatha, sharp and unreadable.

"We were just talking about the Monroe sisters," Lorraine said gently, though without a trace of shame at being caught gossiping.

Rosa exhaled, a soft sound that seemed to carry the weight of sleepless nights. "That's what I came to talk to you about, actually. Celeste mentioned you were here."

Agatha leaned forward, the tea forgotten in her hands. "Did something come back to you? About the two of them together?"

Rosa exhaled slowly, her fingers worrying at the edge of her paper bag. "I've been thinking about it ever since I saw you at the bookstore. It's not that I recognize either of them individually. It's more like a feeling. A flicker. Like I've seen them together somewhere before. The way they move. The way they look at people." She gestured vaguely, as if trying to capture something intangible. "It's not what they say. It's what they don't say to each other."

"Maybe from a film?" Agatha offered. "Or an old premiere? I know the Acadia hosted some special events back in the day."

Rosa shook her head, the motion firm despite her apparent fatigue. "No. Not the movies. Somewhere else. But I can't place it." She tapped her temple in frustration. "It's right there, just out of reach. Like a word on the tip of your tongue."

Emma tilted her head, her expression thoughtful. "Maybe you think you recognize them because you've seen their faces in magazines or online. Vivian was all over the place in the late nineties and early 2000s, right? Those celebrity faces get lodged in our subconscious."

"Maybe." Rosa's tone was noncommittal, bordering on dismissive. Her gloved hands clutched the paper bag tighter. "But it's not the fame. It's something quieter. Something... Odd." She looked directly at Agatha, her gaze suddenly intense. "I'm going to check my old programs and scrapbooks. I kept everything from my days at the Acadia. If I find anything, I'll let you know."

Agatha held her gaze, struck by the urgency in Rosa's voice. "Thanks, Rosa. I'd appreciate it."

Rosa stood abruptly, smoothing her coat with trembling hands. "I'll let you know if I find anything worth sharing." She hesitated, then added more quietly, "Be careful, Agatha. Some memories are buried for a reason."

She didn't wait for a reply before heading toward the door, her heels clicking with quiet resolve against the hardwood floor. The table fell silent as they watched her go.

"Something's really bothering her," Emma said softly once Rosa was out of earshot.

"I know," Agatha replied, watching through the window as Rosa hurried across the street, hunched against the drizzle. "And I think she's right to be bothered."

Mike whined softly from under the table, his nose tracking Rosa until she disappeared from view.

"Did you see how she was clutching that bag?" Lorraine asked, her usual dramatic tone replaced by genuine concern. "Like it contained state secrets."

"Or evidence," Emma added quietly.

"Or memories," Agatha murmured, thinking of her own box of keepsakes from before the divorce, ticket stubs, photographs, birthday cards. Physical reminders of a life that no longer existed except in those fragile paper fragments. "Sometimes the past weighs more than we expect."

They sat in thoughtful silence for a moment, the cheerful bustle of the bakery continuing around them. Eliza slid a fresh plate of cardamom buns onto their table without a word, her eyes questioning.

Agatha shook her head. "No thank you. Maybe later."

"Well," Lorraine said finally, selecting a bun with deliberate care, "if Rosa thinks there's something strange about the Monroe sisters, I'm inclined to believe her. That woman has the memory of an elephant and the instincts of a bloodhound."

"But what could it be?" Emma wondered, absently brushing crumbs from her sleeve. "Even if they're not really sisters, that's hardly scandalous enough to kill over."

"Unless," Agatha said slowly, "whatever Rosa remembers connects to what Henry Maddox was investigating."

The implications of that statement settled over the table like a shadow.

LATER THAT AFTERNOON, the clouds finally parted, allowing watery sunshine to filter through the trees. Agatha walked Mike through the town square, enjoying the brief respite from the rain. Vendors were setting up for the weekend's winter market despite the damp, strings of bunting fluttering gently from lamppost to lamppost like colorful prayer flags.

Bristol Lake was emerging from its shock, returning to its normal rhythms, though conversations still hushed when Agatha passed, and eyes still flicked toward the Acadia Theater with morbid curiosity. Yellow police tape still cordoned off the side entrance, a jarring splash of caution against the theater's elegant façade.

She passed a chalkboard sign outside the community center that read *Trivia Night Canceled Due to Water Main Leak* and waved to Eliza, who was lingering in the bakery doorway, arms crossed against the cold, watching the street.

"Any news?" Eliza called.

Agatha shook her head. "Nothing official."

"Unofficial, then?" Eliza's eyes sparkled with that combination of concern and curiosity that defined small-town relationships.

"Just be careful what you say and who you say it to," Agatha replied. "I think there's more to this story than we know."

Eliza glanced up and down the street. In Bristol Lake, information was currency, and some exchanges were better conducted privately.

By the park, the clouds parted just enough for a weak sunbeam to streak through the treetops, illuminating a solitary figure. Rosa sat on a weathered bench near the gazebo; her small terrier curled beside her. The dog, a scruffy, caramel-colored mix named Pepper, spotted Mike and wagged her tail in greeting but didn't leave Rosa's side.

Agatha approached, deliberately making her footsteps audible on the gravel path to avoid startling Rosa, who seemed lost in thought.

"Mind if I join you?" she asked gently.

Rosa looked up, a brief flash of alarm crossing her face before recognition settled in. "Oh — Agatha. No, of course not."

Agatha settled on the bench, leaving a respectful distance between them. Mike circled once before lying down at her feet, his eyes trained on Rosa with gentle curiosity.

"Nice morning to be out," Agatha said, "in spite of the cold."

Rosa glanced down at Pepper, who had perked up at Mike's arrival, tail going. "She gets restless if I don't bring her. Doesn't matter what the thermometer says."

"Mike's the same," Agatha said, watching the two dogs exchange a polite sniff. "I think he'd drag me out in a blizzard if he had to."

Rosa almost smiled at that. Almost.

They sat quietly for a moment, the hush of the park broken only by a pair of toddlers chasing pigeons across the snow-dusted path, and the distant chatter of vendors setting up their stalls.

"You seem uneasy," Agatha said finally, her voice gentle but direct.

"I am," Rosa admitted, her fingers twisting in her lap.

"There's something strange about those women. Something I can't quite pin down." She stared at the gazebo, its white paint peeling after the long winter. "It's like seeing a face in a dream and then trying to describe it when you wake up. The details slip away."

"You're sure it's not just nerves about the reopening? The Acadia meant a lot to you."

Rosa shook her head firmly. "It's not that. It's..." She paused, searching for words. "It's familiar, but not in a good way. Like déjà vu, but with dread attached. I feel like I've seen them somewhere before, just not on a screen or in a magazine. In real life. But I can't remember when."

Her voice dropped to almost a whisper. "Or why it makes me so uncomfortable."

Pepper whined softly, sensing her distress, and pressed closer to Rosa's leg. Rosa absently stroked the dog's ears, the motion seeming to calm them both.

"Did you check your scrapbooks?" Agatha asked.

"Some of them. I have boxes in the attic I haven't looked through in years." Rosa's expression shifted, a mix of determination and fear crossing her features. "I need to find something. A program, a photo, anything that might jog my memory."

Agatha rested a hand lightly on Rosa's arm, noting how the older woman tensed at the touch before relaxing. "If you do remember something, I hope you'll let me know. I have a feeling whatever you're trying to place might be connected to Henry's death, and I'd hate for you to stumble into something dangerous alone.

Rosa's eyes met hers, suddenly sharp with understanding. "You think they're dangerous."

It wasn't a question.

Agatha chose her words before she spoke. "I think Henry Maddox was investigating something, and now he's dead. I'd hate for history to repeat itself."

Rosa nodded, her lips pressed into a thin line. "I will. I promise."

They sat a moment longer, Pepper dozing against Rosa's ankle while Mike kept a watchful eye on a squirrel making its way along the fence line.

"I should head back," Rosa said finally, gathering herself up with a small effort. "I promised myself I'd get through at least two of those boxes today."

"Good luck with them," Agatha said warmly. "And do call if anything comes back to you."

"I will." Rosa clicked her tongue for Pepper and offered Agatha a small, dry smile. "Though I may just be a woman with too much time and too many old newspapers."

"Between the two of us, I'd trust your instincts over mine any day," Agatha said.

As they headed home, Agatha turned the conversation over in her mind. Rosa struck her as a practical woman — not the sort to lose sleep over nothing. If something felt off to her, that was probably reason enough to take it seriously.

Mike glanced back once toward the park, then looked up at Agatha as if waiting.

"All right," she told him quietly. "We'll look into it."

~

BACK AT THE BOOKSHOP, Emma was waiting with a steaming cup of tea and a worried expression.

"I tracked down Henry's podcast," she said without preamble. "The last three episodes were all about Hollywood scandals from the early 2000s. One specifically mentioned Vincent Cleary and a 'mysterious disappearance' connected to his death."

Agatha hung her coat on the hook by the door, processing this information. "Did he mention Vivian by name?"

"Not directly. But he dropped enough hints that anyone familiar with the case would know who he meant." Emma pushed her glasses up her nose, a nervous habit. "Agatha, I think he was building up to something big. Something he thought would make his career."

"Instead, it ended it," Agatha said quietly.

Outside, snow had begun to fall again, tapping softly against the windows. Inside One Deadly Chapter Books & Brew, Agatha, Emma, and Mike huddled over a laptop, following the digital breadcrumbs of a dead man's investigation, while across town, Rosa Fielding climbed into her attic, searching for memories she wasn't sure she wanted to find.

The storm was just beginning.

9

A VISIT AND A WARNING

The next day, snow started just after noon, soft flakes that quickly grew heavier, blanketing Bristol Lake in white. It wasn't the blizzard kind of snow, but rather the persistent kind that settled in for hours, wrapping the town in hushed quiet that muffled sounds and softened edges. Snow gathered on windowsills and clung to bare tree branches, transforming the cobblestone street into a frosted postcard scene.

The snow had driven away most potential customers, leaving the bookstore in a rare state of quiet. The only sounds were the gentle whisper of falling snow, the occasional turning of pages, and the steady tick of the wall clock.

Agatha stood behind the counter, cradling a mug of chamomile tea between her palms, absorbing its warmth. Mike snoozed beside the till, his small body curled into a tight ball, one ear twitching now and then as he chased dream rabbits. Celeste was out delivering flyers for the mystery book club's "Dead Authors, Live Discussion" night, armed with a down coat and determined enthusiasm. Emma had texted an hour earlier: *Trapped in YA reshelving purgatory. Pray for me. The dystopian romances section has doubled since last month. Send help or chocolate.*

The bookshop felt like a sanctuary on days like this, a safe harbor in a storm. Agatha cherished these quiet moments, even as her mind circled back to Henry Maddox and Vivian Monroe.

She had just reached the final twist in a vintage Ellery Queen paperback, where the murderer was revealed to be the seemingly harmless gardener, when the bookstore door opened, bringing with it a gust of frigid air and the unmistakable scent of snow-dampened wool.

Rosa Fielding stepped inside, shaking snow from her umbrella. Her gray cardigan was damp at the shoulders from melting flakes, and a few wisps of silver hair had escaped from her usual neat bun.

"Rosa," Agatha said, setting her book aside and marking her place. "Did you find something?"

Rosa's expression was tense as she glanced around the empty shop. "I did. Can we talk?"

"Of course. Come sit down." Agatha gestured toward the fireplace seating area, where two overstuffed wingback chairs flanked a small gas fireplace that cast a warm glow even on the dreariest days.

Mike lifted his head from his bed, yawned widely, then trotted over to investigate. Rosa bent to scratch behind his ears.

"Hello again, handsome," she said with a small smile. "Pepper's been asking about you."

"They did get along well at the park," Agatha agreed. "Let me get you some coffee. I just made a fresh pot."

"That would be lovely, thank you."

A few minutes later, they were settled in the wingback chairs, steaming mugs in hand. The snow continued its steady fall past the windows, creating a cocoon of privacy in the otherwise empty shop.

Rosa pulled a manila envelope from her tote bag, her hands unsteady. But before she could open it, the bell above the door chimed.

"Oh, heavens," said Mr. Whitaker, stomping snow from his boots on the mat with more force than his frail frame suggested possible. His tweed jacket was spotted with melting snowflakes, and his bow tie—today a cheerful yellow with blue polka dots—sat crooked. "This snow's doing a number on my knees. Agatha, be a dear and check if my Ellery Queen came in? The 1943 edition with the original dust jacket?"

Agatha smiled patiently. Mr. Whitaker asked the same question every Thursday, and every Thursday the answer was the same. "It's on the hold shelf. Bottom right. Just arrived yesterday."

He gave a cheerful salute and shuffled past their seating area, pausing to tip his hat to Rosa. "Afternoon, Mrs. Fielding. Staying warm, I see."

"Trying to," Rosa replied politely, though her fingers tightened on the envelope.

"Good day for mysteries," Mr. Whitaker declared as he made his way toward the hold shelf. "Nothing like a murder on the page when it's snowing outside."

Rosa winced at the word "murder," a reaction so subtle that only someone watching for it would have noticed.

Mr. Whitaker retrieved his book and waved it triumphantly. "See you next Thursday, Agatha! Keep that hold shelf organized!" Then he was gone, the door swinging shut behind him, letting in a swirl of snowflakes before closing again, leaving Rosa and Agatha alone once more. The shop fell back into its quiet rhythm.

Rosa exhaled slowly, as if she'd been holding her breath. "Now then," she said, opening the envelope. "I went through those boxes in the attic like I said I would. The ones I hadn't looked at in years."

She withdrew a yellowed newspaper clipping. "This is from a 2001 film premiere, just a few months before Vincent Cleary died."

The photo showed a red-carpet scene. A younger woman stood just behind screenwriter Vincent Cleary, smiling shyly at the camera while he spoke to reporters. She wore a simple black dress, her dark hair pulled back in a neat bun, clearly staff rather than celebrity. *Bethany Marks, assistant to Vincent Cleary,* read the caption beneath the photo.

Agatha studied the image. "She does look a bit like Vivian Monroe. Same general features."

"That's what I thought at first," Rosa said. She pulled out a second clipping, this one glossier, printed on better paper. "But then I found this one from a charity gala about a year earlier."

The second photo showed two women in evening gowns, arms linked, smiling together for the press. Agatha recognized Vivian Monroe immediately, younger than she was now, but unmistakably her with that elegant posture and confident smile. She was already famous by then, clearly comfortable in front of cameras. Next to her stood Bethany Marks, wearing a shy expression but comfortable enough in Vivian's presence to link arms. *Rising star Vivian Monroe and friend Bethany Marks attend Children's Hospital fundraiser,* the caption read.

"So they were friends," Agatha said quietly, her mind already working through the implications.

Rosa nodded, wrapping both hands around her mug as if seeking warmth despite the nearby fire. "And here's what I find odd. After Vincent Cleary's death, there's no mention of Bethany Marks anywhere. I went through everything I had—all my old magazines, programs, clippings. She just... vanished."

Agatha set the clippings on the small table between them, studying them side by side. "That is strange. Did she leave the industry?"

"That's just it. I can't find anything. No wedding announcements, no obituaries, no career changes. Nothing." Rosa's voice dropped lower. "Bethany was Vincent's assistant right up until he died, and then she disappeared. Not a word about her anywhere. It's like she was erased."

The fire cast a steady, warm glow across their faces. Outside, the snow fell heavier, blanketing the street in white.

"If Bethany was Vincent Cleary's assistant, she would have known his business," Agatha said thoughtfully. "His secrets, too, probably."

"Exactly." Rosa leaned forward, her eyes sharp. "And if she knew something about his death..."

"Someone might have wanted her to disappear," Agatha finished quietly.

They sat in silence for a moment, the weight of that implication settling over them. Mike shifted at Agatha's feet, sensing the tension in the air.

"May I keep these?" Agatha asked. "I'd like to show them to Detective Dawson."

Rosa hesitated, her fingers hovering over the clippings as if reluctant to let them go. Then she nodded. "Of course.

Just... be discreet. If Vivian found out I was the one asking questions..."

"I will," Agatha promised. She paused. "Rosa, have you mentioned this to anyone else?"

"No. Just you, like you said." Rosa stood, gathering her purse and empty coffee mug. "I should get back. Pepper's probably wondering where I am."

"There's more where these came from," Rosa added. "I have a whole box of scrapbooks from my years at the Acadia. I'll bring them by tomorrow, once I've had a chance to go through them properly."

At the door, Rosa paused with her hand on the knob, glancing back. "Agatha? Be careful. I have a feeling this goes deeper than we know."

After the door closed and Rosa's figure disappeared into the curtain of falling snow, Agatha remained by the fireplace, studying the two photographs laid out on the small table. Mike rested his chin on her knee, his dark eyes watching her face.

Bethany Marks had vanished after Vincent Cleary's death in the early 2000s. Henry Maddox had been investigating that same death. And now, over twenty years later, Vivian Monroe had chosen Bristol Lake—a small town with a theater that just happened to contain old Hollywood film reels from that exact era—to make her grand return.

It couldn't all be coincidence.

Agatha picked up the charity gala photo again, examining it more closely. Vivian looked confident, camera-ready, every inch the rising star. But Bethany... something in her expression told a different story. Not just shyness, but nervousness. The rigid set of her shoulders. The tightness around her eyes despite the smile.

What had Bethany known? What had she seen?

And where had she gone?

The door opened again, and Emma bustled in, shaking snow from her jacket. “Finally escaped the teenage dystopia section,” she announced, then stopped when she saw Agatha's face. “What's wrong?”

Agatha gestured to the photos. “Rosa found something. Look at these.”

Emma crossed to the fireplace, accepting the clippings Agatha handed her. She studied them in silence, her expression growing more serious with each passing moment.

“So Bethany knew Vivian,” Emma said slowly. “And then she disappeared right after Cleary died.”

“No trace,” Agatha confirmed. “Rosa went through everything. It's like Bethany ceased to exist the moment Vincent Cleary was found dead.”

Emma set the photos down, pushing her glasses up her nose—a nervous habit. “What are you thinking?”

Agatha stared into the fire, watching the flames dance behind the glass. “What if...” She hesitated, then continued. “What if Bethany witnessed something? What if she knew Vivian killed Vincent Cleary?”

Emma's eyes widened behind her glasses. “And Vivian killed her to keep her quiet?”

“It would explain why Bethany vanished so completely,” Agatha said slowly, her mind working through the theory. “No obituary, no trace. If someone wanted to make sure she never talked...” She trailed off, letting the implication hang in the air.

“And now Henry starts digging into Cleary's death,” Emma picked up the thread, her voice dropping to a whisper. “Connecting the same dots, asking the same questions...”

"And Vivian has to silence him too," Agatha finished.

They sat in silence for a moment, the theory settling between them like a shadow. Outside, the snow continued to fall, accumulating on the windowsills in soft drifts.

"We need to be very careful," Agatha said finally, gathering the photos and slipping them back into the envelope. "If we're right, if Vivian Monroe really did kill Bethany Marks and is now covering her tracks—then she's extremely dangerous."

She fell silent for a moment, absently stroking Mike's ears as he dozed beside her. "What if Henry Maddox somehow knew about this? What if Vivian couldn't risk him revealing her secret?"

Emma wrapped her arms around herself despite the warmth from the fire. Her voice dropped to barely above a whisper. "Should we go to Detective Dawson?"

"With what? A theory based on two old photographs and the fact that someone disappeared twenty years ago?" Agatha shook her head. "We need more. Concrete evidence. Something that actually connects Vivian to Bethany's disappearance or to Henry's death."

"Then what do we do?"

Agatha looked at her friend, then down at the manila envelope in her hands. "We dig deeper. And we watch Vivian Monroe very, very closely."

Mike lifted his head and let out a low whine, his ears suddenly alert. He stood and padded to the front window, staring out at the snow-covered street.

"What is it, boy?" Agatha asked.

But when she joined him at the window, there was nothing to see but the empty sidewalk, snow gathering in pristine white layers, and the quiet curtain of the storm. Still, the hair on the back of her neck prickled.

Someone was watching. She was sure of it.

"Emma," she said quietly. "Lock the door."

Emma moved immediately, turning the deadbolt with a decisive click. "What did you see?"

"Nothing," Agatha admitted. "But Mike sees something."

They stood together at the window, watching the snow fall, while Mike remained alert at their feet, a low growl rumbling deep in his chest.

Somewhere out there, in the gray afternoon gloom, Vivian Monroe was doing whatever people did when they had something to hide. And Rosa Fielding was walking home through the snow, carrying secrets that someone had already killed to protect.

10

THE PODCAST

Central Avenue was wrapped in a winter fog as Agatha unlocked the door to One Deadly Chapter Books & Brew, Mike trotting eagerly ahead of her. The schnauzer immediately made his usual inspection rounds. Checking the pastry counter, weaving between the cozy mystery shelves, and finally hopping onto his favorite velvet reading chair.

"No customers to charm yet, Mike," Agatha said, hanging up her wool coat. "But give it time."

She flipped the sign to OPEN and started the coffee maker. While waiting for it to brew, she organized the morning's order forms beside the register, humming softly.

Her thoughts drifted to yesterday's conversation with Rosa and that intriguing magazine clipping. The photograph showing Bethany Marks, standing beside Vincent Cleary had certainly raised questions. Rosa's detective skills might be amateur, but her nose for secrets was professional-grade.

"Rosa will probably waltz in sometime today," Agatha

murmured to Mike, "once she's gathered enough evidence to make her case."

Mike's tail thumped against the chair cushion as if in agreement.

Agatha smiled into her mug. "And hopefully with whatever she's been turning over in that sharp mind of hers."

Mike gave a soft huff that sounded almost like agreement.

Celeste was already at work when Agatha arrived, her long brown braid swinging as she arranged fresh pastries in the display case. Her tortoiseshell glasses had slipped down her nose, and she pushed them up absently with one flour-dusted hand. "Morning, Agatha!" she called cheerfully. "Eliza dropped off cinnamon rolls and those cranberry-orange scones you ordered. I've got the coffee brewing and the register counted."

"You're a lifesaver, Celeste," Agatha said, hanging up her coat. "How are your classes going?"

"Finished my essay on Romantic poetry at two this morning," Celeste said with a slight grimace. "But I'm awake now, I promise. Coffee helps." She gestured to the steaming pot.

Mike trotted over to greet Celeste, who bent down to scratch his ears. "Good morning to you too, Mike. Ready to charm customers today?"

"Always," Agatha said with a smile. "I'm expecting Emma this morning. We have some... research to discuss. Could you handle the front for a bit?"

"Of course!" Celeste's eyes lit up with curiosity, but she was too polite to pry. "I'll hold down the fort."

Agatha turned her attention to the new shipment of books waiting to be unpacked. The routine tasks of her bookstore were a welcome distraction from the unsettling events at the Acadia. She had just begun slicing open the first box when the bell over the door jangled sharply. Agatha looked up, expecting Emma or one of her regulars customers, but the figure who stepped inside barely reached the top of the mystery display.

He was maybe seven at first glance, though looking closer she revised that to ten, with a striped scarf wound twice around his neck and a knit hat pulled down so far it touched his eyebrows. Snow dusted his shoulders. He stood in the doorway for a moment, blinking at the warm glow of the shop with wide, serious eyes, as though he needed a second to make sure he'd come to the right place.

Mike lifted his head from the velvet chair and wagged his tail hopefully.

"Good morning," Agatha said. "Can I help you, young man?"

The boy walked up to the counter with careful, deliberate steps. He set both hands flat on the wood and opened them. A crumpled collection of bills and coins tumbled out, slightly damp from being held so tightly.

"I need a book," he announced.

Agatha kept her expression perfectly serious. "Well, you've come to the right place. We have quite a few of those."

He nodded, clearly relieved. "It's for my mom. Her birthday's on Saturday. She really likes the ones with a murder in them, but not a scary murder." He paused, thinking that over. "She said the kind where somebody figures it out and everything's okay in the end."

"Ah." Agatha stepped out from behind the counter and crouched down to his level. "That's a very specific and very good kind of book. What's your name?"

"Ethan."

"Well, Ethan, I'm Agatha. And this is Mike." The

schnauzer trotted over on cue and sniffed Ethan's boot with great interest. The boy broke into a grin for the first time.

"He's small," Ethan said.

"He is. But he has excellent taste in people." Agatha straightened. "Now, tell me about your mom. Does she like tea or coffee?"

Ethan blinked. "What does that have to do with a book?"

"More than you'd think." She smiled and gestured for him to follow her down the center aisle. "Does she like to read curled up with a warm drink, or does she stay up past her bedtime to finish one more chapter?"

Ethan considered this very seriously. "Both," he said. "She falls asleep with her book on her face sometimes. Dad says it's her superpower."

Agatha laughed, soft and genuine. "Then she's exactly my kind of reader."

She led him to the cozy mystery section, pulling out two options and holding them side by side so he could see the covers. One showed a cheerful seaside café. The other featured a quaint English cottage with a tabby cat in the window.

"The cat one," Ethan said immediately.

"Perfect choice." She turned it over and read the back cover summary aloud so he could follow along, his lips moving with the words. When she finished, he gave a firm, decisive nod.

"She'll like that one," he said.

He started gathering his money off the counter, counting it with his tongue pressed between his teeth. Agatha watched him for a moment, then quietly slid the coins and bills back toward him.

"This one's on the house," she said.

Ethan looked up sharply. "What does that mean?"

"It means it's a gift. From the bookstore." She reached beneath the counter for the green tissue paper she kept for wrapping, the kind with the tiny gold stars on it. "A birthday present deserves proper wrapping, don't you think?"

He watched her fold the paper with solemn attention, as though he was memorizing the technique. When she finished and tied a small ribbon around it, he picked it up with both hands and held it like it was something fragile and important.

"Thank you," he said.

"Tell your mom happy birthday from One Deadly Chapter." Agatha walked him to the door and held it open against the cold. "And Ethan? You did a very good thing today, coming all the way here by yourself."

He thought about that for a second. Then he pulled his hat down a little further and stepped back out into the January morning, his gift held close to his chest.

Agatha was still smiling when a girl of about thirteen burst in, pink-cheeked and out of breath, a white paper bag from Eliza's Bakery still clutched in one hand. She spotted Ethan on the sidewalk through the glass and spun back to Agatha with wide eyes. "Was he just in here? By himself?"

"He was," Agatha said pleasantly.

The girl pressed a hand to her forehead. "I told him to wait outside the bakery. I was gone for two minutes." She peered through the window at her brother, who was walking down Central Avenue with his wrapped gift and the calm, unhurried confidence of someone who had absolutely everything under control. Her exasperation softened into something that looked very much like reluctant admiration. "Did he actually buy something?"

“He did,” Agatha said. “A birthday present for your mom. He picked it out himself.”

The girl was quiet for a moment. Then she let out a small breath. “Don't tell him I said this,” she said, “but that's actually really sweet.”

“My lips are sealed.” Agatha smiled. “You'd better catch up with him before he gets too far ahead.”

The girl laughed, tugged her scarf tighter, and pushed back out into the cold. Agatha watched them through the window — the girl falling into step beside her brother, nudging his shoulder with hers, Ethan ducking away with a grin — until they disappeared around the corner.

Mike let out a small, contented sigh from his chair.

“I know,” Agatha said softly. “Me too.”

She was still smiling when Emma pushed through the door a few minutes later, cheeks pink from the cold, already talking before she'd even unwound her scarf. Her copper ponytail escaping its elastic, as if she'd rushed out without her usual careful grooming. Her tote bag sagged with books and what looked like a box of bakery muffins wedged between two hardcovers.

“You will not believe what I found,” she said, blowing on her hands to warm them. There was an urgency in her voice that immediately caught Agatha's attention.

Agatha arched a brow, trying for normalcy despite the knot of worry in her stomach. “If it's another anonymous note slipped inside Murder at the Maple Manor, I'm not ready.” The reference to last fall's mysterious correspondence which had turned out to be Mrs. Finch's letter to her sister in Vermont, packed with enough small-town gossip to keep the whole of New England entertained for a month, accidentally slipped inside the wrong book.

Emma didn't smile. Instead, she unzipped her bag with fingers that seemed to tremble and pulled out her laptop, setting it on the counter with a decisive click. "I couldn't sleep last night. I kept thinking about Henry Maddox, about what Rosa said, about all of it. So I went looking." She glanced up. "He had a podcast website. Active blog posts, episode transcripts, research notes. All of it just... sitting there, publicly available."

Agatha leaned in. "He documented his research online?"

"Podcasters do that," Emma said, already pulling up the page. "Build an audience, share their process. He had a whole series building up to what he was investigating here in Bristol Lake." She turned the laptop so Agatha could see the screen. "But it's his most recent episode that stopped me cold. It was uploaded two days before he died."

"Play it," Agatha said.

Emma clicked the audio file.

Henry's voice spilled into the shop like smoke, low, smug, but softer than usual. There was a strain to it that they'd never heard in his public persona, an urgency that cut through his usual self-importance.

"This is Henry Maddox, and I think I'm finally getting close to blowing the lid off something that Hollywood has kept buried for over twenty years."

Agatha froze. Even Mike lifted his head, his ears perked forward as if he recognized the voice of the dead man.

"There's a name that keeps popping up. Not around Bristol Lake, no, but in the dusty corners of Hollywood's past. Bethany Marks. She was Vincent Cleary's assistant. He's the screenwriter who died in 2001. Official cause? Overdose. My gut? Something darker. There was a trial. Bethany testified. Then she vanished. Poof. Like she never existed."

Emma looked up at Agatha, her eyes wide. "That name. Bethany Marks. It's the same name Rosa mentioned, isn't it?"

Agatha nodded but didn't answer. She was still listening, every nerve ending alert.

"Bethany Marks vanished after that trial like smoke through a keyhole. No forwarding address, no paper trail, nothing. People don't just disappear like that unless someone helps them — or unless they're very motivated to stay hidden. I have a theory about where she ended up, but I needed proof before I said it out loud. That's where the reel comes in. A missing short film Cleary shot before he died. Something personal, never released. If I find it, I find my answer."

The audio crackled faintly, like someone adjusting a mic or moving closer to the recording device.

"There's a local woman who claims to have information. Says she knows something about what really happened to Cleary back in 2001." He paused, amusement creeping into his voice. "Though what someone tucked away in a little town like this could possibly know about Hollywood." He let out a short laugh. "Well, I suppose I'll have to charm it out of her."

Emma looked up slowly. "A local woman with inside knowledge about what happened in 2001."

Agatha met her eyes. "Rosa."

His voice dropped even lower, almost conspiratorial.

The recording wound down, Henry's voice taking on that familiar smug confidence. "Stay tuned, folks. Next episode, I think we'll have something very interesting to share. This is Henry Maddox, and the truth is closer than ever."

The audio ended with his usual sign-off music, cheerful and completely at odds with everything they'd just heard.

Emma closed the player. "He had no idea."

"No," Agatha agreed quietly. "He thought he was about to break the story of his career."

Emma scrolled down the page. "There's more. He kept research notes on his blog. Posted them publicly, like he was daring someone to come after him." She turned the screen so Agatha could read.

The post was titled simply: Questions That Need Answers.

Agatha read the bullet points slowly.

Where is Bethany Marks?

Hidden reel? Projection booth? Archives? Check behind old panels.

Local Woman. Thinks she knows something. Watch her.

Agatha read the list twice, her eyes lingering on the third line. Watch her.

"Emma," she said slowly. "He was watching Rosa. He may have followed her. Asked her questions. She didn't tell me that."

Emma hesitated, biting her lower lip. "Maybe she didn't know? He might have been discreet."

Agatha stared at the counter for a moment. "Or maybe she was trying to protect herself. If she knew someone was following her, asking about the past..."

The implications hung in the air between them, unspoken but unmistakable.

Mike glanced toward the front window, ears perked, then settled back down with a small huff.

Agatha checked her phone. Nothing from Rosa. She set it face down on the counter with a small sigh. "She mentioned she might bring some of her old scrapbooks by if she found anything worth sharing. Haven't heard from her."

Emma glanced out at the gray sky. "Knowing Rosa, she

probably decided her knees weren't up to it and went back to bed with Pepper and a crossword."

Agatha smiled at the image. "You're probably right." She reached for her tea. "I'll check in with her later."

The bell above the door jingled, causing both women to jump. Mike's head shot up, ears alert.

Rosa Fielding stood in the doorway, looking perfectly ordinary in her gray cardigan and sensible shoes. Her silver hair was neatly combed, her purse clutched in both hands in front of her.

"Rosa!" Emma said, unable to hide her surprise. "We were just talking about you."

"Were you?" Rosa's smile seemed stiff, her eyes darting around the shop as if checking who else might be present. "Nothing too scandalous, I hope."

Emma and Agatha exchanged glances.

"Rosa, perfect timing," Agatha said warmly. "Did you manage to dig out those scrapbooks?"

Rosa waved her hand dismissively. "Oh, that. I was being silly. Getting caught up in old memories and making connections that weren't there." She walked to the counter with measured steps. "After a good night's sleep, I realized I was completely mistaken."

Agatha studied her closely. Rosa's hands were steady, her makeup applied with her usual precision, but something in her demeanor seemed rehearsed.

"Mistaken about what, exactly?" Agatha asked.

"All of it, really. Vivian Monroe, the theater, all that old Hollywood gossip. I was making far too much of nothing."

Mike circled Rosa once, then retreated to Agatha's side, pressing against her leg.

"What about Bethany Marks?" Agatha asked quietly.

A flicker of something crossed Rosa's face before her pleasant expression returned. "Bethany who? No, no. I was thinking of someone else entirely. A different actress, different time." She glanced at her watch. "I can't stay. I have a doctor's appointment. Just wanted to let you know not to expect those clippings. It was all a misunderstanding."

She turned to leave, moving with unusual haste.

"Rosa," Agatha called after her. "Are you sure everything's alright?"

Rosa paused at the door, her back to them. For a moment, her shoulders seemed to slump, but when she turned, her smile was firmly in place.

"Everything's fine, dear. Just getting old and confused. You know how it is." She waved once and was gone, the bell jangling in her wake.

Silence filled the shop for a long moment.

"That," Emma said finally, "was odd."

"Yesterday she was absolutely convinced she'd stumbled onto something significant," Agatha said, moving to the window and watching Rosa make her way down the sidewalk at a brisk pace. "People don't just reverse like that. Not without a reason."

Mike whined softly, still staring at the door.

"So much for Rosa's scrapbooks," Emma said. "Whatever she found, she's not sharing it now."

"Then we work with what we have." Agatha turned back to the laptop still open on the counter. "Henry posted everything. His research, his sources, his theories. All of it sitting right there on his blog for anyone to read."

11

VIVIAN'S OUTBURST

Lorraine arrived at the bookstore in a swirl of floral perfume and jangling bracelets. “Mes chéries!” she announced, as if they hadn't seen each other just yesterday. “You will never believe what I just heard!” She paused for effect, glancing between them expectantly.

“Hello to you too, Lorraine,” Agatha said with a smile. “Coffee?”

“No time for pleasantries!” Lorraine waved away the offer, dropping her oversized purse onto the counter with a thud. “I've just come from the bank. Had to order new checks.”

Emma raised an eyebrow. “You still use checks?”

“Of course I do,” Lorraine replied, looking affronted. “How else would people know I have the special series with the Parisian scenes? The Eiffel Tower practically glitters on them.” She adjusted her scarf with a flourish. “Besides, the dry cleaner doesn't take cards, and Monsieur Pierre deserves to see a little culture when handling my transactions.”

Agatha and Emma exchanged amused glances.

"Anyway," Lorraine continued, leaning in conspiratorially, "that's not the important part. Lila. You know, the cashier with that adorable pixie cut who's dating the fire chief's son, well, she couldn't wait to tell me." She lowered her voice to a stage whisper that could probably be heard three shops away. "Rosa Fielding made a huge deposit this morning. Huge! Lila shouldn't have told me, of course. Very unprofessional, but she was simply bursting with the news."

"A deposit?" Agatha repeated, her earlier conversation with Rosa suddenly cast in a new light.

"Cash," Lorraine emphasized, eyes wide. "A stack of bills that barely fit in the deposit envelope. Lila said Rosa looked nervous, kept glancing over her shoulder like she was in a spy movie." Lorraine demonstrated, whipping her head around dramatically and nearly knocking over a display of bookmarks.

Emma steadied the display. "That's... Interesting timing."

"Interesting? It's scandalous!" Lorraine declared. "Where does a retired usher suddenly get that kind of money? Unless..." she gasped, pressing a hand to her chest, "...unless she robbed a bank! Oh, but that can't be right, because she was in the bank." She frowned, momentarily confused by her own theory.

"I don't think Rosa's turned to bank robbery," Agatha said dryly.

"No, you're right," Lorraine agreed. "Her knees are terrible. She could never make a quick getaway."

Mike, who had been dozing in a patch of winter sunlight streaming through the window, raised his head as if following the conversation with interest.

"Rosa was just here," Emma explained. "Acting strangely."

"How strange?" Lorraine demanded, immediately intrigued.

"She came in to tell us she was mistaken about recognizing connections between the Monroe sisters and Bethany Marks." Agatha shrugged, though she didn't look convinced. "Said it was all a misunderstanding."

Lorraine's eyebrows shot up. "After she was so certain yesterday? That doesn't sound like our Rosa. She once maintained for six years that the mayor's wife's lemon bars contained store-bought filling, despite all evidence to the contrary."

"And now we find out she's making mysterious cash deposits," Emma added.

The three women fell silent, the implications hanging in the air between them.

"You don't think..." Lorraine began, her theatrical manner momentarily subdued.

"That she got paid to forget what she saw?" Agatha finished the thought. "I don't know. It seems so... Unlike her."

"Everyone has their price," Lorraine said, suddenly philosophical. "Even Rosa Fielding, apparently."

Mike gave a soft whine from his spot on the floor, as if offering his canine opinion on the matter.

"We shouldn't jump to conclusions," Agatha cautioned. "But it certainly adds another piece to the puzzle."

"A very peculiar piece," Emma agreed.

Lorraine beamed, pleased to have delivered such valuable intelligence. "Well, my work here is done! I've brought vital information to the investigation." She picked up her purse with a flourish. "Now, if you'll excuse me, I need to get to my hair appointment. Jean-Claude is trying something new with lowlights today."

"Jean-Claude is Bill from Scranton and you know it," Emma called after her.

"In my head, he's Jean-Claude," Lorraine replied loftily as she swept toward the door. "And that's what matters!"

The door swung shut behind her as she departed, leaving a lingering cloud of perfume and questions in her wake.

Agatha turned to Emma. "What do you make of that?"

"I think," Emma said slowly, "that someone just paid Rosa Fielding to forget whatever she remembered about the Monroe sisters and Bethany Marks."

"The question is," Agatha mused, "who has that kind of money to spend on keeping secrets?"

They both glanced toward the window, their gazes drawn to the silhouette of the Acadia Theater rising against the gray winter sky.

By late afternoon, a gray chill had settled over Bristol Lake`. Agatha wrapped her scarf tighter around her neck as she crossed Central Avenue, her breath visible in small white puffs. Her boots clacked with purpose against the icy cobblestones, each step deliberate and determined. Mike trotted beside her on alert, his ears flicking at every sound, his paws leaving small prints in the dusting of snow that had accumulated throughout the day.

The Acadia loomed ahead, its freshly painted marquee gleaming despite the somber day. The polished glass doors reflected the gray sky, while sleek chrome handles shone with meticulous care. It was beautiful, a perfect restoration of bygone glamour, but in the fading winter light it looked less like a beacon of revival and more like a glamorous lie, all surface shine concealing rot beneath.

Mike hesitated on the sidewalk. His body tensed, a quiet growl rumbling low in his chest. He planted his feet, reluctant to approach.

"I know," Agatha murmured, crouching briefly to stroke his head, her gloved hand gentle on his fur. "I feel it too."

Inside the theater lobby, the warmth of indoor heating clashed with the empty hush of off-hours. Their footsteps echoed against the marble floor, announcing their presence to whatever ghosts might be listening.

A young woman wearing a headset and an oversized Acadia Theater sweatshirt looked up from her clipboard. Her blonde hair was pulled into a neat ponytail, her expression professionally pleasant but with the faint wariness of someone who'd been told to expect trouble.

"Miss Royale?" she said, squinting. "Miss Monroe is expecting you. Office is down that hallway." She pointed toward a corridor behind the concession stand, then quickly returned to her clipboard, clearly eager to avoid further involvement.

Agatha nodded her thanks, surprised that Vivian had anticipated her visit. Had someone called ahead? Or was Vivian simply waiting for her, knowing that sooner or later, Agatha would come with questions?

She guided Mike across the polished floor, passing under art deco chandeliers that cast a warm golden glow. Between towering poster frames, Agatha caught glimpses of upcoming screenings: *Casablanca*, *Sunset Boulevard*, *The Big Sleep*. Fitting, she thought. All beautiful. All laced with secrets.

The office door stood partially open, revealing a sleek,

modern space that contrasted sharply with the vintage glamour of the theater. Here, everything was clean lines and monochrome elegance. White walls, black furniture, silver accents.

Vivian Monroe stood near the tall window, her silhouette outlined by the fading winter light. She wore a charcoal-gray blazer over a crisp white blouse, both impeccably tailored to her slender frame. A string of pearls gleamed at her throat. Every inch the poised former starlet, except for the way her fingers gripped the back of the chair, white-knuckled.

"Miss Royale," she said without turning. "To what do I owe this unannounced visit?"

Agatha stepped inside, closing the door behind her with a soft click. Mike stayed close, his eyes never leaving Vivian. "I wanted to talk about Henry Maddox."

Vivian turned then, slow and precise. Her icy blue eyes narrowed, unreadable behind the mask of perfect makeup. "I've already spoken to the police. Twice, in fact."

"I know," Agatha said, maintaining a calm she didn't entirely feel. "But I'm not the police."

Vivian's lips curved into a tight, practiced smile that never reached her eyes. "No. You're the town's self-appointed detective. How quaint." The word carried a subtle barb.

Agatha didn't rise to it. "Henry left behind a trail. His podcast, his blog, he documented everything he discovered. About Vincent Cleary's death. About Bethany Marks and her disappearance after the trial. It's all public now. Anyone with an internet connection can listen to his theories."

A flicker of surprise crossed Vivian's face before she masked it, but not quickly enough. Her jaw tightened almost imperceptibly.

"He named you specifically," Agatha continued, watching Vivian's reaction. "Said you were friends with Bethany. That you might know what happened to her after she testified and vanished."

The mention of the name caused a visible shift. Vivian's shoulders squared, her spine straightened, the practiced calm slipping a fraction.

"I'm not accusing you of anything," Agatha said gently. "But you knew her, didn't you? Bethany Marks."

Vivian moved behind the desk and sat with deliberate elegance. She picked up a cut-glass paperweight from the desk, rolled it between her fingers. The crystal caught the light, sending tiny rainbows across the white walls.

"Bethany was..." she paused, choosing her words with care, "a friend. Once."

"And Vincent Cleary?"

A longer pause this time. The paperweight made another circuit between her manicured fingers. "He was brilliant. Troubled. Destructive." Each word seemed carefully selected.

Agatha stepped closer to the desk. "Henry believed there was a missing reel. Something Cleary filmed before he died. He thought it might be hidden somewhere in this building. He mentioned it specifically in his last blog post."

Vivian said nothing, but her fingers tightened around the paperweight, knuckles whitening.

"He also mentioned Rosa Fielding," Agatha continued, watching Vivian's face closely. "That she worked here back when the Acadia first opened. That she might remember things from that time. Did Rosa talk to you?"

Vivian's eyes snapped up, a flash of genuine alarm breaking through her carefully maintained façade. "Why would Rosa come to me?"

"She worked here in the early days. She might've recognized something... Or someone." Agatha let the implication hang in the air between them.

Vivian stood abruptly, the chair rolling back and hitting the wall with a dull thud. "Is that what this is? You're dragging a poor woman's name into your amateur investigation?" Her voice rose, the first genuine emotion Agatha had heard from her.

Mike let out a quiet growl. Not at Vivian, just into the room, as if sensing the charge in the air. His ears were flat against his head, his body tense beside Agatha's leg.

"I didn't kill him," Vivian whispered, her gaze locking with Agatha's. For the first time, the mask slipped completely, revealing something raw and desperate beneath. "You may think I'm cold, Miss Royale. And maybe I am. But I didn't kill anyone."

The vehemence in her voice rang true, or at least, Agatha thought it did. This felt real. Her gaze softened. "Then help me. Who would want to keep that reel hidden? Why was Henry so convinced he knew where Bethany Marks ended up?"

Vivian's eyes drifted to the window, where the last of the winter daylight was fading to dusk. Outside, streetlights were beginning to flicker on, casting a warm glow over the snow-dusted street. "You know what Hollywood does to women who speak up, don't you? They ruin them. Silence them. Or turn them into something else, someone else. Bethany... She tried to disappear before the machine could devour her."

Agatha waited, giving Vivian space to continue if she chose to.

Vivian turned back, her voice hardening even as her eyes

remained vulnerable. "I don't know what Bethany's doing now. But I stayed away for a reason. To survive."

Agatha nodded once, her heart thudding. "And if Rosa recognized someone from those old photographs..."

"She would be mistaken," Vivian said firmly, but something in her eyes wavered.

Agatha reached for the doorknob. Mike stood immediately, ready to follow.

Just as she opened the door, Vivian spoke again, her voice barely audible. "If Rosa says she recognizes me from somewhere in the past... She's either lying or confused."

Agatha paused, glanced over her shoulder. Vivian sat perfectly still, her face half in shadow, looking suddenly older, wearier. For a moment, Agatha could see past the glamour to the woman beneath, someone who had perhaps been running for a very long time.

"Interesting," Agatha said quietly. "I never mentioned Rosa recognizing you or Bianca specifically." She stepped into the corridor, the door closing softly behind her. Mike pressed against her leg as they made their way back through the lobby, past the receptionist, and out into the cold evening air.

The air outside felt cleaner somehow, easier to breathe after the charged atmosphere of Vivian's office. Agatha took a deep breath, letting the cold air clear her head. Snow was falling again, light flurries that caught in the glow of the streetlights.

The streetlights had fully illuminated now as she walked back toward the bookstore, her boots crunching softly in the fresh snow. She found herself replaying Vivian's words. Not what she'd said, but what she hadn't. She hadn't denied knowing where Bethany was. She hadn't expressed shock at the idea that Rosa might have recognized someone. And she had reacted defensively to a question Agatha hadn't even asked.

Agatha pulled out her phone and dialed Emma's number.

"I just spoke with Vivian," she said when Emma answered. "And I think we need to talk to Bianca. As soon as possible."

12

QUIET BIANCA

The morning sun broke through the clouds just after nine, casting weak winter light across Bristol Lake's snow-dusted streets. Inside One Deadly Chapter Books & Brew, the warmth from the radiator and the scent of fresh cinnamon rolls created a cozy haven against the January chill.

Agatha had just finished arranging a new display of vintage Agatha Christie novels when the door opened. Mrs. Delaney from the flower shop shuffled in, her arms full of paper-wrapped bouquets.

"Good morning, dear!" she called out cheerfully, setting the flowers on the counter with a satisfied sigh. "These are for the library's reading corner. Emma asked me to drop them here since you two are meeting this morning." She unwound her scarf, revealing a hand-knitted sweater decorated with tiny embroidered daisies. "Amaryllis. A little preview of spring even though we're buried in snow."

"They're beautiful," Agatha said, admiring the vivid red blooms. "Let me get them in water before Emma arrives."

"Oh, I can do that!" Celeste appeared from the back room, wiping her hands on her apron. Her long braid was coiled into a bun today, held in place with what looked like a pencil. "I just finished restocking the Christie Corner. These are beautiful, Mrs. Delaney!"

"Thank you, dear," Mrs. Delaney said warmly. "You're looking well. How's school?"

"Exhausting," Celeste admitted cheerfully as she unwrapped the flowers. "But I love working here. It's much more interesting than my economics textbook."

Mrs. Delaney settled into one of the reading chairs with a contented sigh. "I've got fifteen minutes before I need to open the shop. Mrs. Patterson is bringing me some of her famous banana bread as a thank-you for the funeral arrangement I made for her sister. Poor thing passed last Tuesday."

She carried the bouquets to the back to find a vase, leaving Mrs. Delany to settle into one of the reading chairs.

MIKE TROTTED over and placed his head on Mrs. Delaney's knee, his tail wagging hopefully.

"And hello to you too, handsome," she cooed, scratching behind his ears. "I heard you've been quite the detective's assistant lately."

Before Agatha could respond, the bell jingled again. Mr. Whitaker bustled in, shaking snow from his galoshes.

"Morning, morning!" he announced, his bow tie. Today a festive red with white snowflakes, crooked as usual. "Agatha, you'll never believe what I saw. That investor fellow, Gordon Lane, coming out of the Acadia at seven in the morning. Seven! What business does an investor have at a theater before the sun's properly up?"

"Maybe he's very dedicated," Agatha suggested, filling a vase with water for Mrs. Delaney's flowers.

"Hmph. Dedicated to what, I'd like to know." Mr. Whitaker tapped his nose knowingly. "Mark my words, there's something fishy about that man. Too slick by half."

Mrs. Delaney leaned forward conspiratorially. "I heard from Lorraine, who heard from Lila at the bank. That he's been asking questions about property values along the waterfront."

"See?" Mr. Whitaker declared triumphantly. "Fishy!"

Agatha smiled, letting the familiar rhythm of small-town gossip wash over her. This was Bristol Lake at its finest. Neighbors caring about neighbors, everyone invested in the community's well-being, even if their methods sometimes involved a healthy dose of speculation.

"Mr. Whitaker," she said gently, "did you come in for a book, or just to warn us about mysterious investors?"

He blinked, momentarily thrown off his investigative track. "Book! Yes, of course. Do you have the new Louise Penny? I've been waiting for it."

"Hold shelf, bottom right," Agatha replied with a knowing smile.

"You're a treasure, my dear." He shuffled toward the shelf, then paused. "But seriously, keep an eye on that Lane fellow. Something's not right."

After Mr. Whitaker collected his book and departed, and Mrs. Delaney left, the shop settled into a peaceful quiet. Agatha stood by the window, watching the morning unfold. Across the street, Eliza was sweeping snow from her doorstep. Two doors down, the antique shop owner was arranging a window display. This was the Bristol Lake she loved. The sense of community, of belonging, of people watching out for one another.

Even with a murder investigation hanging over the town, life continued. It had to.

Celeste appeared from the back room and placed the flower bouquets on the counter for Emma to pick up later. "I'll finish restocking the mystery section," she said, adjusting her tortoiseshell glasses before disappearing back into the shelves.

The door opened again, and Emma entered, her cheeks pink from the cold, her laptop bag slung over one shoulder.

"Sorry I'm late," she said, unwinding her scarf. "I got caught up listening to more of Henry's podcast episodes. There's so much material."

"Mrs. Delaney dropped off those flowers for the library," Agatha said, gesturing to the bright red amaryllis on the counter. "Said they're for the reading corner."

"Oh perfect!" Emma said, glancing at them with a smile. "A little preview of spring. I'll take them with me when I leave."

"Find anything new?" Agatha asked, moving to the counter where Emma was setting up.

"Maybe. But first... " Emma pulled out a thermos from her bag, ". I brought hot chocolate. The real kind, with actual melted chocolate and whipped cream."

Agatha smiled. "You're speaking my language."

They settled into the reading nook by the fireplace, steaming mugs in hand, Emma's laptop open between them on the small table. Mike curled at their feet, content in the warmth.

"Okay," Emma said, pulling up a browser window. "I've been going through Henry's blog archives and earlier podcast episodes. He was obsessed with the Vincent Cleary case for months before he came to Bristol Lake."

She clicked through to a blog post dated six months earlier. "This is where it really starts. He'd gotten access to trial transcripts from Cleary's death investigation. Look at this passage."

Agatha leaned in to read:

"The star witness was Bethany Marks, Cleary's assistant. Her testimony was compelling. She'd found him, called 911, cooperated fully with investigators. But what struck me was how quickly she disappeared after the trial. No interviews, no follow-up, nothing. For someone who'd been at the center of such a high-profile case, her silence was deafening. Where did Bethany Marks go?"

"He was fixated on her disappearance," Emma said. "Every few posts, he'd circle back to it. Where did she go? Why did she vanish so completely?"

Agatha sipped her hot chocolate thoughtfully. "And then he comes to Bristol Lake and dies in a theater owned by women with Hollywood connections."

"Right. But here's what's interesting." Emma scrolled to another post. "He never directly accused the Monroe sisters of anything. He speculated, theorized, asked questions, but he never made direct allegations."

"Smart," Agatha murmured. "Keeps him from being sued for libel."

"Or," Emma said slowly, "maybe he genuinely didn't know. Maybe he was still trying to figure it out when he died."

They sat in silence for a moment, the only sounds the crackling of the fire and Mike's soft snoring.

"I think I need to talk to Bianca," Agatha said finally. "Vivian was defensive, aggressive almost. But Bianca... She's been quiet through all of this. Almost invisible."

"The quiet ones are always the most interesting," Emma observed.

Agatha finished her hot chocolate and stood, her decision made. "Will you be here for a while? In case I need backup?"

Emma nodded. "I'll keep digging through Henry's archives. Call if you need me."

THE WALK to the Acadia Theater took only ten minutes, but it felt longer in the cold. The sky had turned a pale gray, threatening more snow, and Agatha's breath made small clouds in the frigid air. Mike trotted ahead, his nose working overtime as he sniffed at snowbanks and frozen puddles.

When they reached the Acadia's wide front steps, Mike gave a short, alert bark. Not the deep, warning growl he'd given when they'd visited Vivian, this was more curious, questioning.

The heavy glass door swung open before Agatha could reach for the handle.

"Miss Royale," Bianca Monroe greeted from just inside the foyer, her figure silhouetted against the warm interior lighting.

She wore a soft, dove-gray blouse tucked into cream slacks, her dark hair twisted into a low chignon at the nape of her neck. Nothing about her appearance suggested distress or worry. No smudged makeup, no wrinkled clothing, no dark circles under her eyes. Her voice was smooth, feather-light, with no trace of panic or guilt. She smiled as if nothing in the world had gone wrong, as if Henry Maddox hadn't died in this very building.

"I wasn't expecting a visit," she said, though she didn't

look particularly surprised to see Agatha. If anything, there was a calm readiness in her posture, as if she'd been anticipating this moment.

Agatha returned the smile, keeping it neutral, professional. "I thought I'd stop by and ask a few questions. After what happened to Henry Maddox, I'm sure you understand why people are curious."

Bianca's smile faded for just a moment, but her eyes never left Agatha's. Her steady gaze was disconcerting. Not hostile, but unnaturally focused, as if she were memorizing every detail of Agatha's face.

"Of course," she said after a brief pause. "Come in. Would you like some tea? I just brewed a pot of Earl Grey."

Agatha followed her into the small lounge near the back of the lobby, a space clearly designed for private meetings and intimate conversations. Unlike Vivian's stark, modern office, this room felt deliberately cozy. Warm earth tones, overstuffed chairs upholstered in rich velvet, and a low table set with a china teapot and delicate porcelain cups that looked like antiques. Theatrical prints decorated the walls. It Happened One Night, Roman Holiday, All About Eve. All precisely curated for nostalgia, charm, and just enough glamour to distract from any serious conversation.

Mike curled beside Agatha's chair, settling onto the thick Oriental rug with a contented sigh. No growl. Not even a twitch of suspicion. If anything, he looked mildly fond of Bianca, his eyes following her movements with interest rather than wariness.

Bianca poured the tea with graceful ease, her hands steady, her movements precise and practiced. Not a drop spilled as she tilted the pot, the amber liquid streaming into the cups in a perfect arc.

"I heard you spoke to Vivian yesterday," she said, setting the teacup before Agatha. The porcelain made a delicate clink against the saucer. "She mentioned you had some concerns."

"I did," Agatha replied, noting how quickly information traveled between the two women. Had they discussed how to handle her questions? Coordinated their responses?

"And how did that go?" Bianca's tone was light, conversational, but her eyes remained watchful.

"She was tense," Agatha said, deliberately understating Vivian's reaction. "Understandably. Henry's podcast raised some serious questions about her past."

Agatha stirred her tea without drinking it, watching Bianca over the rim of the cup. The tea smelled wonderful. Bergamot and a hint of something floral, but caution kept her from tasting it.

Bianca's expression didn't change, not even a flicker of discomfort at the mention of the dead man. "He tried to interview me once. Caught me in the lobby about a week before the opening. I told him I was just the business side of things. Vivian handled the creative vision. I wouldn't have known anything useful about Hollywood gossip or old scandals."

"Which were?" Agatha prompted.

"Old rumors, mostly," Bianca replied with a slight shrug. "Forgotten dramas from decades ago. I got the impression he was trying to make a name for himself by reviving stories most people had moved on from." She sipped her tea, the picture of composure. "Not my area of expertise."

"You weren't involved in the theater world before this?" Agatha kept her tone casual, curious rather than accusatory.

Bianca gave a soft laugh, the sound musical and light.

"Not unless you count coordinating talent schedules for a few low-budget film festivals. I was much more involved in arts administration, budgets, grants, logistics. The behind-the-scenes work that makes creative visions possible."

It was a perfect answer, specific enough to sound authentic, vague enough to be difficult to verify. And it neatly explained her connection to Vivian without placing her directly in Hollywood's spotlight.

Agatha watched her closely, noting the careful way Bianca held herself, poised but not rigid, friendly but not overly familiar. Everything about her seemed deliberately calibrated to appear normal, approachable, forgettable.

"What made you and Vivian decide to invest in the Acadia?" Agatha asked, changing tack. "Small-town theaters aren't exactly known for their profit margins."

Bianca looked around the lounge with what seemed like genuine fondness, her gaze lingering on the theatrical prints. "Vivian became fascinated when your aunt Edna mentioned Bristol Lake. She and Beatrice had dinner with us one evening, telling stories about this charming town in Maine with its beautiful old theater sitting unused." Her voice softened. "When we looked into it, Vivian seemed almost... Transfixed. She said it reminded her of a theater from her early career, a place that had meant something to her. What started as casual conversation over wine became a serious investment opportunity, and then a passion project." Bianca shrugged with a small smile. "Sometimes opportunity finds you in the strangest ways."

The response sounded rehearsed to Agatha's ears, like a line from a press release polished through multiple tellings.

"Are you two actually sisters?" Agatha asked, watching Bianca's reaction. "I've heard rumors around town..."

For a fraction of a second, Bianca's expression froze before she smiled again. "Not by blood, no. We met in Santa Fe, actually. I was consulting for a gallery opening. Vivian attended, we struck up a conversation, and discovered we had so much in common. By pure coincidence, we even shared the same last name, which felt like fate." She spread her hands in a graceful gesture. "We became so close so quickly that I truly consider her my sister, the family you choose, you know? It seemed easier to let people assume we were related by blood rather than constantly explaining. In Bristol Lake especially, people seem to find comfort in traditional family connections." She shrugged with a small smile. "Does it really matter? Family is what you make it."

The story was plausible, detailed, even charming. But that tiny hesitation. That flash of something before the smile returned, that was real.

Agatha nodded, letting the silence stretch between them. Sometimes silence was the most effective interview technique, creating a vacuum that people felt compelled to fill.

Bianca didn't take the bait. She simply folded her hands in her lap and waited, matching Agatha's patience with her own.

"I know people suspect Vivian," she said finally, breaking the silence on her own terms. "I understand. She can come off as... Guarded. Dramatic. But she's been through a lot. The entertainment industry isn't kind to women, especially as they age."

"And you?" Agatha asked, leaning forward. "What have you been through?"

The question was direct, perhaps even rude, but she asked it anyway.

Bianca laughed lightly, the sound not quite reaching

her eyes. "Not nearly as much. My life has been blessedly ordinary. Though moving to a town like this is its own adventure." She gestured toward the window, where Central Avenue was visible through the falling snow. "Everyone knows everyone. Nothing stays private for long."

There was an edge to her words, despite her light tone.

Agatha took a slow sip of her tea, finally tasting it. It was excellent, perfectly brewed, the right temperature. "Rosa Fielding found something interesting recently," she said casually. "Some old magazine clippings from Hollywood events in the late nineties and early 2000s."

The statement hung in the air between them. Bianca blinked, just once. The only sign that the words had affected her at all. "Oh? From Hollywood events?" Her voice remained steady, but her fingers tightened almost imperceptibly around her teacup.

"Pictures from various galas and premieres. Vincent Cleary appeared in several of them." Agatha paused. "So did a young woman identified as Bethany Marks. She was his assistant."

"How interesting," a smile crossed Bianca's face, pleasant and perfectly measured. "I'm sure Vivian would love to see them. She worked with Cleary on *Midnight Harbor* years ago. She always speaks highly of him."

"There was one picture in particular that caught Rosa's attention," Agatha continued. "A charity gala. It showed Bethany Marks and Vivian Monroe together. They were friends, apparently. Arms linked, smiling for the cameras."

Something flickered across Bianca's face, recognition? Fear? It was gone too quickly to identify.

"That's lovely," Bianca said smoothly. "Vivian had so

many friends in those circles. I'm sure she'd remember Bethany if reminded."

"The thing is," Agatha said slowly, "Bethany Marks disappeared after Vincent Cleary died. There was a trial. He died of an apparent overdose, Bethany testified, and then she vanished completely. No trace of her anywhere."

"How tragic," Bianca murmured. "Hollywood can be overwhelming. Perhaps she wanted a quiet life away from all that scrutiny."

"Perhaps," Agatha agreed. "Henry Maddox certainly thought so. His entire podcast series was built around trying to find out what happened to her. Where she went. Why she disappeared so completely."

Bianca set her teacup down with a delicate clink. "And did he have any theories?"

"Several," Agatha said. "He believed Bethany Marks was still alive, living under a new name somewhere quiet. Somewhere far from Hollywood's spotlight. He thought she might even be here in Bristol Lake."

The silence that followed felt heavy, charged with unspoken implications.

"Well," Bianca said finally, her smile returning but not quite reaching her eyes, "that would certainly make for an interesting story, wouldn't it? Though I can't imagine why she'd choose our little theater for her hiding place."

"Can't you?" Agatha asked softly.

Bianca met her gaze steadily. "Miss Royale, I understand you're trying to make sense of Henry Maddox's death. But sometimes the simplest explanation is the right one. He was a man obsessed with conspiracy theories and unsolved mysteries. Perhaps he simply asked the wrong person the wrong question at the wrong time."

"And who would that wrong person be?"

Bianca stood gracefully, signaling that the conversation was over. "That's for the police to determine, don't you think? I'm just glad they're handling the investigation professionally." She moved toward the door, her movements fluid and unhurried. "I do hope you'll come to our opening night. We're showing Casablanca, a classic for a new beginning."

A reopening, Agatha noted. *As if the first attempt could simply be rescheduled away, along with everything that had happened in that projection booth.*

Agatha stood as well, Mike rising with her. "I wouldn't miss it."

At the door, Bianca paused, her hand resting lightly on the frame. "You know, Miss Royale, Rosa Fielding has quite an imagination. All those years working in theaters, surrounded by drama and performance. Sometimes reality and fiction blur together for people like her. I wouldn't put too much stock in old photographs and half-remembered faces."

"I'll keep that in mind," Agatha said.

As she stepped out into the cold afternoon air, Mike pressed close to her leg. Despite his earlier comfort with Bianca, he seemed eager to leave now, his ears flat against his head.

Agatha looked back at the Acadia, its elegant façade gleaming in the winter light. Bianca stood in the doorway, watching them leave, her expression unreadable. She'd had been poised, pleasant, helpful even. But she'd also been evasive in the most skillful way. Answering questions without really answering them, deflecting with charm and grace.

And she'd never once asked which photographs Rosa had found. Never asked to see them. Never expressed surprise that her supposed sister had been friends with a woman who'd disappeared under mysterious circumstances.

Back at the bookstore, Emma looked up eagerly when Agatha entered, knocking snow from her boots.

"How did it go?"

"She never once asked to see the photographs," Agatha said, unwinding her scarf. "And she never seemed surprised by any of it."

Emma let that sink in. "So she already knew."

"Or she's a very good actress." Agatha settled into the reading chair by the fire. Mike hopped up beside her, curling into a tight ball. "Vivian gets defensive. Bianca just... redirects. Politely. Perfectly."

Her phone buzzed with a text from Lorraine: *Just saw Gordon Lane leaving the Acadia again. Third time this week! Very suspicious!!!*

Agatha showed Emma the message.

"Another thread to pull," Emma said.

"We need someone who knows that building inside and out," Agatha said. "Someone who's been there long enough to know where its secrets might be hiding."

Emma's eyes lit up. "Quentin."

13

MORE THAN A SCANDAL

The Thursday evening book club had been Agatha's first initiative when she reopened the bookstore, and it had become Bristol Lake's most coveted weekly gathering. Never had it devolved into quite such delightful chaos as tonight.

"I'm simply saying," Lorraine declared, waving a chocolate biscotti like a conductor's baton, "that if Miss Marple had access to modern technology, ninety percent of Agatha Christie's mysteries would have been solved by page twelve!"

"Sacrilege!" gasped Mrs. Finch, the retired English teacher whose cardigan collection rivaled the shop's inventory. "The whole point is the psychological insight!"

Emma bit her lip to keep from laughing as she refilled the teacups around the table. The gentle fragrance of steeping tea hung in the air, wrapping the room in warmth.

"Psychological insight?" Octavia Butler snorted, setting down her glass with authority. "Half the time she just happened to remember some village scandal from 1902 that paralleled the current murder."

"That's pattern recognition," Agatha offered, arranging a fresh plate of Eliza's lemon squares on the center table. "It's a legitimate investigative technique."

Eliza, who had closed her bakery early to attend, nodded vigorously. "It's like how I can tell exactly who baked what at the county fair just by looking at the crust pattern."

"That's not investigation, that's your competitive nature," Gladys teased, adjusting her silver-framed reading glasses.

Mike trotted between the chairs, accepting illegal treats from every member despite Agatha's standing "no feeding the detective dog" rule.

"Speaking of pattern recognition," Lorraine stage-whispered, "has anyone else noticed that every time Mayor Crawford wears his lucky blue tie, the town council mysteriously approves his budget proposals?"

"Correlation is not causation," Emma murmured, topping off Gladys's glass.

"Tell that to his dry cleaner," Lorraine shot back. "That tie gets emergency service every third Thursday!"

Celeste, who had been quietly taking notes for the book club newsletter, couldn't contain her laughter any longer. "It's true! I've seen his assistant rushing it to the cleaner's myself!"

The table erupted in laughter just as Mayor Crawford himself stepped inside, looking perplexed at the sudden silence that fell.

"Don't stop on my account," he said, adjusting his tie, bright blue with tiny sailboats. "I just came to pick up that nautical mystery Agatha ordered for me."

Mrs. Finch choked on her wine while Octavia developed a sudden, consuming interest in the ceiling tiles.

"Right here, Mayor," Agatha said smoothly, retrieving a

wrapped package from behind the counter. "Just arrived yesterday."

As the mayor paid and left, the collective restraint of the book club collapsed entirely. Tears of suppressed laughter streamed down Lorraine's face, threatening her expertly applied mascara.

"Third Thursday!" she wheezed, dabbing at her eyes. "Right on schedule!"

"This book club was my best idea ever," Agatha murmured to Emma as they watched Eliza and Celeste comparing notes on their favorite fictional detectives.

"Absolutely," Emma agreed, topping off Agatha's glass. "Though I'm not sure the Bristol Lake Gazette would agree after that discussion about poisoning techniques last month."

"It was strictly academic," Agatha protested with a grin.

"Tell that to Mrs. Peterson. She wouldn't eat her husband's cooking for a week."

For a moment, there were no mysteries to solve except whether Gladys had secretly eaten the last lemon square (she had), and whether Mrs. Finch's new reading glasses were actually the same pair she'd "lost" last month (they were).

And sometimes, Agatha thought as Mike settled contentedly at her feet, those were the only mysteries that really mattered.

"I FOUND SOMETHING," Emma said, waving Agatha over to the back table. Her laptop was open to Henry Maddox's blog, and her notebook was already half-filled with scribbled observations. "I've been going through his older posts. He documented everything."

Agatha pulled her chair closer while a few customers browsed the new releases at the front, their quiet murmurs creating cover for the conversation.

"Look at this." Emma clicked on an image, and a grainy black-and-white photograph filled the screen. A Hollywood event, by the look of it. Vincent Cleary stood in the center, flanked by two men in expensive suits. Vivian Monroe commanded attention on the left, her smile radiant and confident. And there, partially hidden behind one of the executives, stood a young woman in a beige wrap dress. Her face was half turned from the camera, but something about her posture, the tilt of her head.

"Does she look familiar to you?" Agatha asked, pointing at the young woman.

Emma squinted. "Maybe. Something about her. But I can't place it."

Agatha frowned, the recognition nagging at her. "Same here. It's like I've seen her before, but..." She shook her head. "Could be nothing."

"There's more," Emma said, scrolling down. "Another post from the same day. Look at this."

She clicked on a post titled "The Price of Truth." The text was brief:

I received this note yesterday. No signature, no return address. Just slipped under my hotel room door. I'm posting it here in case, well, in case something happens. Someone in Bristol Lake knows the truth about what happened to Vincent Cleary. And they're not afraid to name their price.

Below the text was a photograph of a handwritten note. The scrawl was rushed, uneven:

I know what happened to Cleary. I know what Vivian did. I've stayed quiet until now, but the truth can't stay buried any longer.

Someone else in Bristol Lake knows, too, and they won't stay silent forever. If you're serious about this podcast, meet me. Alone. No recordings. And be ready to pay the price.

Agatha's pulse kicked up. "That changes everything. Whoever wrote this isn't just dredging up Hollywood scandals. They're right here. In Bristol Lake."

"And they were willing to name a price," Emma said, the freckles across her nose stark against her pale skin. "They weren't protecting the truth. They were selling it."

Agatha stared at the anonymous note on the screen. Rosa's sudden cash deposit. Her abrupt reversal, claiming she'd been mistaken about the photographs. Her nervous visit to the bookstore, insisting everything was fine.

"Rosa," she said quietly.

Emma's eyes widened. "You think Rosa wrote this?"

"She recognized something in those old photographs. She was desperate to tell someone about it. And then overnight, she changed her mind completely." Agatha leaned back in her chair. "What if she didn't change her mind? What if she found a buyer?"

Emma was quiet for a moment. "If that's true, then whoever paid her off knew exactly what she had. And what she was willing to do with it."

14

A DAMNING DISCOVERY

The afternoon offered a rare chance to catch up on inventory without interruption, while still having enough browsers to keep the place feeling alive. Winter sunlight slanted through the front windows, weak but welcome after days of gray skies. Agatha was halfway through cataloging a shipment of vintage mystery hardcovers when the bell above the door jingled.

Detective Dawson entered, removing his hat as he stepped inside, snow dusting his shoulders. His tall frame and serious expression seemed out of place among the colorful book displays and cozy reading nooks. "Ms. Royale," he nodded, glancing around to ensure they had relative privacy. "Do you have a moment?"

"Of course," Agatha said, gesturing toward the small office behind the counter. "Coffee?"

"No, thank you," he replied, following her into the back room.

The office was small but organized, a desk with neat stacks of paperwork, bookshelves filled with reference materials, and a window overlooking the snow-covered alley behind the shop. Agatha closed the door partly, leaving it open just enough to hear if a customer needed assistance.

"This isn't an official visit," Dawson said, settling into the chair across from her desk. "But something's come up that I thought you should know about."

Agatha nodded, waiting.

Dawson placed his phone on the desk between them. "We've been reviewing evidence from the night Henry Maddox died. A tourist took video during the theater's opening, capturing the vintage architecture, the restored details." He paused, tapping the screen to life. "They captured something else, too."

He turned the phone toward her and pressed play.

The video showed the theater lobby, panning across the ornate ceiling and down the grand staircase. For a moment, it was just a shaky tourist video, nothing remarkable. Then the camera swept past the small service door tucked beside the concession stand.

Agatha leaned closer. A familiar figure in a muted gray cardigan slipped through the door, glancing over her shoulder before disappearing from view.

"That's... "

"Rosa Fielding," Dawson finished. "Heading up the service stairs that lead directly to the projection booth. The timestamp places her there approximately fifteen minutes before Henry's estimated time of death."

The air seemed to leave Agatha's lungs. "There must be some mistake."

"The facial recognition software confirmed it with 93% certainty," Dawson said. "And she signed the guest register, so we know she was there."

"Did you ask her about this?"

Dawson's expression tightened. "We've been trying to reach her for questioning since yesterday morning. She isn't answering her door or her phone."

Agatha's mind raced, piecing together a timeline against her will. Rosa had shown her that magazine clipping. Rosa had promised more evidence. Rosa had been in the projection booth before Henry died.

"I need to ask you," Dawson continued, his voice flat and professional, "has Rosa mentioned anything to you about being in the projection booth that night?"

"No," Agatha said truthfully. "She never mentioned going up there."

Dawson nodded as if this confirmed something. "There's more to this situation than just the video," he added, his voice lowering further.

For the next fifteen minutes, he shared a series of discoveries that left Agatha increasingly stunned. Each revelation painted a picture of Rosa Fielding that seemed impossible to reconcile with the woman Agatha thought she knew.

When Dawson finally finished speaking, the comfortable familiarity of the bookshop seemed to have receded, replaced by a sense that nothing in Bristol Lake was quite what it appeared to be.

"If you speak with her, please ask her to contact me immediately." He stood, placing his hat back on his head. "Everything I've shared stays between us for now. But I thought you should know what we're dealing with."

After he left, the cheerful sounds of the bookstore. The coffee machine humming, customers quietly chatting, Mike's paws clicking on the hardwood floor, seemed strangely distant. Agatha sat motionless, staring at her desk calendar.

Eventually, she pulled out her phone and sent two identical text messages:

Meet me at the shop after closing. Urgent.

THE LAST CUSTOMER had departed twenty minutes ago, leaving behind the lingering scent of coffee and the comfortable silence of books at rest. Outside, darkness had fallen early, as it did in January, and fresh snow was beginning to accumulate on the windowsills. Agatha had flipped the sign to CLOSED, drawn the blinds halfway, and brewed a fresh pot of coffee. The good beans she kept for emergencies and friends. This qualified as both.

Emma perched on the edge of the window seat, legs tucked beneath her, while Lorraine paced between the mystery section and the front counter, her dramatic emerald cardigan swishing with each turn. The usual post-closing chatter was absent, replaced by a tense silence broken only by the occasional creak of the old building settling.

"Let me get this straight," Emma said after Agatha finished recounting Dawson's visit. She set her mug down with deliberate care. "Rosa was in the projection booth right before Henry died? That can't be right."

"I saw the video myself," Agatha confirmed, leaning against the counter. Mike sat alert at her feet, sensing the shift in atmosphere. "It's definitely her. That gray cardigan she's always wearing, the silver brooch, even that distinctive way she has of glancing over her shoulder."

She replayed the scene in her mind: Rosa's furtive movements, the quick check to ensure no one was watching, the determined set of her shoulders as she slipped through the service door.

"The timestamp on the video puts her there just fifteen minutes before Henry's estimated time of death," Agatha added quietly. "But that's not all. Dawson shared something else. Something that makes this whole situation even more complicated."

Lorraine stopped pacing, her curiosity piqued. "What else could there possibly be?"

"Apparently, they've found evidence that Rosa has been blackmailing several people around town," Agatha lowered her voice despite the empty shop. "Small amounts, but consistent. And Dawson said they believe she's a dealer."

"A dealer?" Emma's eyes widened. "Rosa Fielding? Dealing drugs?"

"That was my reaction too," Agatha said, shaking her head. "But Dawson actually laughed when I asked. He said, 'No, a mink dealer.'"

"A mink dealer?" Lorraine repeated incredulously. "As in, the fur?"

Agatha nodded. "Apparently, Rosa's been running a small-time operation selling vintage mink coats and accessories on the black market. They found a storage unit in her name filled with them. And they've discovered she's been hiding cash to continue collecting her full benefits."

"Oh, the blackmail I knew about," Lorraine said with a casual wave of her hand. "Remember when Pastor Williams suddenly donated that 'anonymous' stained glass window after Rosa caught him sampling communion wine on a Tuesday? Or how Dr. Peterson started offering free dental cleanings to the garden club right after Rosa mentioned she had photos of his boat docked at Clara Winston's lake house, while Mrs. Peterson was visiting her sister?"

Emma and Agatha stared at her.

"What?" Lorraine shrugged, adjusting her scarf. "It was obvious! Rosa has always had a little side business in 'discretion.' I thought everyone knew. Like how we all pretend not to notice that Judge Harris wears a toupee."

"Well, I never," Emma whispered, clearly stunned. "Rosa always seemed so... Ordinary."

"Is she going to be arrested?" Lorraine asked.

"Probably soon," Agatha confirmed. "Dawson said they're just gathering the final evidence they need. He only told me because he thought it might connect to Henry's death somehow."

Lorraine dropped dramatically into the leather reading chair. "Mon Dieu," she murmured, pressing a hand to her chest. "Our blackmailing busybody is not just a potential murderess but a fur-trafficking benefits cheat? I need something stronger than coffee." She glanced hopefully toward the small cabinet where Agatha kept a bottle of brandy for book club emergencies.

"We don't know that she's a murderess," Agatha cautioned, but doubt clouded her voice. She crossed to the cabinet and retrieved the brandy and three small glasses. This definitely qualified as an emergency. "Maybe she went up there for an innocent reason."

"And conveniently never mentioned it to anyone?" Emma raised an eyebrow, accepting the glass Agatha offered. "Not even to you when she showed you that clipping about Bethany Marks? When she was so eager to prove she had valuable information?"

"It makes a disturbing kind of sense," Lorraine said,

sipping her brandy. "If Rosa was already comfortable with blackmail, maybe Henry discovered her little fur empire. Or maybe he found out something else she didn't want revealed."

"But fur coats?" Emma shook her head in disbelief. "It seems so... Oddly specific."

"Vintage furs can be worth thousands," Agatha explained. "And they're increasingly difficult to sell legally. If Rosa had a connection to buyers and a way to source the coats..."

Lorraine took a small sip and shuddered. "Let's look at what we know. Rosa recognized someone, or thought she did. She had access to the projection booth. Henry ends up dead. She has a history of blackmail and underground dealings. She then tries to leverage mysterious information for potential gain." She counted each point on her manicured fingers. "It does paint a rather unflattering picture, doesn't it?"

"But why would Rosa kill Henry specifically?" Emma asked, frowning. "What possible connection could he have to her... Mink business?"

"Perhaps he knew something about her," Lorraine suggested, warming to her theory. "Or she knew something about him. Old secrets have a way of becoming quite combustible when exposed to fresh air."

The three women fell silent, the implications settling between them like dust. Outside, snow fell steadily now, accumulating on the street in the glow of the streetlights. The shadows in the bookshop grew longer, casting familiar shelves in strange new shapes.

"Have either of you tried calling her today?" Agatha asked suddenly.

Emma shook her head. "Not since book club last week."

"I left her a message about the garden committee meeting," Lorraine said. "She never called back, which I found quite rude at the time."

Agatha pulled out her phone and dialed Rosa's number. It rang four times before going to voicemail. "Rosa, it's Agatha. Please call me as soon as you get this. It's important."

She ended the call and looked at her friends. "I think we need to pay her a visit. First thing tomorrow morning."

Emma nodded slowly. "If she's innocent, she deserves a chance to explain. And if she's not..."

"Then we need to know why," Agatha finished.

Mike gave a soft whine from his position by the door, as if sensing the gravity of their decision.

"Eight o'clock, then?" Lorraine asked, draining the last of her brandy. "I'll bring pastries. These situations always require sustenance."

They agreed, none of them giving voice to the worry that had settled in the room. That Rosa's silence might mean something far worse than guilt.

Lorraine and Emma gathered their coats and scarves, bundling against the cold night. They said their goodbyes at the door, promising to meet bright and early the next morning. Agatha watched them disappear into the snowy darkness, then locked the door behind them and began tidying up the glasses and coffee mugs.

SHE HAD JUST FINISHED WASHING the last glass when the door opened. Agatha looked up, startled. She'd locked the door, hadn't she?

Detective Dawson stood in the entrance, snowflakes

melting on his shoulders. He must have tried the door and found it unlocked after all. "Ms. Royale," he said with an apologetic nod. "I saw your lights still on. Hope I'm not interrupting."

"Not at all," Agatha said, though her heart was still racing from the surprise. "I thought you'd gone home for the evening."

"I was heading that way," Dawson admitted, removing his hat and brushing snow from it. "But something's been bothering me all afternoon. Thought I'd run it by you while it's fresh in my mind."

Agatha gestured toward the reading nook. "Of course. Can I get you that coffee now?"

"Actually, yes. It's going to be a long night." He settled into one of the armchairs while Agatha poured two fresh cups from the pot she'd just brewed.

Mike, who had been dozing by the fireplace, lifted his head and gave Dawson a considering look before settling back down with a sigh.

"So what's troubling you, Detective?" Agatha asked, handing him a steaming mug and taking the chair across from him.

Dawson pulled out his notebook, flipping to a bookmarked page. "We've been looking into Vivian's finances as part of the investigation. Standard procedure when someone's involved in a suspicious death."

"And?" Agatha prompted when he paused.

Dawson tapped his pen against his notebook. "For the past twenty five years, she's been making regular money transfers to a bank account in Arizona. Same amount, same day each month. Started right after that screenwriter's death in Hollywood. Vincent Cleary."

"Blackmail?" Agatha asked, the pieces starting to connect in her mind.

"That's my theory," Dawson nodded. "Someone's been bleeding her dry for decades. Makes you wonder what she did that was worth paying to keep quiet all this time."

"You think it's connected to Henry's death?"

"Henry was a podcaster investigating Hollywood scandals," Dawson said, his eyes sharp. "Maybe he uncovered Vivian's secret. Maybe he tried to leverage it himself. Or maybe... "He let the sentence hang for a beat. "Maybe he found the person who's been blackmailing Vivian all these years."

"And got himself killed for his trouble," Agatha finished quietly.

Dawson's expression remained neutral, but something in his eyes told Agatha he was pleased with her insight. "You see why I wanted your thoughts. You know people in this town. Any idea who might have connections to Arizona? Someone who might have known Vivian back then?"

Agatha considered the question carefully, turning it over in her mind. "Not off the top of my head. But I'll keep my ears open."

"I'd appreciate that," Dawson said, rising to his feet and setting his empty mug on the side table. "Just... Be careful who you ask. If I'm right about this, our blackmailer already has one murder on their conscience. They won't hesitate to add another."

As he headed for the door, Agatha called after him. "Detective? Why tell me this? Isn't this confidential information?"

Dawson paused, his hand on the doorknob, a wry smile crossing his face. "Let's just say I've learned to respect your instincts, Ms. Royale. Besides, I've seen how you and your friends operate. Better to give you something real to work with than have you stumbling around in the dark."

Agatha remained seated long after he'd gone, turning this new information over in her mind. Twenty five years of payments to Arizona. A secret worth killing for. And somewhere in Bristol Lake, someone who had been patient enough to wait almost three decades for their moment.

Mike padded over and rested his chin on her knee, his dark eyes watching her face.

"What do you think, boy?" she murmured, scratching behind his ears. "Rosa as a blackmailer and mink dealer, I can almost believe. But whoever has been bleeding Vivian Monroe for all these years? That's a different animal entirely."

Mike gave a soft whine, as if he agreed with her assessment.

Agatha stood and began turning off the lights, her mind already working through the implications. Tomorrow they would visit Rosa and get answers. But tonight, she had a new mystery to consider: who had been systematically bleeding Vivian Monroe for all those years, and what secret was worth killing to protect?

15

COOKIES AND CONSEQUENCES

The next morning broke colder than the day before, a brittle chill that seemed to tap against the windows of the bookshop. The sky stretched above Bristol Lake in washed-out gray.

Agatha arrived at the corner of Hawthorn Drive at precisely 7:55 a.m., Mike trotting beside her with unusual purpose. She spotted Emma already waiting, balancing a tray of coffee cups and wearing her most sensible boots.

"I brought reinforcements," Emma said, offering a cup. "Figured we might need the caffeine."

"Smart thinking," Agatha replied, accepting the warm drink gratefully.

Lorraine appeared moments later, her arrival announced by the jingle of bracelets and a cloud of perfume. Unlike her friends, she'd dressed for a social call rather than an investigation. Bright turquoise coat, matching beret, and carrying what appeared to be a wicker basket.

"Bonjour, mes amies!" she called, waving dramatically.

"I've brought pastries! One cannot confront a blackmailer before breakfast."

Agatha raised an eyebrow. "Pastries?"

"Almond tarts," Lorraine confirmed. "Rosa's favorite. I supervised their creation personally."

"You stood at Eliza's counter giving unwanted advice, didn't you?" Emma asked.

"The creative direction was entirely mine," Lorraine sniffed. "Besides, if we're going to interrogate Rosa about her suspicious bank deposits and mink-dealing ways, we should at least be civilized about it."

As they approached Rosa's cottage, Agatha noted the morning paper still on the step, the porch light burning despite the daylight.

"Odd," Emma murmured. "Rosa always retrieves her paper by seven. Says she can't enjoy her tea without the crossword."

Lorraine stepped forward, her curiosity overcoming caution. "Perhaps she's still sleeping? Though I've never known Rosa to sleep past six, she always claims early risers live longer." She tried the door handle, finding it unlocked. "Oh! It's open."

"Lorraine, wait..." Agatha began, but Lorraine had already pushed the door open with a gentle creak of hinges.

A beat of silence.

Then a scream tore through the quiet morning, high, sharp, and unmistakably Lorraine's.

Agatha and Emma rushed forward.

The kitchen looked like it had been paused mid-morning. A half-full teacup on the table, a napkin folded into a precise triangle, the radio on the counter tuned to the classical station Rosa favored.

And Rosa herself, seated at the table, looking for all the world like she had simply fallen asleep mid-tea. Her cardigan was buttoned neatly, her silver hair perfectly arranged. A plate of cookies sat untouched beside her right elbow. Except Rosa wasn't sleeping.

Lorraine stood trembling in the center of the kitchen, her basket of pastries now on the floor, almond tarts scattered across the linoleum. "Oh, mon Dieu," she whispered, her voice uncharacteristically small.

Emma immediately pulled out her phone and dialed 911 while Agatha approached Rosa carefully. There was no pulse, no breath, just the terrible stillness of absence.

A sheet of paper sat near Rosa's elbow. Folded once, unsealed.

The wail of a siren soon cut through the moment as Sheriff Salinger's cruiser pulled up outside.

"COOKIES," Detective Dawson said grimly, standing on Rosa's front lawn where he'd pulled Agatha aside. "Preliminary tests show they were poisoned. Fast-acting. She wouldn't have suffered."

Agatha nodded, her throat tight. "The ones on the table?"

"Yes. Snickerdoodles. They weren't from Eliza's bakery, different recipe. We're checking all possible sources."

Cookie crumbs. Agatha's mind flashed back to the projection booth. The crumbs near Henry's body. She'd thought nothing of it at the time, assumed they were from the concession stand. But what if...

"The blackmail," Agatha said quietly. "Did you find anything?"

Dawson nodded. "Account books in her desk drawer. She had quite the operation going. Small amounts, but from at least a dozen people in town. And in her closet? A collection of vintage mink pieces that would make a museum curator jealous."

"Rosa Fielding, blackmailer and fur dealer," Agatha shook her head. "Who would have thought?"

"People are full of surprises," Dawson replied, his expression neutral. "Especially in small towns."

Lorraine joined them, having recovered enough to resume her dramatic commentary. "If this turns into one of those tragic-lady-poisoning-her-friend plots, I'm going to need brandy and a chaise lounge," she declared, dabbing at her eyes with a lace-trimmed handkerchief.

"I was going to give her my secret amaretto recommendation that Eliza pretends she invented," she added with a sniffle. "Who will appreciate my impeccable taste in pastries now?"

Despite the gravity of the situation, Agatha found her lips twitching. Trust Lorraine to find the most Lorraine-ish way to process grief.

Dawson approached them, notebook in hand. "Did Rosa mention anything unusual to either of you recently? Any concerns, strange observations?"

Agatha considered her answer carefully. "She showed me some old magazine clippings last week. Photos from Hollywood events in the late nineties and early 2000s. She thought she recognized a connection to the Monroe sisters, something about their past in the film industry."

"Did she mention anyone specific?" Dawson asked, pen poised.

"She showed me photos of Vivian Monroe and a woman

named Bethany Marks together at charity events back then," Agatha replied carefully. "They were friends. Rosa was curious about what happened to Bethany, she disappeared after Vincent Cleary's death. Rosa thought the Monroe sisters might know something about where she went."

"Interesting timing," Dawson said, his expression thoughtful. "Right before her death."

After he moved away, Agatha exchanged meaningful glances with Emma. The unspoken question hung between them: Rosa had been asking questions about Bethany Marks' disappearance, connecting it to the Monroe sisters.

And now she was dead.

AGATHA WALKED HOME the long way, Mike pressed close to her leg. The route took her past the post office and the library, then down Birch Street where the old maples stood bare and black against the January sky. She hadn't wanted to go back to the bookstore. Not yet. The image of Rosa at her kitchen table, buttoned cardigan and untouched cookies, kept replaying behind her eyes.

Emma caught up to her at the corner of Birch and Elm, slightly out of breath. "I figured you'd go this way."

They walked in silence for a block before Agatha spoke. "Dawson told me about the blackmail. Mostly small-time stuff. Dirt on half the town, who was fudging their taxes, who was having an affair. But the mink dealing was something else. Vintage pieces bought at estate sales in other towns and resold through some underground collector's market."

"Rosa Fielding, fur dealer," Emma said, shaking her head. "I would not have guessed that."

“She had nerve. Always did.” Agatha's breath came out in white clouds. “But she picked the wrong target this time.”

Her phone buzzed. Celeste.

“You won't believe who just showed up at the Acadia,” Celeste said, barely containing herself. “I was checking the new movie schedule on my break and this man in an expensive suit walked right past me. Black sedan with tinted windows. He told the receptionist his name was Gordon Lane.”

Agatha stopped walking. Emma, reading her expression, moved closer.

“Was he there to see Vivian?” Agatha asked.

“He had a briefcase chained to his wrist,” Celeste said. “Like something out of a spy movie. And yes, he asked for Vivian by name.”

Agatha thanked her and hung up. She relayed the details to Emma, who let out a low whistle.

“Gordon Lane. Lorraine's mysterious investor.”

They stood at the corner, snow beginning to collect on their shoulders. Mike tugged gently at his leash, eager to keep moving, but Agatha's thoughts had gone still.

“We should warn Lorraine,” she said. “If Rosa was killed for asking the wrong questions, Lorraine needs to keep what she knows to herself.”

Emma already had her phone out. “I'm on it.”

16

ALL EYES ON ELIZA

Snow began to fall again that night, fat flakes drifting down in the windless air and accumulating on the sidewalks in soft white drifts. The windows of One Deadly Chapter transformed into frosted panels, warmth from inside creating delicate patterns of condensation at the edges. Agatha sat at the counter, a warm mug of ginger tea cradled between her palms, staring at the falling snow without really seeing it.

The soft glow of laptop screens illuminated the otherwise dim shop, creating pools of blue-white light in the darkness. Across the room, Emma hunched over her computer, scrolling through the Bristol Lake Gazette archives with the focused intensity only a librarian could muster. Her fingers tapped against the keyboard in a rhythmic pattern that matched the soft whisper of wind against the windows.

Meanwhile, Celeste had her earbuds in, head bobbing to music only she could hear as she scanned through the town council minutes from earlier in the year. Her task: to find any mention of Gordon Lane or hidden permits related to the

Acadia renovation. The occasional click of her mouse punctuated the quiet.

Mike lay under the table, his ears twitching every time the wind rattled the front door, his eyes moving behind half-closed lids as if tracking invisible prey.

It had been a long, heavy day.

Rosa's death had hit the town hard, rippling through Bristol Lake like a stone thrown into still water. Though the official word hadn't been released, whispers of poisoning were circulating with the unstoppable momentum of small-town gossip. The snickerdoodles were now infamous, spoken about in hushed, nervous tones.

AGATHA LOOKED up from behind the counter as a middle-aged woman stepped inside, scraping snow from her boots, her arms full of worn cardboard boxes that looked like they'd been through at least three decades of attic weather.

"Miss Royale?" the woman asked gently. "I'm Rosa Fielding's niece. My aunt left these for you. Said you'd know what to do with them."

Agatha blinked in surprise, her heart pinching at the mention of Rosa's name. "She left these... For me?"

The woman nodded. "She updated her will just last week. Specifically mentioned you should have her collection of vintage gossip magazines." She set the boxes down carefully by the front display table. "All organized by decade. There's even a few old Hollywood clippings in there, I think."

"I'm so sorry for your loss," Agatha said softly, reaching for one of the boxes.

The woman's eyes glistened, but her smile was genuine.

"Thank you. She was quite fond of you, you know. Always said you had a good head for puzzles."

Agatha felt her throat tighten at the memory of Rosa's sharp mind and sharper observations. "Is Pepper being looked after?"

"Mrs. Henderson took her in the same afternoon." The woman's expression softened. "Spoiled rotten already, from what I hear. Pepper's claimed the best spot on her couch and refuses to budge."

Agatha smiled at the image of the little terrier settling into her new home, probably ruling the roost within hours.

The woman gave Agatha's hand a quick squeeze. "Take care of yourself," she murmured, then slipped out with a quiet goodbye.

Celeste emerged from the reading nook, wiping her hands on her book-themed apron. "Did she say vintage gossip magazines?" Her eyes sparkled with curiosity. "What are you going to do with them?"

Agatha stared at the boxes, each one neatly labeled in Rosa's tidy handwriting, 1950s Scandals, Old Hollywood Rumors, Studio Secrets.

"I have no idea," she murmured. "I suppose we should put them in the storage room in the back for now. Maybe I'll donate them to the library later." She paused, then looked at Celeste. "Would you mind helping me carry them?"

Celeste was already lifting a box. "Are you kidding? This might be the best thing anyone's ever left you."

Agatha gave a small smile. "Let's just hope they're not cursed."

Celeste grinned. "Only one way to find out."

They disappeared into the back room, the door swinging

shut behind them with a soft creak, the boxes of secrets in tow.

BY LATE AFTERNOON, poor Eliza Martin's bakery stood nearly empty, shelves still full of untouched pastries. Customers who normally lined up for her morning scones now crossed the street to avoid passing her window. One particularly bold woman had even returned a box of lemon bars with the excuse that "the energy felt cursed." Eliza had accepted them with trembling hands and a brittle smile.

And then there was Gordon Lane.

He had arrived like a ghost, materializing in town without warning. No one remembered seeing him during the theater's renovation, yet there he was now, moving through Bristol Lake with the confidence of someone who belonged. Speaking softly to Vivian. Lurking near Rosa's bungalow. Taking calls in front of the hardware store with a Bluetooth earpiece and an expression that said calculating but calm.

"I still don't trust him," Emma muttered, not looking up from her screen where newspaper headlines from 2001 scrolled past. "Everything about him is just... Off."

"He knew Vivian in Hollywood," Agatha said, rotating her mug slowly between her hands, watching the amber liquid swirl inside. "He's the one who invested in the theater, and yet no one heard his name until yesterday."

Celeste removed one earbud, the faint tinny sound of a podcast leaking from it. "I just looked up Gordon Lane. There's a press release from 2009 where he was listed as a 'consultant' on a stalled documentary about Vincent Cleary's final script."

Emma sat up straighter, her glasses reflecting the glow of her screen. "You're kidding."

"Nope," Celeste said, swiveling her laptop around. "Look at this: 'funding provided in part by industry veteran Gordon Lane.'"

Agatha's heart skipped a beat as she leaned forward to see the screen. The connection was right there in black and white, impossible to dismiss. "So he was connected to Cleary. And now he's here."

Emma bit her lip, a nervous habit she'd had since college. "Do you think Henry found out?"

"I think Henry found out a lot of things," Agatha said quietly, her voice barely audible above the soft whisper of wind. "And someone made sure he didn't tell the rest of us."

Mike barked once, sharp and sudden, his ears perked toward the door.

A knock followed, hesitant and soft.

Eliza stood at the door, her winter coat dusted with snow and her strawberry blond hair damp around the edges where snowflakes had melted. The cold had brought color to her cheeks, but her eyes were reddened. She looked like she'd been crying or like she wanted to and hadn't figured out how yet. "I'm sorry." Her breath caught on the words. "I didn't know where else to go."

Agatha led her inside, guiding her gently toward the fireplace where embers still glowed from the afternoon's fire. Emma fetched a towel from the back room while Celeste disappeared into the kitchen to make hot cocoa, the comforting scent of chocolate soon wafting through the shop.

"They think I did it," Eliza said, voice barely above a whisper. She twisted her hands in her lap, fingers working against each other like she was kneading invisible dough. "The sheriff. People. I saw Martha at the market this afternoon, and she gave me this look, like I had arsenic in my apron."

Agatha sat beside her on the worn leather couch, close but not touching. "No one's accusing you officially."

"But unofficially?" Eliza gave a bitter laugh that sounded foreign coming from her usually cheerful lips. "Come on, Agatha. Rosa died with cookies on the table. Even though Detective Dawson publicly stated they weren't from my bakery, that's not what people are saying." She looked down at her hands, now red and raw from obsessive washing. "Forty years of baking for this town, and now they look at me like I'm some sort of... Witch with a poisoned apple."

"The official report clearly stated they weren't yours," Agatha said firmly. "Dawson made that clear at the press briefing."

"Doesn't matter," Eliza said miserably, accepting the steaming mug of cocoa Celeste offered. "Mrs. Finch returned a box of lemon bars this morning. Said they 'felt cursed.' The Mitchells canceled their standing order for Friday donuts. Three tourists walked in, heard someone whisper my name, and walked right back out." She took a shaky sip. "God, I never thought I'd be afraid to run my own bakery."

Emma sat beside her, her expression gentle but determined. "We'll fix this, Eliza. We know you had nothing to do with it."

Eliza nodded gratefully, her shoulders slumping in relief. "Thank you. I just... I needed someone to believe me." She set down the mug. "This is exactly what happened during the poisoned scone incident. I was arrested for murder and my life nearly fell apart before they finally cleared my name. I can't go through something like that again."

Agatha sat forward, her voice gentle but direct. "Eliza, did you ever see Rosa with anyone unusual in the past few weeks? Maybe someone who looked like they didn't belong?"

Eliza thought for a moment, her brow furrowed, then frowned. "Well, not unusual exactly. But a few days ago, I saw Rosa walking near the back alley behind the theater. She had a manila envelope tucked under her arm."

Agatha's breath caught. "What time of day?"

"Late afternoon," Eliza said, her baker's precision with time kicking in. "Between four and five, because I was pulling the second batch of sourdough from the oven. She looked anxious, kept glancing over her shoulder. I remember because she dropped her keys and didn't even stop to pick them up right away." She took another sip of cocoa. "Rosa never dropped things. She was too careful."

Emma turned to Agatha, excitement sparking in her eyes. "That must have been when she found the scrapbook. Or the clipping."

"She wouldn't have wandered back there unless she thought it was connected," Agatha said, her mind racing. "That alley leads to the side entrance of the projection booth."

Celeste poked her head in from the kitchen, a smudge of cocoa powder on her cheek. "Isn't that where Quentin has been repainting the door?"

Agatha blinked, a new possibility forming. "Quentin. The contractor."

Emma frowned. "Do you think he saw something?"

"Maybe," Agatha said, setting down her tea. "Or maybe someone saw him."

Eliza pulled the towel tighter around her shoulders, shivering despite the fire's warmth. "This town feels different now. Less cozy."

Agatha reached over and squeezed her hand. "We'll fix it. One truth at a time."

LATER THAT EVENING, under snow that fell in steady white curtains, Agatha and Emma made their way to the Acadia Theater. Mike came along, his little red coat making soft rustling sounds with every step, his paws leaving tiny prints in the fresh powder that reflected the streetlights in soft golden halos.

The front doors were locked, the lobby dark except for a single security light. They circled around back, their boots crunching on the snow-covered pavement, breath visible in white puffs.

The alley was empty save for a few bins and a single flickering motion sensor light that cast eerie, jumping shadows across the brick walls. The side door was freshly painted a pale blue, too fresh. The scent of lacquer hung in the cold air, sharp and chemical.

Emma knocked softly, three gentle raps that seemed muffled by the falling snow.

After a moment, Quentin opened the door, wiping his hands on a rag spotted with blue paint. His expression shifted from wariness to recognition.

"Ladies," he said with a nod. "Didn't expect visitors back here."

"Hello, Quentin," Agatha smiled warmly. "Sorry to disturb your work. That blue looks lovely, by the way - perfect for the theater's side entrance."

"Thanks," he replied, his posture relaxing a bit. "Just trying to match the original color from the 1940s. Found some old photos in the archive room that showed the original shade."

Emma nodded appreciatively. "Your attention to detail is impressive. The restoration work you've done is really bringing the Acadia back to life."

Quentin's expression softened with pride. "Just doing my job. What brings you both around to the service entrance tonight?"

"We have a question," Agatha said, her tone gentle but direct. "Did you happen to see Rosa Fielding back here last week? We're trying to piece together her movements before she..." She let the sentence trail off respectfully.

Quentin looked thoughtful, leaning against the door-frame. "Actually, yeah. She was here Tuesday afternoon. Nothing strange, though, she was just coming out of Vivian's office. Didn't carry anything, didn't say much besides hello."

"She was in Vivian's office?" Emma asked, exchanging a quick glance with Agatha.

Quentin nodded. "Yeah, they had some kind of meeting. Rosa didn't look too happy when she left."

Agatha shifted gears. "Quentin, what do you know about film reels at the Acadia? Specifically, any that might have come from Hollywood?"

His face brightened at the question. "Funny you should ask. We've actually got several reels from old Hollywood studios in storage. There's a whole history there."

"Really?" Agatha encouraged him. "I'd love to hear about it."

"Well," Quentin said, clearly warming to the topic, "about fifteen years ago, a man named Harold Jenkins came to town looking to reopen the Acadia. He'd bought an old storage unit in Hollywood that was full of film reels, indie projects, screen tests, some experimental shorts. Real collector's items."

Emma leaned forward. "What happened with his plans?"

"Fell through. Financing issues, I think. But the interesting thing is, he wasn't alone." Quentin glanced at Agatha. "Your aunt Edna was with him. They were partners in the venture."

"My Aunt Edna?" Agatha's surprise was genuine. "She never mentioned anything about trying to reopen the Acadia."

Quentin shrugged. "It was a long time ago. But they left all those film reels here when the deal collapsed. Been in our basement archive ever since, until Ms. Monroe arrived. She's been sorting through them, planning some kind of vintage film festival."

Agatha processed this new information. "Could we see the archive? I'm curious about what kinds of films they acquired."

"Sure," Quentin said, already stepping back and gesturing them inside. "Follow me."

The basement of the Acadia Theater was cooler than upstairs, the air heavy with the faint smell of old paper and wood polish. Their footsteps echoed on the concrete floor as Quentin led them past stacked boxes until they reached a narrow closet door at the end of a dimly lit hallway.

He fumbled with a set of keys and pushed the door open.

Inside were rows of shelves packed with film reels, folders, and theater ledgers dating back decades.

"These are all the reels from that Hollywood storage unit?" Emma asked, scanning the labels.

"Most of them," Quentin confirmed. "Ms. Monroe had some moved to her office for review."

Agatha's eyes caught on a dusty tin can nestled between two reels labeled "1945 Shorts - Acadia Collection" and "New Year's Variety Show 1972." Unlike the others, this one was labeled in careful, faded handwriting:

"Cleary - Final Cut?"

Her heart quickened. Vincent Cleary, the screenwriter from Henry's podcast.

"What's this one?" she asked, pointing to it.

Quentin peered at the label. "Not sure. It's not on my inventory list. Must've been mixed in with the others."

"Mind if I borrow it for a few days?" Agatha asked. "I'm researching the history of independent filmmaking for a display at the bookshop."

Quentin hesitated, then nodded. "Just bring it back in one piece. And don't tell Ms. Monroe I let you take it. She's been pretty protective of the collection."

"I won't," Agatha promised, carefully taking the reel.

BACK AT THE SHOP, Agatha, Emma, and Celeste gathered around the film reel on the table. Outside, snow continued to fall, blanketing Bristol Lake in white silence.

"So your Aunt Edna was involved with bringing Hollywood films to the Acadia," Emma mused. "That can't be coincidence."

"And now Vivian Monroe reopens the theater where these reels have been sitting for fifteen years," Celeste added. "Including one with Vincent Cleary's name on it."

"Do we even have a way to view this?" Emma asked, gesturing to the reel.

Agatha smiled. "Not yet. But I know who does." She

opened her phone and pulled up a contact. “Gladys. Her nephew runs the AV club at the high school. And they love working with vintage formats.”

“Let's hope whatever's on this reel is worth the trouble,” Emma said.

Agatha ran her finger over the faded label. This wasn't just about Henry's murder anymore. The connection between her aunt Edna, the Acadia Theater, and Vincent Cleary's mysterious final film was beginning to take shape.

And somewhere in this small reel might lie the truth that had already cost two people their lives.

17

WHAT ROSA SAW

The bitter January cold had settled over Bristol Lake overnight, transforming the world into sharp edges and frost. Winter in Maine was normally harsh, but this particular morning seemed determined to match the town's somber mood with temperatures that made breath freeze in the air and turned puddles into sheets of ice.

Agatha stood at the edge of Rosa Fielding's garden, one boot on the stepping stone path, the other planted firmly on the frozen ground. Her coat was buttoned tight against the biting wind, and her gloved hands gripped a small flashlight. Mike stood beside her, tail straight as a rod, nose twitching at the cold air.

Sheriff Salinger had officially cleared the scene the night before, the yellow crime scene tape now removed and folded away. Rosa's death was formally classified as a homicide, but they had no suspects. No murder weapon. No motive anyone could point to without sounding like a conspiracy theorist.

But Agatha had a notebook full of connections.

A dead screenwriter. A vanished assistant. A missing reel.

A podcast. A panicked woman who never got to finish her warning.

And now, a film canister labeled *Cleary. Final Cut?* tucked safely in Agatha's desk drawer at the bookshop.

She crouched beside the flower bed where Rosa had planted winterberry bushes the previous autumn. Their bright red berries stood out against the snow, defiantly cheerful against the gray morning light. The earth beneath was frozen solid, the garden dormant and waiting for spring.

Agatha stood, brushing frost from her knees, and turned to check on Mike. Her heart jumped when she realized he wasn't beside her anymore.

"Mike?" She scanned the small yard, then spotted him near the front porch. "Mike! What are you doing?"

He was digging enthusiastically at the base of a snow-dusted juniper bush beside the porch steps, his little paws working furiously, sending up sprays of frozen dirt and ice crystals.

"Mike, stop that!" Agatha hurried over, her boots crunching on the snow. "We can't dig up Rosa's... " She stopped mid-sentence.

As she approached, something caught her eye beneath the juniper's low-hanging branches. A small scrap of paper, crumpled and partially hidden in the mulch and snow. It looked like it had been there for a while, weathered and stained, as if it had been blown under the bush by wind and then dampened by melting snow before freezing again.

Agatha knelt down carefully, pulling Mike back gently by his collar. "Good boy," she murmured, though she wasn't sure if he'd been trying to show her the paper or just enjoying a good dig.

She reached under the juniper, her gloved fingers closing

around the crumpled paper. It was damp and partially frozen, the edges torn and dirty. Carefully, she unfolded it.

Despite the weather damage, she could still make out writing, shaky handwriting she immediately recognized as Rosa's. The ink had bled in places where moisture had seeped in, but the message was still legible.

"What happened to Bethany Marks? Someone will remember."

Agatha's breath caught. She turned the paper over carefully, looking for more, but there was nothing else. No envelope, no address, just this single accusatory question.

"Rosa must have been carrying this," Agatha said quietly to Mike, who had settled beside her, his earlier digging enthusiasm replaced by patient attention. "Maybe she dropped it when she was leaving, or the wind caught it and blew it under the bush. The police would have missed it completely, it's so hidden."

She looked at the note again, her mind racing. Rosa had been planning to confront Vivian about what happened to Bethany Marks. This fit perfectly with what Dawson had said about Rosa's blackmail operation.

"Rosa must have figured out that Vivian knows what happened to Bethany," Agatha murmured, carefully tucking the damaged paper into her coat pocket. "And she was going to blackmail her for it."

She looked down at Mike, who sat watching her attentively, tail wagging. "Good boy. Even when you're just being a pest and digging where you shouldn't, you help solve mysteries."

Mike's tail wagged harder, clearly pleased with himself regardless of whether his digging had been intentional detective work or just typical dog behavior.

EMMA WAS WAITING when Agatha got back, a folder spread open on the counter and two photocopies laid side by side.

"Before you start," Agatha said, pulling the crumpled paper from her coat pocket and smoothing it flat on the counter. "Mike was digging near Rosa's porch and I found this under a juniper bush. It's Rosa's handwriting."

Emma leaned in and read aloud. "What happened to Bethany Marks? Someone will remember." She looked up. "She was going to confront Vivian."

"That's what I think," Agatha said. "And either lost her nerve or never got the chance." Agatha set the note aside. "What did you find?"

Emma tapped the photocopies. "Vivian's business filings for the theater. Her signature on the license application doesn't match the signature on her initial investor documents."

Agatha leaned in. The difference was obvious even at a glance. Different loops, different slant, different pressure.

"Not within a six-month period," Emma said. "Two different people signed these."

Before Agatha could respond, Celeste popped her head around the shelf. "Sorry to interrupt, but Gordon Lane is across the street talking to Martha Peck. They look intense."

Agatha grabbed her coat.

MARTHA PECK WAS DRESSED for battle: wool hat pulled low, puffy coat zipped to her chin, purse slung across her body like a shield. She was pointing her finger at Gordon Lane like he'd just tried to raise her property taxes.

"I'm just saying," Martha huffed, her voice carrying across the quiet street, "Vivian was trouble in the eighties and she's trouble now. And that other one, Bianca, or whatever her name is... Don't think I haven't seen her sneaking around that back alley at night."

Gordon smiled politely, his cashmere scarf wrapped elegantly around his neck. Not a snowflake touched his immaculate shoes. "Mrs. Peck, your concern for your community is admirable."

Agatha crossed the street with Mike trotting beside her. "Mr. Lane, I presume?"

Gordon turned, surprise flickering across his face before his expression cooled. "And you are?"

"Agatha Royale. I run the bookshop across the street."

Martha's eyebrows shot up. "You two know each other?"

"Not formally," Agatha said, then turned to Martha. "I've been meaning to ask. You mentioned seeing someone outside Rosa's house the night before she passed?"

Martha's eyes lit up like Christmas morning. "Yes! A figure, slender, woman's shape, wearing a green coat. Around seven thirty. Rosa had just turned on her porch light. I was walking Stanley's dog and saw someone go up the steps, then leave fifteen minutes later."

"Did you see her face?"

"No," Martha admitted, her shoulders dropping. Then she rallied: "But that coat? Looked just like the one Vivian wears. That sage green wrap thing she's always swanning around in."

Agatha filed that away. "Thank you, Martha. That's very helpful."

Gordon cleared his throat. “Forgive me, but I couldn't help overhearing. You're looking into Rosa Fielding's passing?”

“Just trying to understand what happened. Rosa was well-loved in Bristol Lake.”

“Indeed,” Gordon said. “A tragedy.”

Martha, unwilling to relinquish her spotlight, interjected, “Agatha's not just being nosy. She has a knack for these things.”

“Just some old theater memorabilia Rosa collected,” Agatha said, keeping her tone light while watching Gordon's reaction. “She was quite the film buff.”

“How... interesting,” Gordon replied, his smile not reaching his eyes.

“Speaking of the theater,” Agatha said, “you seem to have experience in the industry. Have you been involved long?”

“Here and there. Various entertainment ventures over the years.”

“It's admirable to help revitalize small-town landmarks.”

A flicker of wariness crossed his face. “Everyone deserves a second chance, Ms. Royale. Wouldn't you agree?”

“Absolutely. Though I've found that running from the past rarely works as well as facing it.”

Gordon studied her for a moment. “Some pasts are better left buried. For everyone's sake.” He glanced at his watch. “If you'll excuse me, I have a call scheduled.”

He stepped away, boots crunching on the packed snow.

Martha watched him go. “That one's got secrets. Mark my words.”

Mike stood rigid beside Agatha, ears high, tail stiff, a low rumble too quiet to be a growl vibrating in his chest.

“I think you're right, Martha,” Agatha said quietly.

Martha patted Agatha's arm with her mittened hand. "Take care, dear. And keep that clever dog of yours close."

Agatha didn't go back to the bookstore. Mike needed a walk, and she needed to think. She turned toward the town square, where the weekly farmers' market persisted despite the cold, a handful of vendors huddled under their tents with thermoses of coffee and grim determination.

She was buying a cup of hot cider when Lorraine materialized beside her, resplendent in a crimson coat with an enormous fur-trimmed hood, a winter arrangement of forced bulbs and evergreen sprigs tucked under one arm.

"Ma chérie! I saw you talking to Gordon Lane just now. Did he say anything useful?"

"He said pasts are better left buried."

Lorraine arched one perfectly drawn eyebrow. "How very guilty of him."

"Maybe." Agatha sipped her cider, watching the steam curl into the cold air. "Or maybe he's just a man who likes sounding mysterious. Either way, I want to know more about him before we write him off as a harmless investor."

Lorraine's eyes sparkled. "Shall I make inquiries? I still have contacts from my theater days who would remember anyone with Hollywood connections."

"Do it," Agatha said. "Quietly."

Lorraine pressed a hand to her chest in mock offense. "Ma chérie, I am the soul of discretion."

Mike sneezed.

"Not a word from you either," Lorraine told him.

18

VIVIAN'S MASK

The next morning began the way most January mornings in Bristol Lake did. Frost painted delicate patterns on the windows, birds huddled in bare branches trying to stay warm, and the comforting scent of cinnamon rolls drifted from Eliza's bakery despite the bitter cold. But inside One Deadly Chapter Books & Brew, things were anything but peaceful.

Agatha stood at the back counter, staring at the clue board, her thoughts swirling like a storm cloud trapped in a teacup. Every thread pointed to Vivian. Every clue whispered the same name.

Bethany Marks.

"I wish we knew more about this Bethany Marks person," Emma said, flipping through a small stack of printouts spread across the table. "Every article mentions her name in connection with Vivian Monroe, but there's hardly any information about who she actually was or what happened to her."

Lorraine swept into the shop with her usual dramatic

flair, a vibrant turquoise scarf streaming behind her like a peacock's tail. She scraped her boots hard against the mat, sending a spray of snow across the entryway rug. "Well?" She glanced around the shop. "What did I miss? Has our little detective club solved the case yet?" She deposited a pink bakery box on the counter. "I brought éclairs. Murder investigations require proper sustenance."

"Bethany Marks does seem to have vanished rather completely," said Celeste, entering the shop behind Lorraine with her ever-present tote bag and a stack of reference books, unwinding her scarf. "Almost like she wanted to disappear from public record entirely." She paused, glancing down at the tote bag slung over her shoulder. "But I think I might have some information that could help."

Agatha arched a brow, momentarily distracted from her thoughts. "Are you saying you figured this out before I did?"

"Not exactly," Celeste said, dropping her bag with a soft thud and settling her glasses more firmly on her nose. "Honestly, I barely knew who Vincent Cleary was before all this. He died before I was born, so it's not like he was on my radar. But I was brushing my teeth this morning and this random memory just hit me — I found this article for a film history project back in college. About his death. The site it was on was pure gossip, like alien abduction in Hollywood levels of nonsense, but this one piece was different. Photos, court transcripts, timeline breakdowns. Super detailed." "Ooh, the plot thickens!" Lorraine exclaimed, hopping onto a stool and propping her chin on her hands. "Go on, darling. Don't spare a single juicy detail."

Emma leaned in, her interest piqued. "And?"

"I printed the article two years ago for my project,"

Celeste continued, "because it was the only one that listed Bethany Marks as a witness and not just a suspect."

Agatha felt her pulse quicken. "Do you still have it?"

Celeste grinned, her eyes lighting up behind her glasses. "Better. I digitized all my school papers into folders. Give me one sec."

She opened her laptop and began typing with the confident speed of someone who had spent their entire adolescence organizing digital archives. Mike trotted over and sat at her feet, offering moral support in the form of a well-timed sneeze that made Celeste laugh.

"Here we go," she said, clicking through a series of neatly labeled folders. "Folder: Film Scandals, Case Studies. Subfolder: Cleary Incident. Subfolder: Gossip Source (Accurate)."

"Mon Dieu, your organization puts my entire life to shame," Lorraine sighed, peering over Celeste's shoulder. "I can't even find matching socks most mornings."

Celeste clicked, and the screen filled with a PDF document.

A dramatic header stretched across the top: "Deadlines and Dead Men: The Vincent Cleary Scandal Nobody Wanted You to Remember." Below it sat a grainy photograph of a young woman in a courtroom, her hands folded tightly on the table in front of her, knuckles white with tension.

"She testified in a closed hearing," Celeste explained, scrolling down. "But one reporter, this woman named Lisette Raines, snuck in. She claimed Bethany looked terrified the entire time. Said her body language was like someone who wanted to run."

Agatha stared at the screen, leaning closer. The photo wasn't clear, blurred by age and poor resolution.

"It could be anyone in this photo, really," she murmured, squinting at the grainy image.

They scanned the headline: "Actress Cleared from Director's Death." According to the article, she had an alibi and was no longer considered a suspect.

The women continued studying the trial photos, each lost in her own thoughts. Emma adjusted her glasses, Lorraine drummed her red-lacquered nails on the table, and Celeste scrolled through the document with methodical precision.

"Wait..." Agatha suddenly sat up straighter. "Do you see this?" Her finger jabbed toward a figure in the background of one of the courtroom photos.

"See what?" Emma asked, leaning in closer.

"This woman in the jury box." Agatha traced the outline of a partially visible face. The photo was grainy, the woman's features blurred by the poor resolution and distance from the camera. "There's something familiar about her."

She pulled the laptop closer, squinting at the screen. The woman was maybe in her forties at the time, with her hair pulled back severely. The angle was unfortunate. Mostly profile, chin tilted down as if she were studying papers in her lap.

"Could be anyone," Celeste said, adjusting her glasses to see better.

"No, look at the posture," Agatha murmured, more to herself than the others. "The way she's sitting, very upright, shoulders back. And see how she's holding that pen? Between her index and middle finger, not the usual grip."

Emma tilted her head. "That is an odd way to hold a pen."

"Rosa holds her pen exactly like that," Agatha said, her pulse quickening. "I remember noticing it when she was filling out a special order form at the shop."

Lorraine leaned in, fascinated. "Mon Dieu, you might be onto something."

Agatha studied the image more intently, her librarian's eye for detail kicking into high gear. "And look at the brooch on her collar. It's hard to see clearly, but it looks like..."

She fumbled for her phone, scrolling quickly through photos until she found what she was looking for. A picture from last month's book club where Rosa had posed with the group. "Here! Rosa's wearing this silver brooch shaped like theater masks. Comedy and tragedy."

She held the phone next to the laptop screen. Even with the grainy quality of the old courtroom photo, the distinctive shape was unmistakable.

"It's the same brooch," Emma breathed.

Celeste zoomed in on the photo as much as the resolution would allow. "The shape matches. And look. Even though it's blurry, you can see the same asymmetry where one mask is higher than the other."

"Rosa wore that brooch every time I saw her. Martha mentioned it once — said it was a gift from Rosa's mother, that she never took it off."

They all stared at the screen in silence.

"So this woman in the jury box..." Emma began.

"Is Rosa," Agatha finished, sitting back slowly as the full weight of the discovery settled over her. "A younger Rosa, but it's definitely her. She was a juror in Vincent Cleary's trial."

They all crowded around the screen, shoulders bumping as they strained to see.

"Oh my..." Celeste breathed, adjusting her glasses. "It's her. A younger Rosa, but it was definitely her."

"It looks like she was a juror in the Cleary trial," Agatha said, her voice tinged with disbelief.

Lorraine gasped dramatically, one hand flying to her throat. "The plot doesn't just thicken, it curdles! Rosa was part of the jury? Magnifique, what a twist!"

The room went quiet for a beat, the only sound the soft hum of the laptop and the ticking of the antique clock on the wall.

Mike let out a low whine from his spot at Celeste's feet, as if sensing the gravity of their discovery.

Agatha sat down slowly in the nearest chair, absorbing it all. The pieces were falling into place too neatly, too perfectly, for it to be coincidence.

"Rosa must have been living in California back then," Emma said slowly. "The trial was in Los Angeles. She would have had to be a local resident to serve on the jury."

"And then she moved to Bristol Lake sometime after," Agatha added. "Started working at the Acadia as an usher. Built a new life here." She paused, turning that over in her mind. Rosa had always presented herself as a Bristol Lake fixture, someone rooted in this town for as long as anyone could remember. She had never once mentioned California, never hinted at a life before the Acadia. An entire chapter of her story that none of them had known existed.

Celeste nodded, tucking a strand of hair behind her ear. "But she never forgot what she saw at that trial. And when Vivian Monroe showed up in Bristol Lake all these years later..."

"Rosa recognized her," Emma finished. "And considering what we found about her history of blackmail, she saw an opportunity."

"I'm floored," Agatha said softly. She looked up at the others, her brow furrowed. "Rosa had a whole other life we knew nothing about."

"It's like one of those Russian nesting dolls," Lorraine declared, waving an éclair for emphasis. "Secrets inside secrets inside secrets. And to think, all this time I thought the most scandalous thing about Rosa was her refusal to share her lemon cake recipe!"

Emma handed Agatha the printout. "So what do we do now?"

Agatha looked up, her expression hardening with resolve. "We watch the reel. Whatever is on it, if Henry thought it was damning enough to die for, it's time we find out what Vivian is so desperate to hide."

Celeste hesitated, glancing at her phone. "I can call the AV club. Gladys's nephew Leo is the president."

"Perfect!" Lorraine clapped her hands together. "I'll bring snacks. Every good film viewing needs proper refreshments."

Two hours later, Agatha stood in the dim, makeshift theater of the Bristol Lake High School's AV lab. The space smelled of popcorn, electrical wires, and energy drinks, an oddly comforting blend that reminded her of late-night study sessions from her college days.

The AV club president, a tall, gangly teen named Leo who wore a vintage Star Wars t-shirt and a blazer for no apparent reason, was setting up the reel with solemn ceremony. His hands moved with surprising delicacy for their size, treating the old film with the reverence usually reserved for ancient artifacts.

"This is really old-school," he said, admiration clear in his voice. "Pre-digital reel-to-reel format. Very delicate. But I've got it."

Celeste beamed with pride. "Leo's the best. He once restored a reel of my grandpa's war documentary using bubble wrap and a shoelace."

Leo nodded without looking up from his work. "True story."

Lorraine had positioned herself in the center seat, a bag of gourmet popcorn balanced on her knees. "I feel like we should have a drum roll or something. This is so deliciously suspenseful!"

They took their seats in the small row of chairs Leo had arranged. Emma sat to Agatha's right, Celeste to her left, with Lorraine beside Emma. The lights dimmed, plunging the room into near darkness.

Agatha settled into her chair, her fingers tapping restlessly against her knee. She'd been turning this moment over in her mind all day — what might be on the reel, what it could finally explain. Now that they were here, the waiting felt almost unbearable.

The reel began to spin, the mechanical sound oddly soothing in its steadiness. The screen flickered once, twice, then filled with grainy black and white images. But instead of revealing Cleary's damning footage, it was simply promotional footage for a 1960s toothpaste commercial.

"That's not right," Agatha murmured, her disappointment palpable.

"Sacrebleu!" Lorraine whispered loudly. "Is this the wrong reel?"

Agatha's stomach sank as she watched cheerful actors smile with impossibly white teeth. "Someone must have switched it," she said quietly. "This isn't Cleary's film."

Leo stopped the projector, looking concerned. "Want me to check the canister?"

Agatha nodded, and he carefully removed the reel, examining it closely. "Yeah, this film stock is definitely from the sixties. See the degradation pattern? The Cleary reel would have been from 2001, totally different."

"Someone got to it before we did," Agatha said, frustration creeping into her voice. "Quentin said Vivian had been reviewing the reels in her office. She had access."

"So when you took what you thought was the Cleary film..." Emma began.

"I was taking a decoy," Agatha finished. "Vivian was one step ahead of us."

"Which means she has the real reel," Celeste said. "Or she's destroyed it."

Lorraine huffed indignantly. "That clever, devious woman! Though one must admire the cunning, even if it is profoundly irritating."

BACK AT THE bookstore later that afternoon, Agatha and her friends settled into their usual spots in the café corner, comparing notes on their disappointing discovery. The smell of fresh coffee filled the air as Emma brewed a fresh pot to help them regroup. Outside, snow had begun falling again, coating the windows in white.

"So much for our big revelation," Celeste sighed, closing her laptop.

"Don't give up yet," Agatha replied, arranging the printed photos and articles they'd collected. "We just need to... "

Martha Peck came in a moment later, brushing snow from her coat as all eyes turned to her.

"Terrible weather," Martha announced to no one in

particular, then spotted their gathering. "Oh, having another one of your little meetings, I see."

Her tone carried a hint of disapproval mixed with curiosity that made Agatha straighten in her seat. Martha Peck had been in town longer than almost anyone. She knew everyone's business, or at least thought she did.

"Just catching up," Agatha said casually, subtly sliding the newspaper clippings into a folder. "What brings you in today, Martha? Looking for a new mystery?"

"Perhaps a mystery that doesn't involve poking into other people's business?" Lorraine suggested with a sweet smile that didn't quite reach her eyes.

Martha sniffed, adjusting her wool hat. "Actually, I came to tell you something. About Rosa."

The atmosphere in the room shifted immediately. Lorraine's eyebrows shot up, and Emma leaned forward.

"What about Rosa?" Agatha asked, keeping her voice even.

"Well," Martha said, clearly enjoying being the center of attention, "I was organizing the church charity committee files. I'm the secretary, you know, and I found something odd. Rosa made a large donation just last month. Anonymous, she requested, but I handle the paperwork." She paused for effect. "Five thousand dollars. In cash."

"That's... unusual," Agatha said, her eyes narrowing with interest.

"More than unusual," Martha continued, lowering her voice conspiratorially. "When I mentioned it to her sister-in-law at the grocery store, she was shocked. Said Rosa lived on a tight budget. Could barely afford her medication some months."

"So where did the money come from?" Emma asked.

Martha shrugged, her expression smug. "That's the question, isn't it? And here's something else peculiar. The donation came right after that Hollywood man, the podcast fellow, arrived in town."

"You don't say," Lorraine murmured, suddenly very interested. "Our Rosa had secrets? How utterly fascinating."

Agatha felt a chill that had nothing to do with the snow outside. "What makes you think there's a connection?"

Martha pulled a folded paper from her purse. "This." She handed it to Agatha. It was a church bulletin from three weeks ago, with a small photo of the congregation at a potluck dinner. In the background, Rosa and Henry Maddox stood together near the dessert table, clearly in conversation.

"They talked at the potluck," Martha said, lowering her voice conspiratorially. "But that's not the interesting part. Ethel Anderson. You know, the one who volunteers in the church kitchen?. She saw them later, talking in the hallway by the bathrooms. Away from everyone else."

"And?" Emma prompted.

Martha leaned in, clearly relishing her moment. "Ethel said she saw Henry hand Rosa a manila envelope. Then Rosa gave him something back. Looked like a brown paper grocery bag with something inside. Not heavy, but bulky."

Agatha exchanged meaningful glances with Emma and Celeste. A film canister would fit perfectly in a grocery bag.

"Ethel thought it was odd," Martha continued, "so she mentioned it to me. I didn't think much of it at the time, but after Rosa's death..." She shrugged significantly.

The room went silent.

"I thought you might want to know." Martha straightened, like someone who had been waiting a long time to deliver news. "Since you're all so interested in poor Rosa's death."

Agatha stared at the church bulletin photo showing Rosa and Henry together, her mind racing. If Rosa had given Henry something in that grocery bag. Perhaps a film reel she'd kept hidden for years, it changed everything. And if Henry had paid her for it with cash in that manila envelope...

"Thank you, Martha," she said softly. "This is very helpful."

"Well," Martha said, adjusting her purse, "I should be going. Bridge club meeting at four." She turned to leave, then paused. "Oh, and Agatha? You might want to know about the cookies."

"What cookies?" Lorraine perked up, always alert to pastry-related conversations.

Martha's expression turned serious. "The ones found at Rosa's house? I made them. I brought them over the day before she died, just being neighborly, you know. Rosa always loved my snickerdoodles." Her voice wavered. "I never thought... I never imagined someone would poison them. That someone would use my cookies to..."

She trailed off, her usual bluster deflating into something that looked like genuine distress.

"Martha," Agatha said gently, "did you tell the police this?"

"Of course I did," Martha replied, pulling herself together. "Detective Dawson questioned me for an hour. But I left those cookies on Rosa's porch in a sealed container, like I always do. I never went inside. Anyone could have tampered with them after I left."

"What time did you leave them?" Emma asked.

"Around six in the evening," Martha said. "Rosa wasn't home, her car was gone. So I just left them on the porch like I usually do when she's out."

Agatha exchanged meaningful glances with Emma and Celeste. That meant the cookies sat unattended on Rosa's porch for who knew how long. Anyone could have swapped them out.

"Thank you for telling us," Agatha said. "I know this must be difficult."

Martha nodded stiffly. "Well. I should go." She turned and left, the bell jangling behind her.

Agatha, Emma, Lorraine, and Celeste exchanged looks.

"So Martha made the cookies, but someone could have switched them before Rosa brought them inside," Celeste said slowly.

"Someone who knew Martha's routine of leaving treats on Rosa's porch," Emma added.

Mike stood up suddenly, his ears perked toward the door where Martha had just exited. A low growl rumbled in his chest.

"What is it, boy?" Agatha asked, watching her dog carefully.

Through the front window, they could see Martha Peck standing on the snowy sidewalk outside, talking on her cell phone. Her expression was urgent, intense. Nothing like the self-satisfied gossip who had just left their shop.

Emma nudged Agatha. "Who do you think she's calling? Look at her face — that's not a casual conversation."

"I don't know," Agatha replied quietly. "But I think we just found our next lead."

Lorraine leaned in, her voice hushed with genuine concern beneath her usual dramatic flair. "Do you think she's dangerous, Agatha? Our Martha Peck, who complains about the hymn selections and organizes the Christmas cookie exchange?"

Agatha watched as Martha gesticulated sharply into her phone, her breath visible in white puffs, her face pinched with an emotion that looked suspiciously like fear.

"I think," Agatha said slowly, "that everyone in Bristol Lake has secrets. And some of them are willing to kill to keep them."

19

THE WRONG REEL

The morning sun broke through the heavy gray clouds that had been blanketing Bristol Lake in snow for days. The sidewalks of Central Avenue had been freshly cleared, leaving neat banks of white along the curbs, and the cold air bit at Agatha's cheeks as she walked toward the Acadia Theater. Mike trotted beside her on his red leash, his thick coat keeping him warm, his breath coming out in little white puffs.

The Acadia's lobby was quiet, the morning light streaming through the tall windows and casting long shadows across the polished floors. Agatha found Quentin in the theater's main seating area, checking the alignment of the restored seats. His flannel shirt was rolled up to his elbows despite the chill, and he had that focused expression of someone who took pride in getting every detail exactly right.

"Morning, Quentin," Agatha called, making her way down the aisle.

He looked up and grinned. "Hey there. Back with my reel, I hope? Ms. Monroe was asking about the inventory yesterday, and I'd rather not have to explain why I let someone walk off with theater property."

Agatha reached into her bag and withdrew the metal canister. "Safe and sound, though I'm afraid it wasn't quite what I expected. Just an old commercial for Sparkle-White toothpaste."

Quentin chuckled as he accepted the reel. "Yeah, well, Harold Jenkins bought that entire storage unit sight unseen at an auction. One of those Hollywood warehouse clearances where they just sell everything in bulk. Could have been anything in there. Major studio outtakes, indie films, or random commercials like this toothpaste ad. Harold figured he'd struck gold, but most of it turned out to be pretty mundane stuff."

"You know what's funny?" Quentin continued, oblivious to Agatha's racing thoughts. "You're not the only one who's been interested in our collection lately. I'm amazed by how many people in Bristol Lake suddenly care about old movies."

Agatha leaned forward. "What do you mean?"

"Well, there was Rosa Fielding, rest her soul. Sweet lady, but she was acting strange the last time she came by. Kept asking to see specific reels, like she was looking for something particular." Quentin's voice took on a nostalgic tone. "She told me she used to work here as an usher during the theater's heyday. Had a real good memory for the films they'd shown."

Agatha's eyebrows shot up. "When was this?"

"Oh, maybe two weeks ago? She seemed nervous, kept glancing around like she was afraid someone might overhear. And then Martha Peck showed up."

"Martha was here too?"

Quentin nodded, his expression darkening. "She was. That's when things got interesting. Martha claimed she was just curious about the restoration work, but she kept asking about the film collection. Wanted to know if we had any reels from the late 1990s or early 2000s. Specifically anything that showed the personal lives of Hollywood actors. Said she was doing research, but the way she asked..." He trailed off, shaking his head.

Agatha's notebook was already in her hands, pen poised. "Did Rosa and Martha run into each other while they were here?"

"Yeah, they did," Quentin said, his voice dropping to match the theater's hushed atmosphere. "Rosa was already in the basement looking through the film collection when Martha showed up. That's when things got weird. They both got real tense, real fast. Rosa tried to leave, but Martha followed her down to the basement. I was working up here, but I could hear voices getting louder."

"They argued?"

"More like... Martha was insisting on something, and Rosa kept saying no. I couldn't make out the exact words, but Martha's voice was getting shrill, you know? Like when she gets worked up at town meetings."

Agatha could picture it perfectly. Martha Peck had a voice that could cut glass when she was agitated, and she'd never been one to take no for an answer gracefully.

"Then what happened?"

"They got even louder. I was about to go down and check on them when I heard Rosa say something like, 'I won't be part of covering this up again.' Then Martha said something I couldn't catch, and there was this crash, like someone knocked over a box."

Quentin rubbed the back of his neck, looking uncomfortable. "I went downstairs to make sure they were okay, but by the time I got there, Rosa was heading for the exit and Martha was standing in the storage room looking like she'd seen a ghost. Rosa left without saying goodbye, and Martha stayed another twenty minutes, going through boxes like she was hunting for buried treasure."

"Did Martha find whatever she was looking for?"

"Hard to say. But she sure didn't seem happy when she left. Stomped up those basement stairs like she had a personal grudge against each step."

Agatha made careful notes, her mind already working through the implications. Martha Peck had admitted giving the cookies to Rosa. She'd had some kind of confrontation with Rosa about covering something up. And now it seemed she'd been searching for something in the film archives.

"Quentin, this might be important," Agatha said. "Can you remember anything else about what they discussed? Any specific films or names mentioned?"

He closed his eyes, concentrating. "She said something about old movies being dangerous, about some people wanting things to stay buried. And Martha kept asking about a specific year, but I can't remember which one. She wanted to know if we had anything from that time period."

Agatha felt a chill of recognition. "I bet she was looking for something from around the time Vincent Cleary died."

"Thank you, Quentin. This has been incredibly helpful."

He stood and stretched, his joints popping after the morning's work. "I hope I'm not getting anyone in trouble. But with everything that's happened. Henry's murder, Rosa's death. I figure the truth's more important than keeping quiet about old arguments."

"You're absolutely right," Agatha assured him.

TWENTY MINUTES LATER, Agatha was sitting in a corner booth at Eliza's bakery, warming her hands around a steaming mug of coffee and trying to organize her thoughts. The lunch crowd hadn't arrived yet, so she had the place largely to herself except for Eliza, who was working behind the counter with flour dusting her apron and a satisfied smile on her face.

Lorraine swept in, her curls bouncing beneath a bright yellow beret that somehow stayed perfectly in place despite the winter wind.

"Agatha! Ma chérie!" Lorraine's voice carried her usual theatrical flair. "I have been looking everywhere for you. There is news, and not the good kind."

She slid into the booth across from Agatha, unwrapping a cherry danish from a paper bag with the careful attention most people reserved for handling explosives.

"What kind of news?" Agatha asked, though she suspected she already knew.

"About Martha Peck, naturally. The woman has been acting stranger than usual, if such a thing is possible." Lorraine took a delicate bite of her danish and sighed contentedly. "Eliza, ma petite, you are an artist. This pastry, it is like sunshine wrapped in sugar."

Eliza beamed from behind the counter. "Thanks, Lorraine. I tried a new recipe for the cherry filling."

"It is magnificent," Lorraine declared, then turned back to Agatha with a more serious expression. "But Martha, she is not magnificent. She is suspicious. Very, very suspicious."

"How so?"

Lorraine leaned forward conspiratorially, her voice dropping to what she probably thought was a whisper but was still audible to half the bakery. "Yesterday evening, I was taking my daily constitutional. You know how I like my evening walks, even in this cold, and I saw Martha sneaking around the back of Rosa's house."

Agatha's coffee cup paused halfway to her lips. "Sneaking?"

"Oui, sneaking. Like a woman with something to hide. She kept looking over her shoulder, and she was carrying this big bag, like she was taking something away rather than bringing something." Lorraine mimed the action, nearly knocking over the sugar dispenser. "When she saw me coming down the street, she practically ran to her car."

"Could you tell what she was taking?"

"Non, but it was heavy. She struggled with it." Lorraine pursed her lips thoughtfully. "And here is the thing that makes me think something fishy is happening. Rosa's house, it has been cleaned. Professional cleaning service, they were there this morning. Very thorough, very expensive looking."

Agatha frowned. "Who arranged for that?"

"No one knows. The cleaning crew, they said it was paid for in advance, cash. Anonymous client." Lorraine's eyes sparkled with the thrill of a good mystery. "But Martha, she was watching from her car while they worked. Sitting there for two hours, just watching."

"How do you know all this?" Agatha asked.

Lorraine leaned back with a satisfied smile. "Mrs. Henderson lives across the street from Rosa, non? She called me this morning, très excited about all the activity. She had been watching through her front window. You know how these retired ladies are, and she saw Martha parked there the whole time. Mrs. Henderson said Martha looked nervous, kept checking her phone."

The door opened, and Emma stepped inside carrying a stack of papers that looked hastily printed, her coat dusted with snow.

"Agatha, thank goodness I found you," Emma said, sliding into the booth next to Lorraine and unwinding her scarf. "I've been researching all morning, and I found something you need to see."

She spread the papers across the table, organizing them with her characteristic efficiency. "Remember how we were trying to piece together the timeline of events from the early 2000s? I went back through the newspaper archives, looking for any mention of Vincent Cleary's death in 2001 or the subsequent trial."

"And?"

"I found this." Emma pulled out a photocopy of what appeared to be a society page from a Los Angeles entertainment magazine. The image quality was poor, but it clearly showed a formal event with several people in evening wear. "This is from a charity gala in Hollywood, February 1995. A few years before Cleary died."

Agatha studied the photograph. In the center was a younger Vivian Monroe, stunning in a silver gown, her arm linked with a man who was identified in the caption as Vincent Cleary. To their left stood another woman, partially turned away from the camera, but with a familiar profile.

"That's Bethany Marks," Emma said, pointing to the woman. "But look who else is in the background."

Agatha squinted at the photograph, and her breath caught. Standing near the edge of the frame, wearing what looked like a server's uniform and holding a tray of champagne glasses, was a much younger Martha Peck.

"Martha was in Los Angeles in early 1995," Agatha said slowly.

"Not just in Los Angeles," Emma corrected. "She was working at events where Vivian, Cleary, and Bethany were present. According to the caption, this gala was held at the Beverly Hills Hotel, and it was catered by Peck & Associates Catering."

Lorraine gasped dramatically. "Peck & Associates! But Martha's maiden name was Peck. She must have been working for family!"

"Wait," Celeste said. "Stanley's last name is Peck too."

Lorraine waved a hand. "Coincidence, ma chérie. She married a man with her own maiden name. It happens."

Emma nodded. "I did some more digging. Martha's uncle owned a high-end catering company that specialized in Hollywood events. She worked for him for about six months in early 2001, right around the time of Cleary's death and the subsequent trial."

"So Martha was there," Agatha said, her mind racing. "She witnessed whatever happened between Vivian, Cleary, and Bethany. She knew the truth from the beginning."

"But why wait until now to act on it?" Lorraine asked.

"Think about it," Agatha said. "Bethany Marks disappeared after the trial, presumably to start a new life. But where did she end up? That's what we need to find out. If Martha recognized someone from that time..."

"Or she was paid to keep quiet," Emma suggested. "And now she's trying to cash in again."

"Maybe," Agatha said. "But now, almost thirty years later, she sees an opportunity. Someone connected to that trial has come to Bristol Lake, someone with money and status. Martha could threaten to expose secrets from the past unless..."

"Unless what?" Emma asked.

"Unless they pay for her silence."

The three women sat in silence for a moment, the weight of the implications settling over them.

"So Martha is blackmailing someone?" Lorraine finally asked. "Vivian, perhaps?"

"Possibly," Agatha said. "Martha and Rosa are both from Bristol Lake. Martha had connections in Hollywood through her uncle's catering company, and Rosa was a juror in the Cleary trial. What are the odds that two women from the same small town in Maine both ended up in Los Angeles at the same time — right when Vincent Cleary died?"

"You think they knew each other back then?" Emma asked quietly.

"Maybe they went out there together. Maybe they reconnected there. Either way, they both came back to Bristol Lake knowing something about what really happened to Cleary." Agatha paused. "And if they were both sitting on that secret all these years..."

"One of them could have decided to cash in," Celeste said.

"Or both of them," Agatha continued. "Maybe they were working together at first, but had a falling out. If Rosa started having second thoughts about keeping quiet, or wanted a bigger cut..."

"Martha would have seen her as a threat," Emma finished.

"But why kill Henry?" Lorraine asked.

Agatha pulled out her notebook and began sketching a timeline. "Henry's investigation threatened everything. If the truth about Cleary's death came out, any blackmail leverage would be worthless."

Emma suddenly looked up from her notes. "What if Martha actually killed Henry to protect her blackmail operation? And then when Rosa became a problem, maybe threatening to confess or demanding more money — Martha killed her too?"

Agatha held up a hand. "That's a stretch. We know Rosa was blackmailing someone. There's evidence for that. And yes, Martha admitted she dropped off the cookies that killed Rosa. But that doesn't make her a murderer. It could just as easily make her a convenient scapegoat. Right now, we need proof, not speculation."

"What kind of proof?" Emma asked.

"Financial records would be a start. Bank deposits, cash transactions, something that shows Martha receiving blackmail payments."

Lorraine's eyes lit up. "I know someone who might help with that. My cousin Paulette, she works at First National Bank. She's not supposed to discuss customer accounts, but she might be willing to confirm if Martha's been making unusual deposits."

"That's a start," Agatha agreed. "Emma, can you keep digging into the historical records? Any other connections between Martha and the Hollywood crowd?"

"Already on it," Emma said, gathering her papers. "The library has access to more newspaper archives. I'll see what else I can find."

As they prepared to leave, Eliza approached their table with a concerned expression.

"I hope you don't mind me overhearing," she said quietly,

"but if you're looking into Martha Peck, there's something you should know."

The three women looked at her expectantly.

"I keep thinking about it," Eliza said, wiping her hands on her apron. "The week before Rosa died, Martha was in every morning buying snickerdoodles. I told you all about it at book club, remember? I thought she'd just developed a sweet tooth." She paused. "But she was also asking detailed questions about my recipe. What kind of cinnamon I use, where I get my flour. Martha's never shown any interest in my baking before." She frowned. "Then one day she asked if I knew where else in town someone could get snickerdoodles that might look similar to mine."

Agatha went still. "Eliza, the cookies that were found at Rosa's house, the ones that contained the poison. Did you ever get a good look at them?"

"The sheriff showed me photos. They looked like snickerdoodles, but something was off about them. The texture looked different, and the cinnamon sugar coating wasn't quite right."

"Someone was trying to make cookies that looked like yours," Lorraine breathed. "To frame you."

"Or at least create confusion about where the poisoned cookies came from," Agatha said grimly.

As they left the bakery, stepping into the cold afternoon air, Agatha's phone buzzed with a text message from Detective Dawson: *"Found something you'll want to see. Can you come to the station?"*

~

THE BRISTOL LAKE POLICE STATION was a modest brick building that had been built in the 1950s and still bore the faint aroma of decades of coffee and worry. Detective Dawson met them in the lobby, his tall frame filling the doorway and his expression more serious than usual.

"Thanks for coming in," he said to Agatha. "I need to show you something we found in Rosa's garden this morning."

He led them to his office, where a clear evidence bag sat on his desk. Inside was a small glass vial with a medical label.

"Potassium cyanide," Dawson said matter-of-factly. "Empty, but it still had enough residue for our lab to identify. Buried under Rosa's winterberry bushes."

"Someone was trying to dispose of evidence," Emma said.

Dawson shook his head. "More like someone dropped it in a hurry. You don't bury evidence in the victim's own garden if you're thinking straight. My guess is whoever did this was rushing and didn't realize they'd lost it." He paused. "But here's the interesting part. This vial has a prescription label. It's from Oxford Hills Veterinary Clinic, dated November 2024."

Agatha leaned closer to read the label. The prescription was for a dog named Duchess, owned by someone named Martha Peck.

"Potassium cyanide is still sometimes used in veterinary euthanasia in specific circumstances," Dawson explained. "The question is, why did Martha Peck's prescription vial end up in Rosa Fielding's garden?"

Agatha looked at Emma and Lorraine, seeing her own thoughts reflected in their faces. The circumstantial evidence against Martha was mounting.

"We're bringing Martha in for questioning," Dawson said. "With the poison vial, her admission about delivering the cookies, the witness statements about her behavior, and now her connection to the Hollywood events from 2001, we have enough to press her hard. But..." He paused, his expression troubled. "We don't have enough for an arrest yet. Everything we have is circumstantial."

"What do you need?" Agatha asked.

"A confession would be ideal. Or physical evidence tying her directly to the murders. Fingerprints on the poison vial before it was buried, witness testimony placing her at the scene, financial records showing motive." He sighed. "Right now, a good defense attorney could explain away everything we have."

The three women exchanged glances of frustration mixed with determination.

"So we keep digging," Emma said firmly.

"Carefully," Dawson warned. "If Martha is our killer, she's already murdered at least two people. I don't want any of you becoming number three."

Agatha nodded, but her mind was already racing ahead. They were close, so close to the truth. Martha Peck had the means, the opportunity, and connections to the past that made her the prime suspect.

But something still nagged at the back of Agatha's mind. Something about the timeline, about the relationships between all the players. Something she was missing.

"Detective," she said slowly, "when you question Martha, can you ask her specifically about what she knows about Bethany Marks? Where she went after the trial, what happened to her?"

Dawson raised an eyebrow. “You think that's relevant?”

“I think,” Agatha said, meeting his gaze, “that Bethany Marks is the key to everything. Find out what happened to her, and we'll know why Rosa and Henry had to die.”

20

BEHIND BARS AND BROKEN ALIBIS

Detective Dawson had called at six-thirty that morning, waking Agatha from a restless sleep.

"We arrested Martha Peck last night," Dawson said without preamble, his voice heavy with exhaustion. "Thought you'd want to know."

Agatha sat up, reaching for the lamp on her nightstand. "What changed? Yesterday you said you didn't have enough evidence."

"Her bank records came through," Dawson replied. "Large cash deposits over the past three months, five thousand here, three thousand there. No explanation for where the money came from. Combined with the poison vial, the cookies, her presence at those Hollywood events, and her confrontation with Rosa..." He sighed. "The DA felt we had enough to hold her."

"Did she say anything?"

"Lawyer'd up immediately. But she'll be arraigned this morning, and bail will be set." A pause. "I know you've been looking into this, Agatha. If you want to talk to her, now might be your only chance before her attorney shuts down all contact."

Which was how Agatha found herself, three hours later, following Officer Bradley down the narrow hallway of the Bristol Lake County Jail.

THE BRISTOL LAKE COUNTY Jail smelled like disinfectant and stale coffee, a combination that made Agatha's stomach turn as she followed Officer Bradley down the narrow hallway. Her footsteps echoed against the polished linoleum, each step feeling heavier than the last.

Martha Peck sat behind the reinforced glass partition in the visitor's room, her usually immaculate gray hair disheveled and her floral housecoat replaced with an orange jumpsuit that hung loose on her thin frame. Dark circles shadowed her eyes, but her spine remained ramrod straight, defiant even in defeat.

She looked up as Agatha settled into the plastic chair opposite her, their conversation conducted through the scratchy intercom system.

"I wondered when you'd show up," Martha sat with her shoulders rounded, the usual sharpness gone from her face. "Come to gloat?"

"I came to listen," Agatha replied gently. "Everyone deserves to tell their side of the story."

Martha's laugh was brittle. "My side? My side is that I'm innocent, and nobody wants to hear that. Detective Dawson thinks he's got his killer all wrapped up with a bow."

"Then tell me what really happened," Agatha said, leaning forward. "Starting with the cookies."

Martha's fingers worried at the hem of her jumpsuit. "I did bring Rosa cookies, just like I told you. Made them myself that afternoon because..." She paused, her usual bluster fading. "Because I felt bad for her. Rosa looked so lost at the theater opening, standing there by herself while everyone fawned over those Monroe sisters."

"But you weren't friends with Rosa."

"No," Martha admitted. "We had our differences over the years. Ancient history now, but still. Doesn't mean I wanted her dead." Her voice grew stronger, more insistent. "I left those cookies on her porch in a sealed container, like I always do when she's out. I never poisoned anyone."

Agatha nodded. "What about the poison vial they found buried in Rosa's garden?" Agatha asked gently. "The one with your name on it."

"I have no idea about that vial... It's not mine," Martha said, her brow furrowed in genuine confusion. "They told me it's dog medication or something." She sighed, shoulders slumping beneath the weight of the accusation.

"I have never had a dog in my life," she continued, a hint of indignation creeping into her voice. "Stanley is super allergic, and to be honest, dogs irritate me." Her nose wrinkled. "All the digging, the panting, and let's not mention that awful slurping sound they make when they drink water..." She shuddered visibly. "I simply can't stand it."

Martha leaned forward, her eyes pleading with Agatha. "I swear, Agatha, I have no idea how that vial ended up at Rosa's house, let alone why my name was on it. Someone's trying to make me look guilty, and they're doing a mighty fine job of it."

"But they found evidence linking you to the poison... "

"Then someone planted it," Martha interrupted, her voice

rising with desperation. "Because I'm telling you the truth. I was afraid people would think I killed Rosa because of our old argument, so I kept quiet about visiting her. But that's all I did, visit and leave cookies. I was there maybe ten minutes."

Agatha studied Martha's face, looking for tells, for the subtle signs of deception she'd learned to recognize over the years. Martha met her gaze, but her eyes gave her away. Something held back. Something she wasn't saying.

"What about the photograph?" Agatha asked quietly. "The one showing you working at the Beverly Hills Hotel gala in 1995. You were there when Vincent Cleary was alive, when Vivian and Bethany Marks were together."

Martha's face paled, and for a long moment she said nothing. When she finally spoke, her voice was barely above a whisper.

"I've never been west of Albany in my entire life," she said firmly. "Stanley and I honeymooned at Niagara Falls and thought we were seeing the world. Whoever that woman is in that photograph, it's not me."

But her hands trembled as she spoke, and she wouldn't meet Agatha's eyes.

Agatha sat back slowly. Martha was lying. The photograph was clear enough, and the family connection to Peck & Associates Catering was documented. But why would Martha deny something so easily proven?

Unless she had something far worse to hide.

"Martha," Agatha said softly, "if you're protecting someone, or if there's something you're not telling me about what happened in California... "

"I wasn't there," Martha repeated, her voice sharp now. "I don't know what that photograph shows, but it's not me.

Maybe it's a cousin, maybe someone doctored it, I don't know. But I was never in Los Angeles."

The lie hung between them, obvious and damning.

"Why did you want the movie reels?" Agatha asked, changing tactics.

Martha's cheeks colored. "Because I'm an old fool who thought if I could impress Stanley with something important, something valuable, maybe he'd stop looking at Vivian." Her voice dropped to barely above a whisper. "Vivian Monroe walks into town looking like she stepped off a magazine cover, and suddenly my husband of forty-three years is straightening his tie every time she passes the hardware store."

The admission hung between them, raw and vulnerable.

"I thought if I could get those reels, maybe convince them to let Stanley help with the projection equipment, he'd see me as someone who mattered. Someone worth paying attention to." Martha's laugh was bitter. "Pathetic, isn't it?"

"It's human," Agatha said softly.

But even as she said it, doubt crept in. Martha was telling the truth about her jealousy, about her motives for wanting the reels. But she was lying about California. And that lie made everything else suspect.

Agatha studied her for a moment. "I want to believe you. But you're not being completely honest with me."

Martha's eyes filled with tears. "I didn't kill anyone. That's the only truth that matters."

Agatha left the visitor's room with more questions than answers. Martha Peck was hiding something. Something big enough to lie about even while sitting in jail accused of murder.

The walk back through the jail corridors felt heavy now, weighted with uncertainty. Agatha pushed through the main entrance doors and stepped into the cold afternoon air, her breath forming white clouds. Snow had begun falling again, light flakes drifting down from the gray sky.

She nearly collided with Vivian Monroe on the front steps.

Vivian looked impeccable as always, her burgundy coat perfectly tailored, not a single platinum hair out of place despite the snow. But her composure cracked when she saw Agatha.

"Oh!" she exclaimed, pressing a manicured hand to her chest. "Agatha. I didn't expect to see you here."

"Visiting Martha," Agatha replied, studying Vivian's face. "What brings you here?"

"Detective Dawson called me." Vivian's voice wavered. "He wanted to ask more questions about the night Henry died. I was just finishing up." She glanced back at the jail entrance, then at Agatha. "I have to say, I'm relieved that woman is behind bars. She's been lurking around the Acadia for weeks, making threatening comments about me and Bianca."

"Threatening comments?"

"Oh yes," Something sharp crossed Vivian's face. "She cornered me outside the theater just two days ago, going on about how Hollywood types don't belong in Bristol Lake, how we're corrupting the town's values. She specifically mentioned that I'd 'get what's coming to me' if I didn't leave town."

Agatha filed that information away. It sounded like Martha, but something about the timing felt off.

A shadow moved in Agatha's peripheral vision, and she turned to see Bianca Monroe emerging from a blue sedan parked at the curb. Even from a distance, Agatha could see that something was wrong. Bianca's usual quiet grace had been replaced by a nervous energy that made her movements seem jerky, uncertain.

"Bianca, darling," Vivian called out, waving her over. "How did your appointment go?"

Bianca approached them slowly, her face pale beneath carefully applied makeup, pulling her coat tighter against the cold. "Fine," she said quietly, but her voice lacked conviction. She looked at Agatha for a moment too long. Concern? Wariness? Whatever it was, Agatha filed it away.

"Are you feeling all right?" Agatha asked gently. "You look a bit under the weather."

"Just tired," Bianca replied, but she couldn't quite meet Agatha's gaze. "It's been a difficult few days. This weather doesn't help."

"Haven't they just?" Vivian agreed, slipping an arm around her sister's shoulders. "All this business with poor Henry and Rosa, and now having to deal with the police asking endless questions. Thank goodness they caught the person responsible."

But Bianca didn't look relieved. If anything, she seemed to shrink into herself, as if she wanted to disappear entirely.

The three women stood in awkward silence for a moment, snowflakes settling on their coats, before Vivian glanced at her watch. "We should get going, Bianca. We have that conference call with the insurance company in an hour."

As the Monroe sisters walked toward their car, Agatha

watched Bianca's retreating figure and felt that familiar tingle at the base of her spine. The one that told her important pieces of the puzzle were still missing.

By the time she returned to the bookstore, Emma and Lorraine were already there, hunched over Emma's laptop at the reading table. Celeste sat nearby with a stack of freshly printed documents.

"Perfect timing," Emma said. "We've been researching Gordon Lane."

Lorraine turned the laptop screen toward Agatha, practically vibrating. "Ma chérie, it turns out our mysterious investor has quite the colorful past. Tell her, Emma."

Emma pulled up a series of newspaper clippings. "Gordon Lane wasn't just Vincent Cleary's business associate. He was engaged to someone named Caroline Walsh back in 1987."

"Caroline Walsh broke off their engagement three weeks before the wedding," Celeste chimed in. "According to the society pages, she eloped with a rising director named Henry Maddox."

"After she left him," Emma continued, "Gordon used his industry connections to systematically destroy Henry's directing career. Blacklisted him from every major studio, sabotaged his projects. Henry spent years doing odd jobs before he reinvented himself as a podcaster."

"And became incredibly successful at it," Agatha said slowly. "Which would have made Gordon's revenge feel incomplete."

"Exactement!" Lorraine exclaimed. "He destroyed Henry

once, but Henry bounced back stronger. So when Henry shows up in Bristol Lake, poking around the same old Hollywood scandal, Gordon sees a chance to finish what he started."

"And Rosa?" Emma prompted. "Where does she fit?"

"She was near the projection booth the night Henry died," Agatha said. "If she saw Gordon tampering with the equipment, she would have used it. That was Rosa. She would have tried to sell what she knew."

"And Gordon couldn't afford a witness," Lorraine said quietly, the excitement draining from her voice. "So he took care of Rosa and planted evidence to frame Martha."

Celeste looked up from her notes. "The poison vial with Martha's name. Making her look guilty without ever pointing at himself."

"An innocent woman sitting in jail," Lorraine said, "while the real killer walks free."

Mike padded to the window and let out a low growl.

Agatha followed his gaze. Across the street, a figure in an expensive coat was walking away from the jail, briefcase in hand, moving with the confident stride of someone who believed he'd gotten away with murder.

Gordon Lane.

21

A FACE IN THE CROWD

Lorraine returned to the bookshop just after lunch. Her normally pristine silk scarf was dusted with snow, and a few flakes were melting on her forehead.

"Well?" Agatha asked, rising from behind the counter where she'd been pretending to inventory new releases while actually jotting theories in her weathered notebook.

Lorraine shook her head, her hat slipping to one side. "Rien, mon cher. I asked everyone at the café and the library. Nobody remembers seeing Gordon Lane the day of the murder." She collapsed into the worn leather armchair by the window. "It's like he vanished into thin air."

Emma looked up from the table where she'd been sorting through Henry's podcast notes. Several colorful sticky notes marked pages of interest. "Or like he never showed up in the first place," she said, adjusting her glasses on the bridge of her nose. "Which means either he's innocent, or..."

"Or he's very, very careful," Agatha murmured, tapping her pen against her lower lip. She glanced at the corkboard where they'd pinned their timeline. Something wasn't adding up. "Someone must have seen him. In a town this small, you can't sneeze without three people offering you a tissue."

Lorraine's eyes widened dramatically. "Peut-être someone did see him, but they're afraid to talk, non? That man has Hollywood connections."

Emma adjusted her glasses with a skeptical look. "Great. This town loves to gossip about everything, but when it comes to actually stepping forward with information, suddenly everyone's too afraid to get involved. Typical Bristol Lake."

LATER THAT AFTERNOON, Agatha slipped Mike's harness on and walked to the hardware store, the earlier snow giving way to watery afternoon sunshine that made the snow-packed sidewalks glisten. Mike trotted beside her with surprising energy despite the cold, his nose working overtime at each lamppost and shrub.

Inside the store, the scent of fresh lumber and motor oil greeted her, along with the familiar creak of the old wooden floorboards. Stanley's Utility & Hardware had been a fixture in town since long before Agatha moved to Bristol Lake, and it remained stubbornly unchanged in an era of big-box stores.

She was browsing the gardening gloves, comparing the durability of leather versus synthetic options for spring planting, when she heard a familiar voice from the next aisle.

"Watch your step there. That shelf's wobbly," Quentin said to a clerk as he grabbed a can of sealant and a roll of duct tape. His theater maintenance uniform. Khaki pants and a navy polo with the Acadia Theater logo, was splattered with what looked like fresh paint.

"Quentin!" Agatha called, waving as she rounded the corner, Mike's leash looped around her wrist.

He turned and gave her a friendly smile, though she noticed the dark circles under his eyes. "Hey, Ms. Royale. Stocking up for some theater maintenance. Never ends, y'know? Just patched up the lobby ceiling, and now the bathroom sink is leaking." He gestured at his supplies with a weary sigh.

"Quick question, if you don't mind," Agatha said, lowering her voice and stepping closer. Mike sniffed at Quentin's shoes with interest. "Did you happen to see anything unusual the day Henry died? Anyone out of place or sneaking around? Any detail might help, no matter how small."

Quentin scratched the back of his neck, his eyes drifting to the ceiling as he thought. "Hmm. Not really. Just the usual folks. Ms. Vivian looking frazzled about the refreshments, Ms. Bianca arriving fashionably late as always, Henry fussing with his slides right up until showtime, the staff running around." He shrugged. "I didn't think much of it. Just another screening day, you know? Until... Well, until it wasn't."

Agatha nodded, trying to hide her disappointment. "Thanks anyway. I figured it was worth asking. Every piece helps complete the puzzle."

Quentin turned to leave but paused mid-step, his brow furrowing. "Oh, wait! I almost forgot." He snapped his fingers. "I did see Mr. Gordon."

Agatha froze, her hand tightening on Mike's leash. The miniature schnauzer looked up at her, sensing the sudden tension. "Gordon Lane? Are you sure?"

"Yeah, positive. He's hard to miss with that silver hair and those fancy shoes that probably cost more than I make in a month." Quentin leaned closer, lowering his voice. "He wasn't at the actual screening, but I saw him earlier in the evening, near the back exit. Looking kind of... I don't know, antsy? Checking his watch, peering around corners. He disappeared after that. Figured he left or something."

Agatha felt a chill despite the warm interior of the store. The hair on her arms stood up. "Thanks, Quentin. That's... Helpful. Very helpful."

"No problem. Hope it helps with whatever you're working on." He hesitated. "It's about Henry, isn't it? And maybe Rosa too? The police don't seem to be doing much since they arrested Martha."

"Just connecting some dots," Agatha said vaguely. "Thanks again."

AGATHA WAS STILL TURNING over what Quentin had told her when she pushed open the bookstore door, Mike trotting in ahead of her.

Emma looked up from the reading table. "You've got that look."

"Gordon Lane was at the Acadia the night Henry died," Agatha said, unwinding her scarf. "Quentin saw him near the back exit before the screening."

Lorraine emerged from the true crime section with an armful of books. "The back exit that leads to the projection booth?"

"The very one."

Emma tapped her pen against the table. "But revenge

seems like such a weak motive for murder. What else could Gordon gain from Henry's death?"

Before Agatha could respond, the door swung open with such force that the bell nearly flew off its hook. A blast of cold air rushed in, and Mike barked once in surprise.

Bianca stepped in, pale and wide-eyed, snowflakes melting on her coat. Her normally immaculate wrap dress was wrinkled beneath her winter coat, and her usual poise was completely gone. Her handbag dangled from her fingertips, and her carefully styled hair had come partially undone.

"Agatha," she said, breathless, clutching the doorframe. "I need to talk to you. I heard you're good at solving crimes." She swallowed hard, tears welling in her eyes. "I think Gordon killed Henry."

"What makes you say that?" Agatha asked, moving toward her.

Bianca's hand trembled as she reached into her purse and pulled out her phone. "Because I found this voicemail on Vivian's phone."

She pressed play and turned up the volume. Gordon Lane's unmistakable voice filled the quiet bookshop, trembling with rage.

"I won't rest until I destroy Henry completely. He'll pay for what he did to me. No matter what it takes."

Bianca stared at the phone. "This was left the day before Henry was killed."

The shop door swung open again.

Mrs. Willoughby bustled through the entrance, arms full of shopping bags. "Agatha, dear! I'm here to pick up my special order. You said those new Agatha Christie reprints came in?" She paused, finally noticing the tense atmosphere and Bianca's tear-streaked face. "Oh my. Is everything alright?"

"Everything's fine, Mrs. Willoughby," Agatha said, moving toward the counter. "Just helping Bianca with some theater business. Let me get those books for you."

"Wonderful! I'll just browse while you finish up," Mrs. Willoughby said, though her curious gaze lingered on the group as she wandered toward the cozy mystery section.

Agatha caught Emma's eye and tilted her head toward the back room.

22

VOICES FROM THE PAST

The shop door closed behind Mrs. Willoughby with a gentle jingle, her new Agatha Christie reprints tucked safely in her shopping bag. Agatha waited until the elderly woman disappeared down the snowy sidewalk before flipping the sign to "Closed" and turning the deadbolt.

"Back room," she said to Emma and Lorraine, nodding toward Bianca who sat perched nervously on a stool by the counter, clutching her purse like it contained something dangerous.

Mike trotted alongside them, his nails clicking against the hardwood floors as they retreated to office.

Agatha cleared off her desk with a sweep of her arm, sending pens and paper clips scattering. Emma winced but said nothing.

"Play it again," Agatha said once they were settled, leaning forward intently.

Bianca's fingers trembled as she set her phone on the desk and pressed play. Gordon Lane's voice filled the small space, the anger in his tone unmistakable even through the tinny speaker.

"I won't rest until I destroy Henry completely," Gordon's voice snarled. "He'll pay for what he did to me. No matter what it takes."

A chill settled over the room as the message ended. Mike's ears perked up, his head tilted as if trying to understand the human emotions swirling around him.

"That's definitely Gordon Lane," Emma confirmed, adjusting her glasses. "I'd recognize that voice anywhere."

"When was this left?" Agatha asked again, her detective instincts honing in on the timeline as she studied Bianca's face closely for any reaction.

"The day before Henry died," Bianca replied, her voice unsteady. She tucked a strand of hair behind her ear, a nervous gesture that made her seem more vulnerable than the composed business partner Agatha had met at the theater opening.

"Mon Dieu!" Lorraine exclaimed, throwing her hands up dramatically. "He practically confessed! Why hasn't Detective Dawson arrested him yet?"

"Because a threatening voicemail isn't enough evidence," Agatha said, tapping her pen against her notebook. "Though it certainly establishes motive."

Bianca bit her lower lip, hesitating before she spoke. "Henry was digging into Gordon's past. His Hollywood connections. I overheard them arguing at the theater the day before the screening."

"Including his connection to Bethany Marks," Agatha said quietly, watching Bianca's reaction closely.

Something flickered across Bianca's face. Surprise, fear,

something else Agatha couldn't quite identify, before her expression settled back into concerned neutrality.

"I don't know who that is," Bianca said, but her fingers twisted the strap of her purse a little tighter.

Agatha made a mental note of the reaction. "We need to find what Henry discovered about Gordon. I bet he kept notes somewhere."

"He was staying at the Bristol Inn," Emma offered. "Room 207. I heard him mention it when he came into the library asking about old newspaper archives."

"Should we tell Detective Dawson about the voicemail?" Lorraine asked.

Agatha shook her head. "Not yet. We need more than this. Dawson would just say Gordon has a temper but that doesn't make him a killer."

"So what's the plan?" Lorraine asked, leaning forward eagerly.

"We split up," Agatha said. "Bianca and I will check Henry's room at the inn, if we can get access. Emma and Lorraine, try to find Vivian. Ask her about this voicemail and why Gordon would leave such a threatening message about Henry."

"Why would Gordon want to destroy Henry?" Emma wondered aloud.

"That's exactly what we need to find out," Agatha replied. "Two hours. Then we meet back here."

THE BRISTOL INN stood three stories tall at the edge of Central Avenue, its brick facade and black shutters dusted with snow, giving it a timeless New England charm despite the winter chill. A small brass plaque by the entrance proudly proclaimed "Established 1887," though the modern key card locks on the doors told a different story.

Agatha and Bianca hurried across the parking lot, their breath forming white clouds in the cold air. Inside, the warmth was immediate and welcome.

Agatha approached the front desk, where a young woman with curly hair and tortoiseshell glasses looked up from her computer.

"Welcome to the Bristol Inn," she said with a practiced smile that immediately warmed when she recognized Agatha. "Oh! Ms. Royale from the mystery bookshop! I loved that Agatha Christie collection I bought from you last month."

"I'm glad you enjoyed it," Agatha smiled. "We just got in some new Dorothy L. Sayers first editions you might like."

"I'll definitely stop by," the clerk said, then lowered her voice. "I don't usually see you on this side of town. How can I help you?"

"We're helping collect Henry Maddox's belongings for his family," Agatha explained. The lie came easily, a necessary evil in the pursuit of truth. Beside her, Bianca fidgeted with her purse strap but said nothing.

The desk clerk's smile faltered. "Oh, Mr. Maddox. Yes, such a tragedy. The police already took some of his things, but they said the rest could be packed up." She hesitated, glancing between them. "Do you have authorization from his family?"

"His producer sent us," Agatha said smoothly. "They want his podcast equipment and notes specifically. Time-sensitive material, you understand."

After a moment's consideration, the clerk nodded and

reached for a spare key card. “Room 207. Just sign here, please.”

HENRY'S ROOM was exactly what Agatha would have expected. Expensive clothes strewn across the bed, toiletries scattered across the bathroom counter, and a makeshift recording setup on the desk. A laptop sat closed beside a professional microphone and headphones. Several notebooks lay stacked haphazardly next to an empty coffee cup.

“Let's start with the notebooks,” Agatha suggested, pulling on a pair of thin gloves she'd brought from the shop. “You check the laptop.”

Bianca hesitated. “I'm not sure I should... “

“It might be password protected anyway,” Agatha conceded. “Check the drawers instead.”

They worked in silence for several minutes, the only sound the rustling of papers and the occasional creak of the old building. Outside, snow had begun falling again, the flakes drifting past the window in the fading afternoon light.

Agatha flipped through Henry's notebooks, finding mostly podcast outlines, interview questions, and random observations about Bristol Lake. Nothing incriminating.

Until she reached the third notebook.

“Look at this,” she said quietly, holding up a page filled with Henry's hurried scrawl.

G.L. - Hollywood fixer? Trail of money from Cleary estate → offshore accounts → Acadia Theater renovation. Connection to B.M. Disappearance? Same pattern - creates new identities for people who need to disappear. Who is he protecting now?

“Looks like Henry found a connection between Gordon's

current financial activities and something from his Hollywood past," Agatha realized, pieces clicking into place. "He was following the money."

"But why would Gordon kill Henry over financial irregularities?" Bianca asked, her voice strained. "Wouldn't that just bring more attention to whatever he was hiding?"

"Unless what he was hiding was worth killing for," Agatha said grimly. "People have killed for far less than money."

As they continued searching, Agatha found a small voice recorder tucked inside Henry's jacket pocket hanging in the closet. She pressed play, and Henry's voice filled the room:

"Gordon Lane connection to Bethany Marks confirmed. Sources say he helped her disappear after Cleary's death. Follow-up: Where did the money go? And what's Vivian Monroe hiding? Her story about leaving Hollywood doesn't add up. According to my sources, she was at Cleary's house the night he died, despite her alibi. Gordon is protecting her, but why?"

Agatha glanced at Bianca, who was methodically searching through the desk drawer, seemingly unaware of the bombshell recording.

"Find anything over there?" Agatha asked casually, slipping the recorder into her pocket.

"Nothing important," Bianca set the papers down with deliberate calm. "Just travel receipts and hotel stationery."

EMMA AND LORRAINE found Vivian at Eliza's bakery, sitting alone at a corner table with an untouched cappuccino. Through the frosted window, they could see snow continuing to fall on Central Avenue. She looked perfectly put together as always, but Emma noticed the slight shadows beneath her eyes, expertly concealed but visible if you knew to look.

"May we join you?" Emma asked, approaching the table, unwinding her scarf.

Vivian glanced up, surprise registering briefly before her features settled into their usual elegant mask. "By all means," she said, gesturing to the empty chairs. "Though I can't imagine I'll be good company today."

"We wanted to ask you about Gordon Lane," Emma said, adjusting her glasses as she sat down.

At the mention of Gordon's name, Vivian's composure slipped. Her fingers tightened around her cup, her shoulders tensed almost imperceptibly.

"What about him?" she asked, her voice carefully neutral.

"Did you know he threatened Henry?" Lorraine asked, leaning forward with none of Emma's tact.

Vivian looked genuinely surprised. "Threatened? Gordon? That seems unlikely."

"We have proof," Emma said. "A voicemail he left on your phone. 'I won't rest until I destroy Henry completely. He'll pay for what he did to me.'"

The color drained from Vivian's face. "You accessed my voicemail?" She turned to Lorraine. "Was this your idea of amateur detective work?"

"It was found accidentally," Emma said quickly, giving Lorraine a warning glance. "The question is, why did you keep a threatening message like that instead of reporting it?"

Vivian sighed, some of the tension leaving her shoulders. "Oh, that." She waved her hand dismissively. "Gordon and Henry had some ridiculous falling out years ago over a woman they both dated in Los Angeles. Ancient history. They were always posturing like that, all drama, no substance." She traced the rim of her cup with one manicured finger. "Gordon has been my financial backer for years. Without his investment, the Acadia renovation would never have happened. He's dramatic and prone to grand statements, but he wouldn't actually hurt anyone."

"He sounded pretty serious," Lorraine remarked, her French accent thickening with suspicion.

Vivian's gaze drifted to the window, watching snowflakes swirl past outside. "Men like that always sound serious when their egos are bruised. You should have heard Henry's messages to Gordon after that whole fiasco." She shook her head with an air of worldly amusement. "Hollywood types never quite grow up. They just get better suits and bigger bank accounts."

As they stood to leave, pulling their coats back on against the cold, Vivian caught Emma's wrist, her grip surprisingly strong. "Be careful," she said quietly. "Gordon protects his investments. And sometimes his investments include people."

As Agatha and Bianca left the inn, stepping out into the snowy afternoon, a silver Mercedes pulled up to the curb. Gordon Lane stepped out, his face darkening when he spotted them.

"What were you doing in there?" he demanded, blocking their path to the sidewalk, his breath visible in the cold air.

"Looking into why Henry died," Agatha said honestly, meeting his gaze without flinching.

Gordon stepped closer, his expensive cologne failing to

mask the scent of whiskey on his breath. "Stay out of this, Ms. Royale. This goes beyond a small-town murder."

"Two people are dead," Bianca lifted her chin and met his eyes. "And Martha's been arrested for something she didn't do."

Gordon's expression hardened. "Some secrets are better left buried. For everyone's sake."

"Is that a threat, Mr. Lane?" Agatha asked calmly.

"It's advice," he replied. "Free of charge." He moved past them toward the inn entrance, then paused. "Tell Vivian I know about the film reel. We need to talk."

Agatha and Bianca exchanged glances as they hurried back toward the bookshop, their boots crunching on the snow-packed sidewalk. "What film reel do you think he's talking about?" Bianca asked.

"I'm not sure," Agatha admitted. "But I have a feeling it's connected to Vincent Cleary somehow."

THEY WERE HALFWAY BACK from the inn, the four of them walking close together against the cold, when Agatha's phone rang. Detective Dawson.

"Someone broke into Rosa's house," he said, his voice clipped. "Came in through the back window. Didn't trip the sensors until they were leaving."

Agatha stopped walking. Emma, Lorraine, and Bianca clustered around her on the snowy sidewalk. "That house is a sealed crime scene," Agatha said. "Someone broke into a police-sealed crime scene?"

"Whoever it was knew what they were doing. The place wasn't ransacked. They were after something specific."

Dawson paused. "Keep your eyes open, Agatha. This isn't someone panicking. This is someone with a plan."

She ended the call. For a moment, none of them spoke. Their breath rose in white clouds under the streetlight.

"That takes nerve," Emma said quietly. "Breaking into a house with police tape on the door."

"Not nerve," Agatha said. "Desperation. Whatever Rosa had, someone still needs it badly enough to risk a felony."

Lorraine pulled her coat tighter, her usual bravado dimmed. "Or they're cleaning up loose ends. Making sure Rosa can't tell us anything else, even from the grave."

Mike pressed against Agatha's leg and growled, low and focused, his attention locked on something across the street.

A figure stood half-hidden behind a parked van, watching them through the swirling snow.

"Don't turn around," Agatha murmured. "We're being watched."

The figure held position for another breath, then slipped into the darkness between two buildings and was gone.

Lorraine let out a shaky exhale. "Well. That's new."

23

THE PAPER TRAIL

The next morning, Agatha checked her watch as she approached the bookstore. Eight o'clock, and Mrs. Finch was already waiting at the door.

"You're late," Mrs. Finch announced, though Agatha was right on time.

Agatha smiled, unlocked the door, and headed behind the counter to start Mrs. Finch's weekly latte. Extra foam, dash of cinnamon, served in the blue mug with the chipped handle because she insisted it tasted better that way. Some things in Bristol Lake were as reliable as the tides.

"Murder or no murder, a woman needs her routine," Mrs. Finch declared, smoothing her cardigan with one hand while adjusting her reading glasses with the other. She'd been Bristol Lake's third-grade teacher for forty years before retiring and still carried herself with the air of someone who could silence a room with a single raised eyebrow. Snow dusted the shoulders of her wool coat, which she'd draped over the back of her chair.

"I couldn't agree more," Agatha said, carefully creating a

leaf pattern in the foam. She slid the mug across the counter, along with a small plate containing a blueberry scone from Eliza's bakery.

"How is Eliza holding up?" Mrs. Finch asked, her voice dropping to a concerned whisper. "People can be so cruel with their gossip."

"She's managing," Agatha replied. "The official statement from Detective Dawson cleared her bakery, but you know how small towns are with rumors."

Mrs. Finch sniffed. "Don't I just. Why, Stanley Peck was telling everyone at the hardware store that those cookies were definitely from Eliza's, no matter what the police said." She took a sip of her latte and made an appreciative sound. "Perfect as always, dear."

Mike trotted in from the true crime section, where he'd been napping between the shelves. He gave a perfunctory sniff at Mrs. Finch's snow-dampened boots before settling beside Agatha's feet, ever the loyal companion.

The shop was quiet for a Tuesday morning in January. A handful of regulars browsed the shelves, the soft rustle of pages turning and occasional murmurs creating a comforting ambient soundtrack. In the reading nook by the window, Gladys was engrossed in the latest Louise Penny novel, occasionally making notes in her small leather-bound notebook. Her "murder journal," as she called it, where she tracked clues and suspects in every mystery she read.

These everyday moments were what Agatha loved most about her bookshop, the simple, predictable rhythms of small-town life. Even with two murders hanging over Bristol Lake like storm clouds, people still needed their books, their coffee, their quiet corners to escape into different worlds.

But beneath this veneer of normalcy, Agatha's mind was

racing. Last night's break-in at Rosa's house. The mysterious watcher outside her shop. The threatening voicemail Gordon had left for Henry.

Emma hurried into the bookstore, her red ponytail bobbing with each step, a manila folder clutched to her chest. Her cheeks were pink from the cold.

"Sorry I'm late," she said, breathless, unwinding her scarf. "Library board meeting ran long. Mrs. Harrington had opinions about the upcoming reading programs. Many, many opinions."

Agatha smiled. "I saved you a scone."

"Bless you," Emma said, placing the folder on the counter and accepting the offered pastry. "I've been up since five researching Gordon Lane. You won't believe what I found."

Mrs. Finch, sensing gossip, leaned in.

"Why don't we talk in the office?" Agatha suggested, catching Emma's eye with a meaningful glance toward Mrs. Finch.

"Oh, don't mind me," Mrs. Finch said airily, opening her paperback with exaggerated focus. "I'm completely absorbed in my book."

Agatha led Emma to the small office behind the counter, Mike padding along behind them. Once the door was closed, Emma spread the contents of her folder across the desk.

"Financial records," she said, tapping a stack of printouts. "Gordon Lane made substantial donations to the Acadia Theater renovation fund through three different shell companies."

"How did you find these?" Agatha asked, impressed.

Emma adjusted her glasses with a small smile. "Let's just say I called in a favor from my cousin who works at First National. The point is, Gordon has been funneling money through these companies for years, long before he officially appeared as an investor in the theater."

"So he's been financially involved with Vivian and Bianca for much longer than he's admitted," Agatha mused, examining the documents.

"Exactly," Emma confirmed. "And here's the kicker. One of the shell companies, Cleary Arts Foundation, was established just weeks after Vincent Cleary's death in 2001."

Agatha felt a chill despite the office's warmth. "He's been covering his tracks for decades."

"There's more," Emma said, pulling out another sheet. "You know how people talk at the library? Mrs. Morrison was there this morning and mentioned her cousin who works dispatch at the police station. Apparently they found something at Rosa's house during the break-in investigation." "What kind of something?" Agatha asked.

"A note," Emma said. "Handwritten, on theater stationery. It says, 'Rosa, we need to talk about what you saw. Meet me at the theater tomorrow, 8 PM. Come alone.'" Emma paused dramatically. "It's signed with the initial 'G.'"

"Gordon," Agatha whispered.

"That's not all," Emma continued. "According to Mrs. Morrison's cousin, the note was dated, written the day before Rosa died."

Mike gave a soft whine from his spot under the desk, sensing the tension in the room.

"Did they say if anything was taken during the break-in?" Agatha asked. Emma shook her head. "Mrs. Morrison's cousin didn't know, they're still inventorying Rosa's belongings. But apparently they found a receipt in Rosa's kitchen drawer for a safe deposit box at Bristol Lake Savings and Loan." "Do they know what's in it?"

"Not yet. The cousin said they're getting a warrant."

Agatha leaned back in her chair, absorbing this new information. "Gordon arranges to meet Rosa, presumably about something she saw at the theater. The next day, she's poisoned. Then someone breaks into her house, possibly looking for something she left behind. Something that might be in that safe deposit box."

"It's all connected to the film canister," Emma said confidently. "Rosa must have found something on that reel that incriminates Gordon. Something worth killing for."

Before Agatha could respond, there was a soft knock at the office door. Celeste poked her head in, her thick braid draped over one shoulder.

"Sorry to interrupt," she said, "but Lorraine just called. She says it's urgent and she'll be here in five minutes."

LORRAINE ARRIVED in a flurry of floral perfume and jangling bracelets, her dramatic entrance causing several customers to look up from their books. Snow melted on her fur-trimmed hat as she swept it off. Today she wore a vibrant teal dress with a matching headscarf, looking like she'd stepped off the set of a 1960s film.

"You will not believe who I just saw at the bank," she announced without preamble, sliding onto a stool at the counter.

"Good morning to you too, Lorraine," Agatha said dryly, wiping down the espresso machine.

Lorraine waved away the greeting. "Gordon Lane. Looking incredibly nervous. He was trying to access a safe deposit box."

Emma and Agatha exchanged startled glances.

"Whose safe deposit box?" Emma asked.

"That's the interesting part," Lorraine said, leaning forward conspiratorially. "I was at the bank depositing a check from my insurance company. You remember, for that ridiculous fender bender last month, when who should come storming in but Gordon Lane himself."

She paused for dramatic effect, smoothing her headscarf. "He marched straight to the manager's office, but the door didn't close properly. I may have... Adjusted my waiting position to hear better." She shrugged unapologetically. "He claimed he had power of attorney for Rosa Fielding. Had documents and everything. But the bank manager wasn't buying it."

"Gordon was trying to access Rosa's safe deposit box?" Agatha repeated, making sure she understood correctly.

"Exactement," Lorraine confirmed. "And when they refused him, mon Dieu, the look on his face! Like he'd swallowed a lemon whole. He stormed out muttering something about 'legal consequences.'"

"He's getting desperate," Emma observed.

"But why would Gordon have power of attorney for Rosa?" Celeste asked, looking up from the new release display she was arranging.

"He wouldn't," Agatha said firmly. "It must be a forgery. He's trying to get whatever Rosa left in that box before the police do."

The door opened again, and they all turned to see Eliza entering, carrying a pink bakery box, shaking snow from her coat. Her usual cheerful demeanor seemed subdued, her smile not quite reaching her eyes.

"Thought you all might need a pick-me-up," she said,

placing the box on the counter. "Fresh cinnamon rolls. Just out of the oven."

"Eliza, you're an angel," Lorraine declared, immediately opening the box and inhaling the sweet, spicy aroma.

"How are you holding up?" Agatha asked gently.

Eliza sighed, leaning against the counter. "Better, I suppose. Detective Dawson came by the bakery this morning to publicly buy a dozen cookies. I think he was trying to show everyone they're safe to eat."

"That was kind of him," Emma said.

"It helped," Eliza admitted. "Though I still noticed some customers whispering and giving me side-eye. Stanley Peck came in for his usual morning danish and barely made eye contact." She shook her head. "I've been baking in this town for eight years. I catered his grandson's birthday party, for heaven's sake."

"People are scared," Agatha said. "They're looking for someone to blame."

"Well, they should be looking at Gordon Lane," Lorraine said through a mouthful of cinnamon roll. "The man practically oozes suspicion."

Eliza's eyes widened. "Gordon? Really? He seems so... Polished."

"A polished stone can still be used as a weapon," Emma pointed out.

The conversation was interrupted by Agatha's phone ringing. Detective Dawson's number flashed on the screen.

"Dawson," she answered, stepping away from the counter for privacy.

"Agatha," his voice came through, sounding grimmer than usual. "We opened Rosa's safe deposit box. You might want to see what we found."

An hour later, Agatha found herself in Detective Dawson's office at the Bristol Lake Police Station, a small, neat space with framed diplomas on the wall and a desk notably free of clutter. Unlike the cluttered chaos of some police offices, Dawson kept his space meticulously organized.

"I shouldn't be showing you this," Dawson said, sliding a clear evidence bag across his desk. "But given your... Unconventional assistance in past cases, I thought you might have insights."

Inside the bag was a yellowed newspaper clipping from early 2001, with the headline: "SCREENWRITER'S DEATH UNDER INVESTIGATION; FOUL PLAY SUSPECTED." Below was a photo of a crime scene, with police tape cordoning off what appeared to be an upscale home. In the background of the photo, partially blurred but still recognizable, was a much younger Gordon Lane talking to a uniformed officer.

"That's not all," Dawson said, pushing another evidence bag forward. This one contained a handwritten letter on Acadia Theater stationery.

G. I know what happened to Bethany Marks after the trial. I know where she's been all these years, and I know you've been helping her hide. I have proof. The film reel from Cleary's house shows what really happened that night, and I've traced the bank records showing where you've been sending money all these years. Meet me tonight or I go to the police with everything. R

Agatha stared at the letter, her heart racing. "Rosa found out what happened to Bethany Marks. She was blackmailing Gordon about knowing where Bethany is."

"That's how it looks," Dawson agreed, his expression serious. "Rosa somehow found out where Bethany Marks has been hiding all these years. Maybe she uncovered Gordon's role in helping her disappear, maybe she traced financial records. Either way, she was blackmailing him about it. We believe he killed her to keep that secret buried, but we need more concrete evidence to make it stick."

"And there's more," Dawson continued. "We found traces of the same poison that killed Rosa on an envelope in Gordon's hotel room. The lab confirmed it this morning."

"You searched his room?"

"With a warrant," Dawson confirmed. "After the break-in at Rosa's house. We also found this." He produced a third evidence bag containing a small brass key. "It matches Rosa's safe deposit box."

Agatha sat back, processing this information. "So Gordon had a key to Rosa's box. She was blackmailing him about recognizing Bethany Marks. And he had poison matching what killed her."

"It's circumstantial," Dawson admitted, "but it's adding up. We're bringing him in for questioning this afternoon."

"What about the film canister?" Agatha asked. "The one from Rosa's note. Did you find it?"

Dawson shook his head. "Not yet. But we're still looking."

As Agatha stood to leave, pulling her coat back on, Dawson added, "Be careful, Agatha. If Gordon Lane is behind these deaths, he's not going to stop until he gets what he wants."

"And what does he want?" Agatha asked.

"To bury the truth," Dawson said simply. "Whatever it is."

~

Back at the bookshop, Agatha found Emma, Lorraine, and Celeste waiting eagerly for news. Outside, snow had begun falling again, the flakes drifting past the windows. She filled them in on what Dawson had shown her, watching their expressions shift from curiosity to shock.

"So it really is Gordon," Celeste said, wide-eyed. "He killed them both."

"It certainly looks that way," Agatha agreed, though something still nagged at the back of her mind. A piece that didn't quite fit.

"Well, I for one am relieved," Lorraine declared. "Once they arrest him, this town can start returning to normal. Though I must say, the drama has been invigorating." She fanned herself dramatically.

"What's bothering you?" Emma asked, noticing Agatha's distracted expression.

"I'm not sure," Agatha admitted. "Something about this feels too... Neat. Too perfectly tied up."

"Criminals make mistakes," Emma pointed out. "Maybe Gordon just isn't as clever as he thinks he is."

"Maybe," Agatha said, unconvinced.

The afternoon passed in a blur of customers, coffee orders, and quiet conversations about the latest developments. Word had spread quickly about Gordon being brought in for questioning, and the bookshop buzzed with speculative whispers. Outside, the winter afternoon darkened early, the snow continuing to fall.

At closing time, Agatha found herself alone in the shop, Emma having left for a library board meeting and Celeste heading home to study for finals. She was just locking the register when Mike suddenly sat up, ears alert, a low growl building in his throat.

"What is it, boy?" Agatha asked, instantly on guard.

A shadow moved past the window, too quickly to identify. Mike barked sharply, rushing to the door.

Agatha peered out into the snowy twilight. The street appeared empty, but she couldn't shake the feeling of being watched. She double-checked the locks, then moved through the shop, turning on extra lights and drawing the blinds.

As she reached to close the blinds in the reading nook, she froze. Across the street, partially hidden by the maple tree in front of the post office, stood a figure watching the bookshop. Snow swirled around them, but Agatha could make out enough to know it wasn't Gordon, the build was wrong, smaller, more delicate.

The figure stepped back, disappearing into the shadows as a car drove past, its headlights cutting through the falling snow.

Agatha's phone rang, startling her. Detective Dawson again.

"Agatha," his voice was tight with urgency. "Gordon Lane has disappeared. He never showed up for questioning, and his hotel room has been cleared out. We've issued an APB, but I wanted to warn you directly."

"Thanks for letting me know," Agatha said, trying to keep her voice steady as she continued to scan the darkened, snowy street.

"There's something else," Dawson added. "We found the missing film canister."

Agatha's heart jumped. "Where?"

"In a ventilation duct in the projection booth at the theater. But here's the strange part, it's empty. Whatever film was inside is gone."

As Agatha ended the call, she couldn't shake the feeling

that despite all the evidence pointing to Gordon, they were still missing something crucial. The case wasn't solved, it was only getting more complicated.

And somewhere in Bristol Lake, a killer was watching, waiting, and planning their next move.

24

WHAT GORDON LEFT BEHIND

Agatha hadn't slept a wink. Her mattress felt like rocks, and her mind raced with questions about Gordon Lane's sudden disappearance. People didn't just vanish in Bristol Lake. Not without leaving ripples in the town's gossip pond.

A cold January morning greeted Bristol Lake as Agatha flipped the bookstore sign to OPEN. Frost coated the windows, and fresh snow from the night before blanketed Central Avenue. The brass bell above the door clinked softly against the glass, a familiar sound that usually brought her comfort. Today, it only emphasized the unsettling quiet that had settled over the town since the news broke.

Emma was already there, curled in the window nook with a blueberry scone that left a trail of crumbs on her oversized cardigan, her breath occasionally fogging the cold glass.

"Still no sign of our mysterious benefactor?" Emma asked, looking up from a stack of town permit filings she'd been scrutinizing.

Agatha shook her head, her tousled light brown hair

shifting as she frowned. "He's gone. Not at the hotel. Not at the Acadia. His car's still parked behind the hotel, but there's frost on the windshield that hasn't been cleared. I checked it myself this morning."

"That's peculiar," Emma said, brushing pastry crumbs from her lap. "Gordon struck me as the type who makes grand exits, not silent escapes."

Before Agatha could respond, the bell over the door chimed its cheerful greeting, letting in a blast of frigid air. The sound clashed with Detective Dawson's grim expression as he stepped inside. His coat was dampened by melting snow, and the lines around his eyes seemed deeper than yesterday.

"Good morning, ladies," he said, his voice carrying the weight of unwelcome news. "You might want to sit down for this."

Emma straightened in her seat. Agatha remained standing, her fingers gripping the edge of the counter.

"We found Gordon Lane," Dawson said, removing his hat. "Or rather, we traced his movements. He's already gone. Flew out last night on a private jet to Vietnam. No extradition treaty with the U.S."

Agatha's stomach dropped like a stone in a well. "He ran?"

"Because he had plenty to run from," Dawson said, his weathered face tightening. "Gordon was laundering money through the theater restoration fund. Shell companies, fake invoices, phantom contractors, he'd been orchestrating this scheme for years. That generous grant he dangled in front of Vivian and Bianca? Nothing but dirty money in need of cleaning."

Emma let out a low whistle, her eyebrows shooting upward. "Well, that explains his interest in our little town theater. But..." her voice dropped to a near whisper, "did he kill Henry?"

Dawson shook his head, removing a small notebook from his pocket. "No. We've confirmed he was in Oxford Hills at the exact time Henry died. Security footage from three different locations places him there, and we spoke with a woman named Claire Winters who confirmed they were together that evening." He flipped a page in his notebook. "She made quite a point of emphasizing their relationship was 'physical only.'"

"What about Rosa?" Agatha asked. "Was he with this Claire woman when Rosa died too?"

Dawson nodded. "Same alibi holds. He was in Oxford Hills both nights. We've verified it six ways to Sunday. Gordon Lane didn't kill anyone. He's a financial criminal, not a murderer."

"So he's a crook with impeccable timing," Agatha said, crossing her arms over her chest. "But not a killer."

"Precisely," Dawson said. Then he leaned forward, lowering his voice. "Listen, we found something you should know about. There was a manila envelope in Gordon's room at the hotel. He left instructions with Mrs. Peterson to mail it to you if anything happened to him."

Agatha's eyebrows rose. "What was in it?"

"That's the thing," Dawson said, looking uncomfortable. "It's technically evidence in an ongoing investigation, but the contents... They're not related to any financial crimes. It's about an old Hollywood scandal. The department's focus is on the money laundering, not decades-old gossip." He hesitated. "I've documented everything, photographed each page. Officially, I'm here to ask if you have any insights on why he'd want you to have this information."

Emma and Agatha exchanged looks.

"Why would he leave this for me?" Agatha asked, genuinely puzzled. Dawson shrugged.

"You've been asking questions. Maybe he thought you'd know what to do with it. Maybe he wanted the truth to come out even if he couldn't stick around to face it himself." He slid a thin folder across the table. "Look, I can't leave the original documents with you, but these are copies. Consider this a professional courtesy. If you find anything that connects to our murder cases, I expect a call." He stood, straightening his coat. "And Agatha? Whatever you're digging into, be careful. People who run usually have good reasons." The door swung shut behind him, letting in one last swirl of cold air.

Agatha opened the thin folder carefully. Inside were photocopied documents, including a letter with handwriting that had been preserved in the copy. Even in black and white reproduction, she could see how the rushed, all-caps handwriting slanted urgently to the right.

Later that day, she and Emma sat together at the front table, the fire crackling in the background as snow continued to fall outside. Agatha carefully examined the contents. Inside was a neatly typed letter, several photocopied documents with age-yellowed edges, and a black-and-white photograph. The letter came first.

"Read it aloud," Emma whispered, leaning forward.

Agatha cleared her throat and began:

"Agatha,

If you're reading this, I'm likely somewhere over the Pacific by now. I know how this looks. I didn't kill Henry Maddox or Rosa Fielding. I had no reason to, and I have solid alibis for both deaths. But I'm guilty of something else that's haunted me for decades.

Years ago, I helped two women disappear. One out of fear, the other out of ambition. I forged contracts, paid off a studio representative, and made a film reel vanish into thin air. I thought it was enough to keep the past buried. Then Henry started asking questions about the Acadia's history, and I knew it wouldn't stay hidden forever.

Vivian was there the night Vincent Cleary died. So was Bethany Marks. They lied for each other, and I made it easier for them both.

If anything happens to anyone else in Bristol Lake, start with Vivian Monroe. She knows everything.

-G.L."

Agatha looked up, her face pale. Emma's eyes were wide as saucers.

"Good heavens," Emma breathed. "Vivian was at the murder scene. Here, let me see the rest."

Agatha passed over the next page. A heavily redacted nondisclosure agreement with Bethany Marks' name faintly visible through the black lines. Another document showed a witness list from the Cleary case investigation, and in the margin, the initials V.M. had been circled repeatedly in red ink.

But it was the photograph that made Agatha's breath catch in her throat. A glamorous studio gala from another era. Vincent Cleary stood laughing in the center, champagne glass raised high. To his left stood Bethany Marks. Young, beautiful, with an unreadable expression in her eyes. And next to her, draped in a sequined dress and luxurious fur stole, was Vivian Monroe.

On the back of the photo, someone had written in faded ink: *"Vivian Monroe, Bethany Marks, Vincent Cleary - Industry Gala, February 2001"*

"My stars," Emma whispered, tapping the photo. "He

wasn't just covering for them. He was complicit in whatever happened. Vivian was there when Cleary died."

Agatha nodded slowly, piecing it together. "Gordon helped them both escape. Bethany disappeared after the trial, and Vivian... Vivian stayed but changed her identity somehow. And now he's gone, but he left us breadcrumbs to follow."

"But Vivian already told us she didn't know anything," Emma said quietly.

Agatha's jaw tightened. "Apparently she lied."

THE BELL over the door jingled wildly as Celeste burst through, windblown and breathless, a folder clutched to her chest like precious treasure. "I found it!" she exclaimed, still catching her breath. She waved the folder above her head. "I couldn't sleep last night after everything that happened, so I went digging through the town hall archives as soon as they opened this morning."

"What did you find?" Agatha asked, making room at the table.

Celeste slapped down the folder, flipping it open to reveal a yellowed document. "The original business license application for the Acadia Theater from 2002, right after it was purchased following Cleary's death. Look at this."

Agatha scanned the top page. Two signatures graced the bottom. One had been scratched out and replaced. The original, still partially visible beneath the correction, read: *Vera Martin.*

Agatha frowned, her forehead creasing. "Who in the world is Vera Martin?"

Emma adjusted her glasses, leaning closer to the document. "This signature was replaced later with Vivian Monroe's. Could Vera Martin be connected to her somehow? Or maybe..." She hesitated, then lowered her voice. "Maybe it's an alias she used after the Cleary case?"

Celeste nodded vigorously, her earrings swinging with the motion. "My film studies professor said nearly everyone in old Hollywood had fake names or used aliases to hide from scandals. Norma Jeane became Marilyn Monroe. Marion Morrison became John Wayne. Maybe Vivian Monroe changed her name after Cleary died to distance herself from the case."

"Or maybe," Agatha said slowly, tracing her finger over the scratched-out signature, "she's hiding something far more damaging than a screen name. Gordon's letter said he helped her disappear after Cleary's death. Maybe Vera Martin was who she was before, and Vivian Monroe is the new identity he created for her."

The three women fell silent, each lost in thought. Agatha looked out the window toward the Acadia Theater. It stood majestic and silent beneath the winter sky, its marquee unlit, snow gathering on its awnings, its secrets still locked behind those ornate doors.

"The truth is in there somewhere," she murmured, a spark of determination igniting in her eyes. "We just need to set the perfect trap and lure it out into the light."

THE AFTERNOON STRETCHED LONG into evening, and still the women lingered. Emma had pulled out her laptop to keep digging through old Hollywood archives, Lorraine had produced a tin of shortbread from somewhere in her enormous handbag, and Agatha was just sliding the last of the day's receipts into the register drawer when the bell above the door jingled.

Celeste stepped inside, but there was nothing ordinary about the way she moved. Her face was pale, her scarf half-unwound, and the hand holding her keys trembled so badly they rattled against each other.

"Celeste?" Agatha came around the counter immediately. "What's wrong? I thought you'd left for the night."

"I did. I had." Celeste closed the door behind her and leaned against it, as though she needed something solid at her back. "I locked up the side entrance, the one that opens into the alley, and when I turned around there was a man. Right there. Close enough I could've touched him."

Emma shut her laptop with a snap. "Did he hurt you?"

"No. No, he didn't do anything. That's the strange part." Celeste pressed a hand to her chest. "I thought he was going to. With everything they've been saying on the news about Petunia Heights, that man who attacked those two women last month, I thought, this is it, this is how it happens. I couldn't even scream. My throat just locked up."

"Sit down, ma chérie." Lorraine steered her to a café chair, bracelets jangling softly. "Breathe. You're safe now. Agatha, tea. Lots of it."

Agatha set the kettle on. Mike padded over and laid his chin across Celeste's knee.

"Tell us everything," Emma said, scooting her chair closer. "From the moment you turned the key."

Celeste took a shaky breath. "He looked at me, right in the face. Then he put his finger to his lips. Like this." She demonstrated, pressing her index finger against her mouth.

"Telling me to be quiet. And then he just walked past me, out the other end of the alley, like he was never there."

Lorraine's hand flew to her raspberry felt hat, the cardinal ornament wobbling precariously. "Mon Dieu. It's the Petunia Heights Strangler. He's moved on to Bristol Lake. I said this would happen, didn't I, Emma? I said it just last week at the post office."

"You said a psychic warned you about bad energy from the north," Emma said.

"And what is Petunia Heights if not north of here? The psychic knew. The psychic always knows."

"Lorraine." Agatha's voice was gentle but firm as she poured the tea. "Let's not get ahead of ourselves."

"I am not getting ahead of anything. A strange man in a dark coat, lurking in alleys, pressing his finger to a young woman's lips? That is a serial killer's calling card if I've ever heard one. Celeste, dear, have you updated your will?"

"She is twenty-two years old, Lorraine," Emma said.

"It is never too early, ma chérie. I had mine drafted at nineteen. One cannot predict when tragedy strikes."

A small, watery laugh escaped Celeste, and the tight line of her shoulders eased just a fraction. Agatha shot Lorraine a grateful look over the rim of her teacup. For all her theatrics, Lorraine knew exactly what a frightened young woman needed, even if she'd never admit to doing it on purpose.

"What did he look like?" Agatha asked, settling across from Celeste.

"I couldn't see much. A dark coat. A hat pulled low. He was tall, I think. Maybe my father's age, maybe older. It was so fast, and the alley light's been out for a week."

Agatha's mind was already working the angles. It wasn't a robbery. He hadn't demanded anything, hadn't even spoken.

He'd wanted her quiet, which meant he didn't want to be seen. Not by Celeste, and not by anyone else.

"Could it have been Gordon?" Emma asked, lowering her voice.

For a moment the possibility hung in the room. Agatha turned it over, testing the fit. The height was right. The coat. The air of a man trying not to be noticed.

Then she shook her head. "Dawson told us this morning. Gordon flew out on a private jet last night. He's in Vietnam by now, where we can't touch him."

"Unless Dawson is wrong," Lorraine said darkly, reaching for another shortbread.

"Dawson doesn't guess, Lorraine. He had flight records. Security footage. Gordon is gone."

"Then who was it?" Celeste whispered.

Nobody had an answer. Outside, the wind rattled the shop windows, and somewhere down Central Avenue, a car door slammed and echoed through the cold.

"From now on," Agatha said finally, "none of us leaves through the side door after dark. We use the front, together, with Mike, until we know what we're dealing with."

"A pact." Lorraine raised her teacup solemnly. "Sensible. Tragic, but sensible."

Emma and Celeste clinked their cups against hers.

Agatha walked Celeste to her car herself, Mike trotting alongside. The alley was empty, lit only by the pale wash of streetlight from Central Avenue. But as she watched Celeste's taillights disappear around the corner, Agatha couldn't quite shake the feeling that whoever had stood face to face with her young assistant was still out there, closer than any of them wanted to believe.

Snow began to fall again, soft and silent over Bristol Lake.

25

A ROLE SHE NEVER AUDITIONED FOR

It was a gray afternoon in Bristol Lake, the kind where heavy clouds pressed low and threatened more snow. The sky hung pale and colorless, turning shop windows into little glowing lanterns against the winter gloom. Fresh snow from the morning had been packed down on the sidewalks, and the scent of woodsmoke drifted through Central Avenue. Inside the bookstore, the espresso machine let out a soft hiss of steam, and someone's order of cinnamon scones sent waves of buttery sugar through the air.

Agatha paced slowly between the classic mystery shelves, Mike at her heels and a steaming cup of Darjeeling in hand. She was turning over the words "Vera Martin" in her mind like a puzzle piece that didn't quite fit. "Maybe she was never really Vivian," she said aloud.

Emma, sitting at the front table with a stack of old theater programs and a cinnamon scone half-gone, looked up. "Do you think Vera Martin is her real name?"

Agatha nodded. "We know she scratched it out. People

don't usually hide a name unless they're running from something."

"Or reinventing themselves," Celeste offered, joining them with a refill of her coffee and the town archive app open on her phone. "Actors do that all the time. Marilyn Monroe was Norma Jeane. Judy Garland was Frances Gumm."

The door flew open and Lorraine staggered in, one hand pressed to her chest. "Mes chéries, I was nearly flattened by that delivery truck from Delia's Deli! The man drives like he thinks he's in the Grand Prix!"

Agatha smiled despite herself. "You're just in time. We were discussing aliases."

"Oh! Are we uncovering secret spy identities now? Because I always suspected Mrs. Tolliver from the post office of being a retired MI6 agent. She's far too precise with her stamps."

Emma laughed. "We think Vivian Monroe might have used Vera Martin's name at some point. Maybe she stole her identity."

Lorraine gasped and pressed her hands to her chest like she'd just heard that her favorite film noir was being remade. "Not the Vera Martin from Dusk Over Catalina? The one who dropped off the map sometime around 2001?"

Three heads swiveled toward her.

"Wait," Agatha said. "You know that name?"

"Mais oui! I used to collect gossip magazine articles about her. She was all cheekbones and mystery. Vanished right around 2001." She paused. "Now that I think about it, it was right after that director's death. If the timeline Henry was talking about was correct, everyone thought she skipped the country or joined a cult in Italy."

Celeste was already tapping her phone. "She disappeared after 2001. No death record. No comeback. Just poof."

Emma furrowed her brow. "Wait, this doesn't make sense. Vera Martin and Vivian Monroe were both working actresses around the same time, weren't they?"

Lorraine nodded, tapping her chin thoughtfully. "Vera was already starring in psychological thrillers by the late '90s. Vivian appeared in smaller roles around the same time, background work, minor parts. Both were in LA, both moving in the same circles."

Agatha looked back at the scratched-out name on the license form. "Then Vivian couldn't be Vera. They were different people working at the same time. But what if Vivian used Vera's name after Vera disappeared? An alias? A cover to hide her own identity after Cleary died?"

"You think she stole her identity?" Celeste asked. "What if... She did more than borrow a name?"

Emma whispered, "You mean, what if she killed Vera Martin? Made her disappear so she could use her identity?"

No one spoke for a long moment.

Agatha slowly sat back, the implication hanging in the air like smoke. "We don't have proof. But if she used that name on official paperwork after Vera disappeared... It means something. She wanted to hide who she really was by taking on a dead woman's identity."

Lorraine, ever the dramatic one, whispered, "And maybe she made sure Vera disappeared permanently."

"Gordon's letter said Vivian was at Cleary's house the night he died," Agatha said quietly. "What if she killed both Cleary and Vera Martin? And then later, when Henry started asking questions..."

"She had to kill him too," Emma finished.

They sat in silence for a moment, the clink of coffee mugs and the soft whirr of the espresso machine grounding the moment in cozy reality.

Then Celeste leaned forward, her eyes lit with curiosity. "Remember the restoration inventory from the Acadia? One of the film reels was logged but never archived. It was listed under 'B.M.' and checked in during the initial cleanout."

Agatha's brows rose. "Bethany Marks. That reel could be the one Gordon mentioned, the one that shows everything."

"If it exists," Emma added.

"Then we need to find it," Agatha said. "But if we go digging, they might panic."

Lorraine waggled her eyebrows. "Then let us not go digging. Let them bring it to us."

AN HOUR LATER, the plan was hatched over chai lattes and Lorraine's impromptu monologue about the tragic demise of her favorite scarf. They would host a "Hollywood Nostalgia Night" at the Acadia Theater. It would be a public tribute to the golden age of film, and to Henry, of course.

Emma and Celeste would create a short documentary-style video from public domain film clips, set to dramatic music and spliced with carefully chosen audio from Henry's podcast drafts. It wouldn't point fingers, but it would hint. Subtly. Just enough to rattle the right nerves.

"We'll call it a celebration," Agatha said, jotting notes in her spiral-bound planner. "A way to honor Henry's legacy and love for truth. And if Vivian is hiding something, she'll feel it."

"Ooh! We should serve cocktails with starlet names,"

Lorraine said. "I could whip up a `. 'Murder on Mulholland Mojito.'"

Emma snorted. "Only if you promise not to wear your feather boa again."

"Darling, the boa makes the night."

THAT EVENING, Agatha walked downtown, Mike trotting beside her, the sidewalks slick with packed snow and ice. The town felt quiet but watchful. Stanley Peck was closing up the hardware store for the night, giving her a knowing nod despite his wife being in jail. Mrs. DeLuca in the florist shop waved through the glass while arranging pale roses. The glow from streetlamps cast a soft halo over everything, the snow reflecting the light and giving the town a faint silver-screen shimmer.

As they passed the Acadia, Agatha stopped. The marquee lights flickered lazily, casting golden reflections onto the snowy sidewalk. The theater looked serene, even innocent. But something inside it was festering.

Mike let out a low, muffled growl.

Agatha followed his gaze.

Across the street, parked half in shadow, was a familiar car. Snow covered its hood and roof.

Behind the wheel sat Vivian Monroe. Her hands rested calmly on the steering wheel. She was staring directly at Agatha.

Agatha took a slow step forward, heart skipping, her breath forming white clouds in the cold air.

Vivian didn't move. Her face unreadable, the picture of icy composure.

Then, just as Agatha stepped off the curb, the car's engine started and it pulled away, tires crunching on the snow.

Mike barked, sharp and clear, his paws scraping at the icy pavement.

Agatha stood in the snowy evening, watching the taillights disappear into the winter darkness.

"She's scared," she whispered.

Or worse.

"She knows what's coming."

26

THE SCRAPBOOK

Snow fell lightly over Bristol Lake the next morning, the flakes drifting down in lazy spirals and dusting the streets with fresh powder. The snow tapped against the bookshop windows with a gentle persistence that matched Agatha's mood, quiet but determined. At One Deadly Chapter Books & Brew, Agatha sat with Emma and Lorraine around the corner table, swirling honey into her tea with a methodical motion while Celeste closed her laptop with a dramatic sigh that seemed to echo through the nearly empty shop.

"Well," Celeste said, pushing her tortoiseshell glasses up her nose, "Bianca called. She asked Vivian about the tribute idea. Vivian said no." She mimicked Vivian's clipped tone with surprising accuracy: "'The Acadia wasn't some sentimental town square' and that it wasn't open for 'gimmicks.'" Her fingers made air quotes around the last word.

Emma groaned, slumping forward until her forehead nearly touched the table. "So much for luring them into slipping up. Back to square negative three."

“We have nothing concrete to go to Detective Dawson with,” Agatha said, frustration settling in her chest like a stone. “No proof of what Vivian might be hiding, no evidence she even knew Henry beyond their arguments. Just theories and hunches.”

“And yet, criminals tremble when they hear the words 'theories and hunches,'“ Lorraine declared, stirring her chai latte with a cinnamon stick. “Sherlock Holmes operated entirely on hunches and the occasional pipe-smoking session. Hercule Poirot solved cases with nothing but his 'little gray cells.'“

“I don't think that's the example we want to follow,” Emma said dryly.

Lorraine waved her hand dismissively, nearly sending her cinnamon stick flying. “Details, darling. The point is, we need to think like the great detectives. What would Miss Marple do?” She struck a pose, squinting her eyes and stooping dramatically as if impersonating an elderly woman. “She would knit something terribly complicated while extracting confessions from unsuspecting villagers.”

Celeste snorted into her hot chocolate.

Lorraine tapped her chin with a manicured finger, each nail painted a different shade of blue in an ombré effect. “Then we need something that connects her. Something personal.” Her eyes brightened suddenly. “Didn't Rosa say she had old clippings? A scrapbook?”

Agatha sat up straighter, nearly spilling her tea. “You're right. Rosa mentioned she thought she recognized something about Vivian's past. Maybe she kept notes, old clippings. Something that connects Vivian to her Hollywood days.”

“Dawson might let us look,” Emma said, straightening in

her chair. "It's worth asking. He seems to respect your instincts, even if he pretends not to."

"Oh, he respects more than her instincts," Lorraine said with a theatrical wink that involved her entire upper body. "I've seen the way he looks at you, Agatha. Like a puppy who's found the only person who understands his complex inner life."

"Lorraine!" Agatha felt her cheeks warm despite herself.

"What? I'm merely stating observable facts. I have two eyes and thirty-seven years of experience watching men try to hide their feelings behind badges and grimaces." She sipped her latte primly. "Besides, he's single, you're divorced. It's practically a mathematical equation at this point."

"Can we please focus on the potential murder investigation and not my nonexistent love life?" Agatha asked, though she couldn't help the small smile that tugged at her lips.

"Fine," Lorraine sighed dramatically. "But I'm making a note in my mental diary: 'Agatha denies attraction to handsome detective, film at eleven.'"

Mike, who had been dozing near the register, lifted his head and gave a small whine as if offering his own commentary on the situation.

"Even Mike agrees with me," Lorraine said triumphantly.

"Mike agrees with anyone who might have treats in their pocket," Agatha replied, but she reached down to scratch behind his ears affectionately.

SNOW STILL DRIFTED down when Agatha stepped outside with Mike an hour later. The sidewalk was covered in fresh powder, and her breath formed white clouds in the cold air.

Mike was already nosing at the mailbox with exaggerated curiosity as if important correspondence awaited his personal inspection. At the end of the walk, Detective Dawson's cruiser idled quietly, windshield wipers pushing aside the accumulating snow in a hypnotic back-and-forth motion that matched Mike's wagging tail.

"Morning," Dawson said, rolling down the window. His face looked tired, the lines around his eyes deeper than usual. "You still thinking about Rosa Fielding?" The question wasn't accusatory, but knowing.

Agatha gave a faint nod, snowflakes catching in her hair. "I think there's something in her house we missed. Something personal. A clue." She hesitated. "She mentioned a scrapbook from her theater days. It might help connect some dots."

Dawson looked at her for a long moment, then sighed, his breath fogging in the cold morning air. "I can authorize a search. Her sister's the executor and already cleared most of the place out for donation. But if there's anything left, it's yours to look through." His expression turned serious. "Just be careful, Agatha. Whoever's behind this has already killed twice."

"Thank you, Detective."

"Edgar," he corrected quietly, then immediately looked as if he regretted the familiarity. "Call if you find anything. And take someone with you."

"I will," Agatha promised, already mentally selecting her team.

~

By midday, Agatha, Emma, and Lorraine stood outside Rosa Fielding's small blue cottage on Hawthorn Lane, the quaint home looking forlorn with its empty bird feeder and snow-covered flower boxes. Icicles hung from the eaves, and the porch steps were slick with ice. The wooden steps creaked under their weight, as if the house itself was sighing.

Lorraine peeked through the front window, cupping her hands around her eyes. "I feel like I'm trespassing. At least let me pretend to be wearing all black." She straightened and struck a dramatic pose. "Lorraine Dubois, international woman of mystery."

"You wore leopard print, Lorraine," Emma pointed out, gesturing to Lorraine's winter coat, which featured a pattern that would make any safari guide nervous.

"It's my stealth pattern," Lorraine insisted, patting the coat fondly. "Big cats use it in the wild. No one ever sees them coming."

"I'm pretty sure people see leopards coming," Emma muttered, stamping her boots to shake off the snow.

"That's because they're not wearing sensible flats and Chanel No. 5 like me," Lorraine said with an imperious sniff. "It's my one luxury splurge - throws off the predator-prey dynamic completely."

Agatha bit back a laugh as she unlocked the door with the key Dawson had given her. The house smelled faintly of potpourri and dust, the air still and expectant, like it had been waiting for someone to return. They walked quietly through the living room with its faded floral sofa and collection of porcelain figurines, and into a narrow hallway that led to Rosa's bedroom and den.

"Look for anything out of place," Agatha pulled the door closed behind them. "Notes, letters, a journal maybe.

Something that might tell us what Rosa knew about Vivian."

Emma moved toward the kitchen, her practical nature drawing her to the most organized room in any house. Lorraine veered into the living room, her flats padding softly on the hardwood floor. She stopped in front of a low cedar trunk tucked beneath the window, running her fingers along its carved lid.

"Oh, this has scrapbook written all over it," she said, lifting the lid with a flourish. "And also maybe mothballs. Eau de Grandmère, as we say in French."

Agatha joined her, kneeling beside the trunk despite her protesting knees. Inside were several photo albums bound in faux leather, a few plastic sleeves stuffed with newspaper clippings, and a stack of yellowed envelopes tied with faded ribbon.

Lorraine pulled out a dusty scrapbook labeled *Theater Years* in curling silver marker. "Voilà!" she exclaimed, blowing dust from the cover in a theatrical gesture that sent her into a brief coughing fit. "Oh dear," she wheezed, "mystery-solving is hazardous to one's respiratory system."

She opened the scrapbook, each page turning with a soft crackle of age. They flipped past programs from local productions, flyers for community theater shows, and several ticket stubs from Broadway performances, all meticulously arranged and annotated in Rosa's neat handwriting.

"She certainly was thorough," Emma said, rejoining them from the kitchen. "Look at these notes. She even recorded which actors flubbed their lines on opening night."

"The original theater critic," Lorraine said admiringly. "I would have loved to gossip with her over martinis."

As they turned another page, something fluttered loose

and landed in Lorraine's lap. She picked it up gingerly between two perfectly manicured fingertips. "Ooh. What do we have here? Secret love letters? Theater rivalries? A recipe for the world's best lemon squares?"

Agatha leaned in, her heart quickening. The paper was from a small notebook, with Rosa's distinctive handwriting scrawled across it:

January 10th - Vivian's secret from 2001. She's hiding something big. All that money, that fancy theater - she's desperate to keep her past buried. If I can prove what she really did that night, I'll be set for life. Time to make my move.

Lorraine's eyes widened as she read over Agatha's shoulder. "Mon Dieu, she was planning this carefully. Look at the date - just two days before Henry died."

Agatha went cold. "This shows Rosa was actively planning to blackmail Vivian about whatever happened in 2001. And timing-wise..."

"If Vivian found out Rosa was digging into her past right when Henry was also asking questions," Emma said grimly, "she might have panicked. Killed them both to keep her secrets buried."

They continued searching through the scrapbook, finding more notes in Rosa's handwriting. Some appeared to be random observations about people in town and their secrets, others seemed like calculations of amounts she might demand. But this entry about Vivian was different. It was more focused, more deliberate, as if Rosa had been building her case carefully.

Emma examined the journal entry again. "She doesn't specify exactly what she knew. Just that she knew something from 2001 and that Vivian was desperate to keep it buried."

"Smart," Agatha said. "Even if Rosa was bluffing, just

fishing to see if Vivian would pay. It would have terrified someone with real secrets to hide."

Lorraine's expression sobered, though her voice maintained its theatrical lilt. "If Rosa pushed too far with her little blackmail scheme, she might've signed her own death warrant. A tragic final act."

"We need to document everything," Emma said, pulling out her phone to take photos. "This could be the evidence we need."

As they carefully sorted through the rest of the trunk, Lorraine unearthed a small address book bound in red leather. She flipped through it, stopping suddenly with a gasp worthy of a daytime soap opera.

"Oh. Mon. Dieu." Each word punctuated with dramatic emphasis. "Look at this!" She thrust the book toward Agatha, her finger pointing to a name written in Rosa's neat script: *Vera Martin (?)* followed by what appeared to be an old Los Angeles phone number.

"Vera Martin," Agatha breathed. "The name on that business license application Celeste found."

"The plot thickens to the consistency of my aunt Mildred's holiday gravy," Lorraine said, her eyes sparkling with excitement. "We have a connection!"

They packed the scrapbook and address book carefully into Emma's tote bag and took one last look around the quiet house. Outside, the snow had intensified, swirling around the picket fence in white gusts.

Emma hesitated at the door, glancing back at the tote bag. "Is it legal to just... take that? The scrapbook?"

"We're not taking it," Agatha said, shouldering the bag. "We're borrowing it."

"Does Dawson know we're borrowing it?"

Agatha headed for the door. “He will. Let's go talk to Vivian.” She pulled her coat tight and stepped onto the icy porch. “I think it's time she told us who she used to be.”

“And who she pretends to be now,” Emma added, pulling her coat tighter against the cold.

Lorraine adjusted her leopard-print coat with a flourish. “Ladies, we're about to star in the final act of this little drama. And unlike the theater, there are no rehearsals for confronting a killer.” She paused dramatically, then added with a wink, “But my performance will still be flawless. It always is.”

Mike, waiting patiently in the snowy yard, gave a single bark that sounded strangely like agreement.

27

FINAL CLUE FALLS INTO PLACE

Sunday morning arrived cold and quiet, as if Bristol Lake had been blanketed in fresh snow overnight. The town yawned awake slowly, streets covered in white powder that sparkled like scattered diamonds in the soft early light. Storefronts stood sleepy-eyed and half-shuttered along Central Avenue, their windowpanes frosted at the edges, snow piled against their doorsteps. Only Eliza's bakery and Mabel's Corner Diner showed signs of life, their windows glowing with warm yellow light, the comforting aroma of fresh coffee and cinnamon rolls curling through the frigid air like a familiar embrace.

Inside One Deadly Chapter Books & Brew, Agatha sat in her favorite armchair near the front window, flipping through Rosa's scrapbook for what felt like the hundredth time. The leather binding was growing soft from handling, its edges frayed. She traced her finger over the pages, hunting for any detail she might have missed, any thread that might unravel the entire mystery if pulled just right.

Mike rested at her feet on the braided rug, occasionally

twitching as his paws moved in tiny running motions. Agatha smiled down at him, wondering what suspects he might be chasing in his doggy dreams. The shop felt particularly quiet this morning, as if the books themselves were holding their breath, waiting for the final chapter to be written.

Emma nudged the door open with her hip and stepped inside, balancing a pink pastry box and a manila folder stuffed with newspaper clippings. Her cheeks were flushed from the morning chill, snow dusted her shoulders, and her red hair was disheveled from the wind. "Lorraine's already halfway to the Acadia," she announced, unwinding her scarf as she crossed to the reading table and set everything down. Pastry flakes scattered across the polished wood surface as she opened the box to reveal still-warm croissants. "She insisted on wearing her red trench coat. Said if she's going to confront a former starlet, she might as well dress the part."

Agatha gave a weary smile, reaching for a croissant. "Of course she did. I'm surprised she didn't bring a director's megaphone."

"Don't give her ideas," Emma warned, pouring coffee from the thermos she'd brought, her fingers still cold from the walk. "The costume shop on Willow Street has one in the window display."

They fell into companionable silence, the only sounds being the occasional turning of pages and Mike's gentle snoring. There was little left to theorize now. The scrapbook. Rosa's dramatic and oddly methodical collection, had offered everything they needed. The journal entry wasn't one of Rosa's usual observations. This one had the raw, desperate edge of someone who knew too much and got too bold for her own good.

Agatha opened the book again, flipping to the page they'd nearly memorized, the one containing Rosa's planning notes:

January 10th - Vivian's secret from 2001. She's hiding something big. All that money, that fancy theater - she's desperate to keep her past buried. If I can prove what she really did that night, I'll be set for life. Time to make my move.

"It's motive," Agatha said softly, the steam from her coffee cup rising in the cool air. She removed her glasses, wiping the lenses with the edge of her cardigan. "It might not be proof beyond a shadow of a doubt, but it's motive. And Vivian had means and opportunity."

Emma nodded, brushing a stray crumb from her lap. "And she had something to hide. That much we know." She pushed her folder of clippings toward Agatha. "I found three more mentions of Vera Martin in old Hollywood trade magazines from the late '90s and early 2000s. Always as a footnote, never in the spotlight. Then she vanished completely after 2001."

Agatha stood, her chair scraping softly against the hardwood floor. Mike's eyes opened briefly before he settled back into sleep. "We may not have Gordon anymore to question... "

"Not unless we want to book a trip to Vietnam," Emma muttered, sipping her coffee.

Agatha's lips quirked into a half-smile. ", but Vivian's still here. And she has some explaining to do." She glanced at the wall clock, its brass pendulum swinging with quiet precision. "We should get moving. Lorraine's patience is inversely proportional to her excitement level."

"Which means she's already tapping her foot and checking her watch," Emma said, gathering their evidence into her tote bag.

Agatha clipped Mike's leash to his collar, rousing him from his nap. "Come on, detective. Time to close this case."

THE ACADIA THEATER looked less glamorous in the thin morning light than it did during evening performances. Snow covered the awnings and piled against the walls. Without the glow of marquee lights or the chattering crowd to mask its imperfections, it seemed older, more vulnerable, like an aging actress caught without her makeup. Frost clung to the red velvet awnings, and ice had formed on the brass handles of the wide double doors, which creaked as Lorraine pushed them open with dramatic flair, her breath forming white clouds.

"Vivian said to meet her in the lounge," she whispered, though no one else was around to hear. She waved them in with an exaggerated gesture worthy of a spy film. "And yes, she knows we found the scrapbook. I may have... Hinted."

"Subtle as ever," Agatha said, stepping into the dimly lit foyer, grateful for the warmth inside. The smell of furniture polish and old carpet greeted them, along with the faint hint of Vivian's signature perfume hanging in the air.

"I prefer to think of it as 'effective communication," Lorraine replied, adjusting the belt of her trench coat, which was indeed a shade of red so vibrant it almost glowed in the shadowy interior. "Besides, the element of surprise is overrated. I prefer the element of anticipation, so much more dramatic."

They made their way through the lobby, past the empty concession stand with its gleaming popcorn machine, and toward the private lounge reserved for special guests and theater donors. Mike trotted alongside them, his nails clicking softly on the marble floor.

The lounge was dimly lit by a single crystal chandelier, its light refracted into a thousand tiny rainbows across the walls. The room smelled faintly of dust and old upholstery, with undertones of the lemon oil used to polish the antique bar that dominated one wall. Vintage movie posters in ornate frames adorned the walls. Classics from Hollywood's golden age, each signed by the stars who had once graced the screen.

Vivian Monroe stood near the back wall, arms folded across her chest, her icy blue eyes unwavering as they entered. She wore a pale silk blouse and perfectly tailored slacks, her dark hair styled in a smooth, elegant bob that framed her face like a picture. She looked as if she'd stepped out of another era entirely. A living remnant of old Hollywood glamour displaced in their small New England town.

"I was wondering when you'd come," she said coolly, her voice perfectly modulated. No hint of emotion, no crack in the veneer.

Agatha held up the scrapbook, its worn cover catching the dim light. "We found this in Rosa Fielding's house."

Vivian's gaze didn't move, didn't even flicker. "Did you."

Not a question, Agatha noted. A dismissal dressed as acknowledgment.

"One of the pages had notes about you," Agatha continued, stepping further into the room. "Rosa was planning to blackmail you. She thought she knew what you did in 2001, and she believed you'd pay to keep it quiet."

"She wrote a lot of things in that scrapbook," Vivian said, her tone flat. She gestured vaguely with one perfectly manicured hand. "The woman had an active imagination."

Emma stepped forward, clutching her folder of evidence.

"But the note about you didn't read like the others. It wasn't playful. It was calculated. She was building a case against you."

Vivian was quiet. The hum of the overhead lights filled the silence, punctuated only by the soft sound of Mike sniffing intently at the baseboards, following some scent only he could detect.

"You could have walked away," Agatha said, watching Vivian's face carefully for any reaction. "But Rosa threatened to expose you. Just like Henry did. That's two people with knowledge of your past, your real past. Your life before you became Vivian Monroe."

Still no reaction. Just that same porcelain mask, perfect and impenetrable.

Lorraine tilted her head, her earrings catching the light as she moved. "You used Vera Martin's name when you registered the business. That wasn't a coincidence." She paced slowly, her red coat swishing dramatically with each step. "You wanted to hide behind her identity, didn't you? Make your own past disappear."

Vivian finally moved. She crossed her arms tighter over her chest and took a long breath, the first sign of any emotion they'd seen. "I didn't kill Henry," she said.

"Then who did?" Agatha asked simply.

Vivian looked away, her gaze finding one of the movie posters. Midnight Alibi, starring a younger version of herself, radiant in black and white. Her voice was quieter now, almost reflective. "I was in the projection booth that night, yes. But it was early, hours before the screening started. I checked every detail of the reopening. The equipment, the sound system, everything." She turned back to them, eyes hardening again.

"By the time Henry died, I was downstairs in the theater with dozens of witnesses."

Agatha stepped closer, close enough to see the fine lines at the corners of Vivian's eyes that her expensive makeup couldn't quite conceal. "Who is Bethany Marks to you?"

Vivian hesitated, her expression flickering like a candle caught in a draft. For a moment, the mask slipped, revealing something vulnerable underneath, fear, perhaps, or regret. Then it was gone, replaced by the same cool composure.

"Bethany is... Someone I would rather forget," Vivian said, measuring her words. "We knew each other, back in the day. Worked on the same sets. But I haven't seen or spoken to her since 2001."

Emma's heart pounded as she pressed further. "What was on the reel? The one Henry was looking for before he died?"

Vivian met Agatha's eyes, her voice calm but clipped. "I don't know anything about a reel. There are too many reels in this theater to keep track of." She straightened, smoothing an invisible wrinkle from her immaculate blouse. "Now, if you'll excuse me, I have a theater to run."

As Vivian turned to leave, Mike suddenly barked sharply, once, the sound echoing in the quiet room. Everyone froze.

The dog was standing near the vintage movie poster for Midnight Alibi, his nose working furiously at the wall behind it. He barked again, more insistent this time.

Agatha moved toward him, gently easing the frame away from the wall. Behind it was a small wall safe, its metal door gleaming dully in the chandelier light.

"Interesting place for a safe," Agatha remarked, letting the poster fall back into place. "Most people don't hide them behind removable wall decorations."

Vivian's expression didn't waver. "Wall safes are more common than you'd think. This one came with the building."

"Did it?" Emma asked, consulting her notes. "Because according to the renovation permits, that wall was completely rebuilt six months ago."

Lorraine stepped forward, her eyes bright with excitement. "What's in the safe, Vivian? What are you hiding?"

The silence that followed was heavy, oppressive, like the moment before a summer storm breaks. Vivian looked between the three women, calculating, assessing. Then, with a small sigh that seemed to deflate her entire being, she reached into her pocket and pulled out a small key.

"Not here," Vivian touched Agatha's arm briefly, urgently. "Not like this." She glanced toward the door, as if expecting someone to burst in at any moment. "Meet me at the bookstore tomorrow. I'll bring everything. But you need to know..." she paused, her eyes suddenly intense, almost pleading. "I'm not the one you should be afraid of."

With that cryptic warning hanging in the air, Vivian slipped past them and out of the lounge, her footsteps fading into the quiet of the empty theater.

"Well," Lorraine said after a moment, breaking the tense silence. "That was suitably dramatic. Do you think she'll actually show up?"

Agatha looked down at Mike, who had settled back at her feet, mission apparently accomplished. "I think she will." She reached down to scratch behind his ears. "Good boy, Mike. You found the final clue."

As they walked back through the lobby toward the exit, Emma leaned close to Agatha. "Do you believe her? That she didn't kill Henry?"

Agatha pushed open the heavy door, letting in a rush of cold winter air that smelled of snow and possibility. "I'm not sure. But I think we're about to find out who did."

28

THE CONFESSION

Snow tapped against the bookstore windows in a gentle, irregular rhythm, the flakes accumulating on the sills like nervous fingers drumming on glass. Agatha arranged a tray of teacups on the reading table. Her grandmother's china with the delicate blue flowers, while Emma reorganized their evidence into neat, logical piles. The handwritten timeline. The newspaper clippings. Rosa's scrapbook with its damning journal entry. Everything in its place, just as a proper investigation should be.

Lorraine paced by the window, her reflection ghosting across the frost-edged glass. "She's late," she announced, checking her watch for the third time in five minutes. "That's either very dramatic or very suspicious. I can't decide which."

"Give her time," Agatha said, though she felt the same unease crawling up her spine. "She said an hour."

Mike had abandoned his usual napping spot for a vigilant position near the door, ears perked forward, body unusually still. Even he seemed to understand the gravity of the moment.

"Do you think she'll actually tell us the truth?" Emma asked, adjusting her glasses as she reviewed her notes one final time. "About Bethany Marks? About the reel?"

"I think..." Agatha began, but the door opened before she could finish, cutting her off mid-thought, letting in a blast of cold air.

It wasn't Vivian.

Bianca Monroe stood in the doorway, snowflakes glistening on her camel-colored coat. Her face was pale, her normally perfect makeup smudged beneath one eye, as if she'd wiped away a tear. She glanced nervously over her shoulder at the snowy street before stepping inside and closing the door behind her with deliberate care.

"Is she here?" Bianca asked, her voice barely above a whisper. When Agatha shook her head, Bianca's shoulders sagged with visible relief.

"Tea?" Agatha offered, gesturing to the waiting pot. Keep it normal, she thought. Keep it calm.

"Please," Bianca said, shrugging off her coat, snow melting on the shoulders. "I hope I'm not interrupting."

"Not at all," Emma said, carefully sliding the most incriminating evidence beneath a folder. "We were just catching up on some paperwork."

Lorraine, for once, seemed to understand the need for subtlety. She merely smiled and pulled out a chair for their unexpected visitor. "Dreadful weather, isn't it? My hair is absolutely destroyed. Not that I mind. I think the disheveled look adds character." She patted her still-perfectly-styled curls.

Bianca accepted the cup Agatha offered, but made no move to drink. Instead, she stared into the amber liquid as if seeking answers in its depths. The clock on the wall ticked heavily into the silence. Mike, unusually alert, watched Bianca with an intensity that seemed to unnerve her further.

"Is everything alright?" Agatha asked finally, settling into the chair across from her. "You seem troubled."

Bianca's eyes darted to the door again, then back to Agatha. "No," she admitted, her voice catching. "Nothing is alright. And it hasn't been for a very long time."

She set down her untouched tea and opened her handbag with trembling fingers. From within, she extracted a folded piece of paper, creased from repeated handling.

"I can't do this anymore," she said, smoothing the paper on the table. "I thought I could, for the theater's sake. For my own sake. But after what happened to Rosa..." She took a deep breath that seemed to shudder through her entire body. "I found this in Vivian's private email. She doesn't know I have access."

Emma leaned forward as Agatha picked up the paper. It was an email, printed and dated three days before Henry's death:

Henry, Your silence isn't worth $250,000. I won't be blackmailed over something that happened decades ago. Your "investigation" into my past ends here. If you think you can extort me and ruin everything I've built, you've tragically miscalculated. This ends now. -V

Agatha felt the weight of the words sink into her chest. "This is a threat."

"It's more than that." Bianca sat back, something settling in her expression. "It's motive."

Lorraine, who had been reading over Agatha's shoulder, gasped with dramatic flair. "Mon Dieu! You're saying Vivian... "

"Yes," Bianca interrupted, leaning in. "Vivian killed Henry. But not the way everyone thinks."

The snow intensified outside, the flakes swirling against the windows in white gusts, a fitting backdrop to the darkness of her words.

"She poisoned him first," Bianca continued, her words spilling out in a rush now. "The electrocution was staged, afterward. Rosa helped her. She was the one who actually arranged the body, made it look like an accident."

Emma's pen hovered over her notepad, momentarily forgotten. "Rosa was involved?"

Bianca nodded, a strand of hair falling across her face. "Vivian paid her well, very well, to help stage the scene. But then Rosa got greedy. She wanted more money to keep quiet. She even wrote one of her blackmail notes." She gestured to the scrapbook peeking out from beneath Emma's folder. "I know you found it."

"And so Vivian killed Rosa too," Agatha said, the pieces clicking into place with terrible clarity. "To silence her."

"Yes." Bianca looked down at her hands, now clasped tightly in her lap. "Vivian told me everything three nights ago. We were alone in the theater after closing. She'd been drinking, more than usual. She thought I would understand, that I would keep quiet to protect our business." Her voice broke. "But I can't live with this anymore. Not after Rosa."

She looked up, her eyes wide, glassy. "What if she decides to take me out too, now that I know everything? I'm afraid for my life, and that's why I'm here telling you everything."

Mike suddenly growled, a low rumble that seemed to vibrate through the floorboards. Agatha placed a calming hand on his head, but his eyes remained fixed on Bianca, unblinking and wary.

"I need to make a call," Agatha said, rising from her chair. "Emma, would you mind getting our guest some more tea?"

Emma nodded, understanding immediately. "Of course. Lorraine, could you help me with the pastries in the back?"

Lorraine opened her mouth as if to protest being removed from the drama unfolding, then caught Emma's pointed look. "Ah, yes. The pastries. Very important, pastries. Can't have a confession without proper sustenance."

Once in the small office at the back of the store, Agatha dialed Detective Dawson's number, her fingers steady despite the gravity of the situation.

"Dawson," he answered on the second ring, his voice gruff.

"It's Agatha. I need you to check something." She kept her voice low, aware of Bianca sitting just beyond the door. "Henry Maddox's autopsy, was he tested for poison?"

A pause. "Not specifically. Cause of death was clearly electrocution. Why?"

"I have reason to believe he was poisoned first, the electrocution staged after death. Can you check?" She hesitated. "And quickly."

Another pause, longer this time. "This isn't just one of your theories, is it?"

"I have a confession and documentary evidence sitting in my bookstore right now."

"Don't move. Don't let anyone leave. I'll call the medical examiner and be there in twenty."

The line went dead. Agatha returned to find Emma making pleasant small talk about the weather while Lorraine, in a display of unexpected tact, refilled Bianca's teacup and offered her a lemon square.

"Detective Dawson is checking into it," Agatha said simply, resuming her seat.

Bianca nodded, a strange relief washing over her features. "Thank you. I should have come forward sooner, but I was afraid."

"Of Vivian?" Emma asked.

"Yes," Bianca replied, but something in her tone struck Agatha as odd, a discordant note in an otherwise convincing performance.

The next fifteen minutes stretched like taffy, sticky and uncomfortable. Lorraine filled the silence with increasingly improbable stories about her time in "Paree" (which Agatha strongly suspected was actually a weekend in Montreal), while Emma continued making notes and Bianca sat in tense silence, jumping at every sound from the street outside. Snow continued to fall steadily, accumulating on the sidewalk.

The door opened again, and there stood Vivian Monroe, elegant despite the snow that had darkened her silk blouse at the shoulders. She carried a small leather portfolio under one arm. Her eyes narrowed immediately at the sight of Bianca. "What are you doing here?" she asked, her voice sharp with suspicion.

Before Bianca could answer, Vivian noticed the printed email on the table. Her face drained of color. "Where did you get that?"

"It's over, Vivian," Bianca said, rising to her feet. "I told them everything."

For a moment, no one moved. The only sound was the soft patter of snow against the windows and Mike's low, continuous growl. Then, with deliberate calm, Vivian placed her portfolio on a nearby shelf and smoothed her hair.

"I see," she said quietly. "And what, exactly, is 'everything'?"

Bianca opened her mouth to respond, but the bell chimed a third time as Detective Dawson entered, accompanied by a uniformed officer, both shaking snow from their boots. His jacket was dark with melting snow, his expression grim.

"Vivian Monroe," he said, not bothering with preliminaries, "the medical examiner just confirmed traces of digitalis in Henry Maddox's tissue samples. It was missed in the initial autopsy because no one was looking for it."

Vivian's face remained impressively impassive. "I don't know what that means."

"It means," Dawson continued, "that Henry Maddox was poisoned before he was electrocuted. The poison would have killed him within minutes. The electrocution was staged."

"Just as I told you," Bianca interjected, looking at Agatha with wide, earnest eyes.

Dawson turned to Vivian. "We already had records of cash withdrawals from your personal account. Fifteen thousand dollars the day after Henry's death, which matched a deposit into Rosa Fielding's account. And another ten thousand two days before Rosa died." He paused. "At the time, we thought they were unrelated transactions. But now, with Ms. Monroe's statement about Rosa helping you stage the scene and then demanding more money, it all connects."

The silence that followed was absolute. Even Mike had stopped growling, watching the scene with canine intensity.

"Vivian Monroe," Dawson said formally, "you're under arrest for the murders of Henry Maddox and Rosa Fielding." He recited her rights as the uniformed officer stepped forward with handcuffs.

As the officer secured the handcuffs, Vivian stood

perfectly still, her back straight, her chin lifted with the same regal bearing she'd maintained since arriving in Bristol Lake. Only her eyes betrayed any emotion. Not guilt or remorse, but something Agatha couldn't quite identify. Knowledge, perhaps. Or resignation.

"Let's go," Dawson said, guiding Vivian toward the door.

As they passed Bianca, Vivian paused, her eyes locking with her business partner's. Something passed between them, a look that contained volumes. Bianca was the first to look away.

Once they had gone, the little bell jingling with incongruous cheerfulness as the door closed behind them, letting in one last blast of cold air, a strange silence fell over the bookstore.

"Well," Lorraine said finally, exhaling dramatically. "That was the most excitement this shop has seen since Mrs. Finch discovered we shelved cozy mysteries next to true crime."

Emma shook her head, still processing. "So it's over. Vivian killed them both."

"Is it?" Agatha murmured, almost to herself.

Bianca gathered her things with curious haste. "I should go," she said, not quite meeting Agatha's eyes. "It's been... A difficult day."

As she headed for the door, Mike finally moved from his watchful position. He stepped directly into Bianca's path, not growling now, but staring up at her with unwavering focus. Bianca hesitated, then carefully stepped around him.

"Thank you for listening," she said, pulling on her coat. "For believing me."

~

After she left, Emma turned to Agatha. "Do you think Vivian's really guilty?"

Agatha was quiet for a long moment, watching the snow fall outside. "The evidence points to her. But..."

"But what?" Lorraine prompted.

"Bethany Marks." Agatha turned to face them. "We've been so focused on Vivian that we forgot, where is Bethany Marks? Gordon's letter said he helped both women disappear. Vivian stayed in plain sight with a new identity. But Bethany?"

Emma flipped back through her notes. "The Arizona bank account. Vivian's been sending money there for thirty years."

"What if Bethany is still involved somehow?" Agatha said slowly. "What if she's not just hiding in Arizona collecting payments? What if she's been here all along, or recently came back to Bristol Lake?"

"Pulling strings?" Lorraine's eyes widened. "Using Vivian as a scapegoat?"

"Or," Emma said quietly, "what if Bethany Marks has been right under our noses this entire time, and we just didn't see it?"

The three women exchanged uneasy glances. Mike, still near the door, let out a low whine.

Someone came in, and all three women glanced toward the door. Quentin stood in the doorway, his work clothes damp from melted snow, his expression a mixture of concern and determination. In his hands, he carried a battered metal movie reel case.

"Ms. Royale." Quentin pressed a hand to his chest for a moment, collecting himself. "I came as soon as I could. This is the movie reel everyone's been talking about." He placed it carefully on the table. "I found it hidden behind a false panel in the old projection booth. We were installing new equipment and had to remove some of the original wood paneling. It was tucked away in a space that wouldn't show up on any standard inspection. I didn't think much of it until I heard about Ms. Vivian's arrest."

Lorraine gasped, her hand flying to her heart with theatrical precision. "The missing reel! The plot thickens!"

Agatha carefully opened the case, Emma and Lorraine leaning in close. Their collective breath caught as they realized the reel itself was missing. Instead, nestled in the center where the film should have been, lay a small brass key attached to a faded tag that read "Los Angeles First National, Box 247."

"I don't understand," Quentin said, frowning at their reaction. "It's just a key."

"It's more than that," Agatha replied, turning the key over in her palm. "It might be the key to everything."

She glanced toward the door where Bianca had exited. Mike was still watching it, his posture alert and wary.

"What is it, boy?" she asked softly. "What did you sense?"

The snow continued its steady accumulation against the windows, covering footprints on the sidewalk outside, erasing evidence with each passing minute. But some truths, Agatha knew, couldn't be so easily dissolved. They remained, hidden perhaps, but waiting. Like the contents of a safe deposit box in Los Angeles, to be discovered.

29

THE NEXT MOVE

Agatha rubbed her tired eyes and checked the wall clock. Barely seven, and she'd already reorganized the new releases display, restocked the mystery shelf, and read every news article about Gordon Lane's disappearance twice. The business journal article smiled back at her. "Philanthropist Funds Historic Theater Restoration", but the headline now felt like a lie. "Vietnam," she muttered, scrolling through the news reports. "Why Vietnam?"

"Ma chérie, you will not believe what has happened." She pressed a hand to her chest, her cardinal ornament bobbing on its felt perch. "Eliza's is in absolute uproar."

Agatha set down her coffee. "What happened?"

"Patricia Howe — you know Patricia, she volunteers at the library on Wednesdays — she was helping Eliza take the trash out to the alley behind the bakery when she saw a man standing at the far end. Tall, dark coat, perfectly still in the cold. She called out and he didn't answer, didn't move, just stood there watching her." Lorraine's bracelets jangled as she pressed a hand to her heart. "She screamed. By the time Eliza came running, he was gone."

Agatha felt a small chill that had nothing to do with the January air still clinging to Lorraine's coat. "That sounds like the man Celeste saw in the alley."

"That is exactly what everyone is saying." Lorraine's voice dropped. "And once someone mentioned Petunia Heights strangler, mon Dieu, there was no stopping it. Mrs. Calloway refused to let her grandchildren walk home. Frank Briggs called the sheriff's office twice."

Agatha glanced toward the window. Central Avenue looked exactly as it always did — quiet, snow-dusted, perfectly ordinary. But ordinary, she had learned, had a way of hiding things in plain sight.

"Could it really be him?" she murmured, almost to herself.

Lorraine spread her hands. "Since when has Bristol Lake ever waited for answers before jumping to the worst possible conclusion?"

EMMA STEPPED inside carrying two steaming coffees and a paper bag that filled the air with the heavenly scent of fresh-baked pastries. Her cheeks were pink from the morning chill, and snow clung to her coat. Her red hair was twisted into a messy bun that somehow looked both accidental and intentional.

"Breakfast delivery," she announced, setting everything down on the counter. "The cinnamon walnut scones you like. Eliza made them fresh this morning. Said they were 'therapeutic baking' after all the excitement."

Agatha looked up from her laptop, where she'd been reading a thread of news stories about Gordon Lane's sudden disappearance. The screen's blue light reflected in her glasses as she rubbed her tired eyes. "You're a saint. I've been up since five."

"I know. I could practically hear your brain working from my house." Emma pulled up a stool and peered over Agatha's shoulder, unwinding her scarf. "What are you reading that's so important it interrupted your sleep cycle?"

Agatha sighed and turned the screen toward her. "I've been re-reading everything about Gordon's escape. The more I think about it, the less sense Vietnam makes." She tapped a paragraph in the article. "Why there specifically?"

Emma took a bite of her bagel, considering. "You've been stuck on the Vietnam question all morning, haven't you?"

"Because it doesn't make sense," Agatha said, breaking off a corner of her scone. "Why Vietnam? Why not somewhere more predictable, like the Caymans or Switzerland? Places known for banking discretion and wealthy fugitives?"

Emma shrugged. "Maybe he had connections there. Or maybe he just picked a country at random from a travel blog. 'Top Ten Nations That Won't Send You Back for Trial.'"

Agatha didn't smile. The joke fell flat against the seriousness of her expression. "No. Gordon never did anything by accident. Something's off." She brushed crumbs from her fingers. "The timing is too convenient. Right when the investigation into the murders was heating up, right when questions about the theater's finances were surfacing, suddenly Gordon is halfway around the world?"

"You think they were working together?" Emma asked, her voice lowered even though they were alone in the shop.

Agatha was quiet for a moment, turning her coffee cup

slowly in her hands. "Dawson said his involvement was purely financial, and that he had an alibi." She paused. "But Gordon Lane didn't strike me as the kind of man who lets someone else run his risks for him. He funds things. He shapes things." She looked up. "And then he disappears the moment it all unravels."

Emma held her gaze. "You think Dawson got it wrong?"

"I think," Agatha said carefully, "that alibis can be bought. And Gordon Lane had more than enough money to buy a very good one."

Before Emma could respond, Detective Dawson entered the store looking more relaxed than usual. His coat was unbuttoned despite the morning chill, his usual stern expression softened somehow, and he held a manila folder in one hand.

"Ladies," he greeted, nodding to them both. "Mind if I interrupt your caffeine ritual?"

"We insist," Agatha said, gesturing toward a chair. "Can I get you a coffee? We just made a fresh pot."

"Thanks, but I've had my quota for the morning." Dawson sat, placing the folder on the table with a quiet tap. His fingertips lingered on it for a moment, as if weighing whether he should have come at all. "Vivian confessed."

Agatha raised a brow, her scone forgotten. "To everything?"

He nodded, that single movement containing a strange mix of professional satisfaction and personal weariness. "She admitted to both murders. Poisoned Henry, staged the electrocution. Paid Rosa to help, then silenced her when Rosa demanded more." He opened the folder, revealing a neatly typed confession statement with Vivian's elegant signature at the bottom. "It's all here. Clean and tidy."

Emma leaned forward, her glasses sliding down her nose as she peered at the document. "What about Gordon and Bianca? Were they involved?"

"Vivian claims they knew nothing," Dawson said, running a hand through his hair. "And the evidence backs that up. She told me herself that Gordon was laundering money through the theater, but it was unrelated to the murders. And Bianca was in the dark about it all."

Agatha nodded slowly, but her expression was unreadable, a mask of polite interest that revealed nothing of her thoughts. She didn't mention the key still sitting in her coat pocket, its weight a constant reminder of unanswered questions.

"The Acadia will stay open," Dawson continued, as if sensing her silent skepticism. "Bianca's taking over operations. Said the town deserves to have its theater after all this trouble."

"How thoughtful," Agatha murmured, her tone neutral.

They chatted for a few more minutes. About the upcoming town council meeting, the weather forecast, Sheriff Salinger's retirement announcement. Topics that floated on the surface while deeper currents moved beneath. Finally, Dawson departed with a promise to keep them updated on any developments, the bell jingling cheerfully behind him.

Once he was gone, Emma turned to Agatha. "You don't believe it, do you? Vivian's confession."

Agatha sipped her now-lukewarm coffee. "I don't know what to believe yet. But I do know that people confess to crimes they didn't commit all the time. Sometimes to protect someone else."

"Like who?" Emma asked.

"Gordon, maybe. Or Bethany Marks." Agatha shrugged. "We still don't know where she is or if she's even involved at all."

Emma nodded slowly. "We need more information."

"Exactly," Agatha said. "Which is why we need to find out what's in that safe deposit box."

THE DAY PASSED with unusual slowness, as Mondays often do after eventful weekends. The regular customers trickled in. Mr. Finch for his weekly mystery, Mrs. Ogilvy to browse the new releases, Gladys to gossip under the pretense of buying a birthday gift for her nephew. Each carried questions about Vivian's arrest, and each left with some small nugget of information they would no doubt share over bridge games and garden club meetings. The Bristol Lake gossip network operated with the efficiency of a well-oiled machine.

By closing time, Agatha felt the weight of the day pressing down on her shoulders. She flipped the sign to CLOSED with unusual weariness, and Mike seemed to sense her mood, staying closer than usual as she tidied up.

That evening, Agatha, Emma, and Lorraine met at Mabel's Diner. The familiar neon sign buzzed and flickered in the growing dusk, casting a warm pink glow over the snowy sidewalk. The smell of frying onions and freshly baked rolls greeted them at the door, and the clatter of forks against ceramic plates filled the cozy space. Waitresses in crisp aprons navigated between tables with practiced grace, balancing plates piled high with comfort food.

They slid into their usual booth by the window, where the checkered curtains fluttered in the breeze from the ancient heating vent. The vinyl seats squeaked beneath them, worn smooth by generations of Bristol Lake residents. Outside, snow continued to fall gently, coating the parked cars along Central Avenue.

"I think I'm finally hungry again," Lorraine announced, scanning the menu with dramatic flair. Today she wore a turquoise sweater with an oversized brooch shaped like a peacock, its rhinestone tail catching the light whenever she moved. "A murder confession really takes it out of a girl. I've been positively wasting away."

"You had two lemon bars and a croissant today," Emma reminded her, adjusting her glasses as she studied the daily specials board. "I saw you at the bakery when I was dropping books at the library."

"Emotional calories don't count," Lorraine declared, waving away the observation with a bejeweled hand. "Besides, stress causes weight loss. It's science. Or French. One of those."

Mabel herself took their orders. Burgers all around, with chocolate milkshakes for Emma and Lorraine, and vanilla for Agatha. The diner owner had been serving Bristol Lake for thirty years, her once-black hair now steely gray but her memory for regular customers' preferences still razor-sharp.

"Extra pickles for you," she said to Emma without asking. "And a side of those sweet potato fries you pretend not to like but always steal from Agatha's plate."

Emma blushed. "Am I that predictable?"

"Honey, in this town, we're all creatures of habit," Mabel replied with a wink. "That's why we notice when something's off." She glanced meaningfully toward the table nearest the door, where Bianca Monroe sat alone, picking at a salad and checking her phone every few minutes. "Some folks just don't quite fit the pattern."

As Mabel walked away, Lorraine leaned in, her voice a theatrical whisper. "She's been there for an hour. Hasn't eaten more than three bites. Just watches the door like she's expecting someone."

"Or waiting for something," Agatha murmured, her gaze drifting to Bianca's tense posture.

They settled into the soft murmur of the diner, the familiar soundtrack of their Monday evenings providing a sense of normalcy that felt both comforting and strangely surreal after the weekend's events. Around them, life continued. Gladys and her bridge club sat by the jukebox, arguing over pie flavors and the merits of different celebrity detectives. Stanley Peck sat at the counter nursing a coffee, looking tired and worried. A group of high school students crowded around a corner booth, textbooks forgotten as they debated the latest superhero movie.

It was, for a moment, perfectly, beautifully normal. As if Vivian Monroe hadn't just confessed to double murder. As if Gordon Lane hadn't fled the country. As if everything was just as it should be in their little corner of the world.

But Agatha couldn't relax into the comforting rhythm of diner chatter and clinking silverware. The questions kept circling in her mind, like birds that refused to land. She reached into her coat pocket and pulled out the small brass key that Quentin had discovered in the movie reel case. It glinted under the diner lights, innocuous yet somehow heavy with significance.

"You're still thinking about it," Emma said, not a question but a statement. She knew Agatha too well to mistake her distant expression for anything but the wheels of detection turning.

"I am," Agatha replied, setting the key on the table between them. "Hard to forget about a safety deposit box key that was hidden inside a movie reel. A box in Los Angeles."

"What's in it, do you think?" Lorraine asked, sipping her milkshake and leaving a perfect crescent of red lipstick on the straw. Her eyes sparkled with the excitement of mystery, the thrill of secrets yet to be uncovered.

"Hard to tell... But it's probably something important. Maybe even revealing," Agatha murmured, turning the key over with her fingertip. "Something worth hiding. Something worth finding."

The table grew quiet, each woman lost in thought as their food arrived, the plates steaming in the cool evening air.

Emma stirred her shake with her straw, creating a miniature whirlpool of chocolate. "You think whatever's in that box is connected to Gordon?"

Agatha nodded, her expression thoughtful as she squeezed ketchup onto her plate in a neat circle. "I don't know if Vivian even knew it was there. But someone wanted us to find it. And if it leads back to Gordon, then maybe he's not as innocent as Dawson thinks."

Lorraine set down her glass with a soft clink, more serious than usual. "Are you suggesting a road trip? Because I have a cousin in Malibu who owes me a favor, and I've been dying to see if California really does have superior avocados."

Agatha met their eyes, seeing the loyalty and curiosity reflected there. Friends who had stood by her through previous investigations, who understood her need to find the truth, however complicated or messy it might be. "I think I need to go to Los Angeles. Find that safe deposit box. See what's inside."

Mike, who'd been curled up beneath the table, lifted his head and gave a soft, approving chuff, as if adding his vote to the expedition.

Emma sighed and grabbed a napkin, scribbling something that looked suspiciously like a packing list. "Fine. But I'm picking the playlist. If I have to spend hours in a car, it's not going to be with your true crime podcasts and Lorraine's French pop albums."

Lorraine clapped her hands, her numerous bracelets jingling like wind chimes. "And I'm packing snacks! Trail mix, granola bars, those little cheese wheels that don't need refrigeration. We're going on an adventure!"

Agatha smiled at last, the first genuine smile of the day, though it was tinged with determination. "Not we. Me."

"Oh no," Lorraine said, wagging a bejeweled finger. "You're not doing this without backup. If there's a dusty mystery in California, I'm coming with my sunhat and a suspicious attitude. Besides, someone needs to make sure you actually eat regular meals."

"And someone needs to keep Lorraine from spending all her money on Hollywood Boulevard," Emma added. "Which means I'm coming too. The library can survive without me for a few days."

LATER THAT EVENING, Agatha found herself alone at the bookstore, catching up on paperwork long after closing time. The street outside had grown quiet, most of Bristol Lake's shops dark except for the security lights that cast long shadows across the snowy street. Celeste had left an hour earlier, eager to get home to finish a paper for her online literature course.

The gentle tick of the old wall clock and Mike's occasional sighs were the only sounds accompanying the scratch of Agatha's pen as she updated the inventory ledger. When the sudden noise came. A soft thud against the front door, she froze, pen poised mid-sentence.

Mike lifted his head, ears pricked forward, a low growl building in his throat.

"Easy, boy," Agatha whispered, moving cautiously toward the window. She peered through the blinds just in time to see a figure in a dark coat running away down the snowy sidewalk, face hidden, moving with urgent purpose, leaving footprints in the fresh snow.

Her heart beating a little faster, Agatha unlocked the front door and looked down. There on the welcome mat, partially covered by fresh snow, lay a single red rose, its stem wrapped in black tissue paper. Attached was a small card, the message written in block letters that betrayed no handwriting style:

RETURN THE KEY TO WHO IT BELONGS. STOP SNOOPING.

Agatha picked up the rose carefully, brushing off the snow, feeling the weight of the threat beneath its beauty. The thorns had been left intact.

"Well, Mike," she said, locking the door firmly behind her, "I think someone's nervous about our trip to Los Angeles."

Mike gave a soft woof of agreement, pressing against her leg protectively.

And Agatha Royale wasn't done yet.

30

BOOK CLUB CONFIDENTIAL

"Nobody is going to Los Angeles," Agatha announced the next morning, gathering her friends in the office at the back of One Deadly Chapter.

Lorraine's face fell dramatically, her hand pressed against her heart. "But I've already planned my entire Hollywood wardrobe! The oversized sunglasses, the flowing scarf, the air of mystérieuse sophistication!" She draped an imaginary scarf around her neck with a flourish.

"I'm sorry, Lorraine," Agatha said, trying not to smile at her friend's theatrical disappointment. "But we need to stay right here in Bristol Lake. That's where we'll find our answers."

"What happened?" Emma asked, her practical nature immediately sensing something was wrong. "You seemed set on checking that safety deposit box yesterday."

"I found this on the welcome mat last night," Agatha explained, reaching into her pocket. "Right after I spotted someone in a dark coat watching the store. When I went to the window, they ran off down the sidewalk." She withdrew a single red rose, its stem wrapped in black tissue paper, a small note card still attached, and passed it to Emma.

Emma read it silently, her eyes widening. "They're threatening you about the key."

"Oh my goodness," Celeste gasped, adjusting her glasses nervously. "Do you think it's connected to the key Quentin brought in?"

"It has to be," Emma said, examining the note without touching it. "They're specifically mentioning the key."

Lorraine leaned forward, her earlier disappointment forgotten. "First mysterious figures lurking in shadows, now threatening roses with ominous notes? This is getting positively sinister!"

Despite her dramatic tone, Lorraine extended one finger toward one of the thorns that had been deliberately left intact, stopping just short of touching it. "Mon Dieu," she murmured. "How very gothic."

"Have you told Detective Dawson?" Emma asked, always the practical one.

Agatha nodded. "I called him this morning about the rose and the figure I saw. He wanted me to bring the key to the station, but I convinced him my plan might work better. He wasn't thrilled, but he agreed to keep an eye on things from a distance."

"A plan?" Celeste's eyes widened behind her tortoiseshell frames.

"Yes. Whoever left this is afraid of what we might find in that safety deposit box. So instead of actually going to Los Angeles, we're going to make them think we're going."

Emma nodded slowly, understanding dawning on her face. "You want to flush them out."

"Exactly." Agatha pulled the safety deposit box key from her pocket, turning it over in her palm. "Someone's been watching us since we found this key, and they're getting nervous."

"So what's the plan?" Celeste asked, nervously adjusting her tortoiseshell glasses.

"We make them think we're leaving town to check this safety deposit box, then watch to see who reacts." Agatha spread a map of Bristol Lake across the table. "Tonight's book club is the perfect opportunity to plant the seed."

"But who would care about an old key?" Emma wondered aloud, helping Agatha arrange chairs in the reading nook.

"Someone who knows what it opens," Agatha replied. "And I think that someone is connected to whatever happened to Vincent Cleary twenty-five years ago."

"Martha Peck will be back at book club tonight," Celeste arranged the last of the cookies on the plate. "It must be a relief for her to be cleared of suspicion."

"Vivian's testimony confirmed she wasn't involved in Rosa's death," Emma nodded, straightening a stack of bookmarks. "Though I doubt Martha will ever forgive us for suspecting her in the first place."

"Speaking of Martha," Lorraine said, peering through the curtains at the street outside, "isn't that her coming this way now? Good heavens, she walks like she's perpetually disappointed in the sidewalk."

Sure enough, Martha Peck was approaching the bookstore, bundled in her winter coat, her thin lips pressed together in their familiar expression of dignity. She carried a covered plate in her hands.

"Right on schedule," Agatha murmured. "I sent her a note about book club tonight. If anyone's going to spread news about our 'trip' to Los Angeles, it's Martha. No one has a faster gossip network."

Emma and Celeste both stared at Lorraine.

Lorraine looked between them. "What?"

"Agatha is wrong there," Emma said dryly. "Nobody spreads gossip faster than Lorraine."

Agatha paused, then smiled. "You're right." She turned to Lorraine. "But you're absolutely forbidden to talk about this trip. Not a word to anyone."

"Of course, ma chérie," Lorraine responded, placing a hand over her heart with mock solemnity. "My lips are sealed. Like a tomb. A very fashionable, discreet tomb."

Martha entered the bookstore, a swirl of cold following her in. She brushed a few stray snowflakes from her sleeves, her gaze sweeping critically around the shop as she unbuttoned her coat. "I brought chocolate chip cookies," she announced, setting the plate on the counter. "Since I heard you were having book club tonight. Despite everything that's happened."

There was an unmistakable stiffness to her voice. Not quite forgiveness, but perhaps a tentative step toward normalcy.

"Thank you, Martha," Agatha said warmly, refusing to be intimidated. "How nice of you to think of us. We're so glad you could make it tonight."

Martha's lips thinned further, if that was possible. "Well, someone has to maintain standards in this town. Even after being falsely accused." She straightened her cardigan with a sharp tug. "I assume you've selected something appropriate for tonight's discussion?"

"Actually, yes," Agatha said, holding up the novel they'd

chosen: *The Silver Key Mystery*. "I thought it was rather fitting."

Martha's eyes narrowed, and Agatha could have sworn she saw a flicker of something, recognition? concern?. Before the older woman's face settled back into its mask of disapproval.

"I'll just help Emma set up the refreshments," Martha said, moving toward the reading nook with surprising quickness.

Lorraine sidled up beside Agatha. "Did you see that? She practically flinched when she saw the book title."

"I saw," Agatha confirmed quietly. "And by tomorrow morning, half of Bristol Lake will know we're headed to Los Angeles."

By seven o'clock, the bookshop was filled with the comfortable buzz of conversation. The evening darkness had settled over Central Avenue outside, the windows frosted at the edges. Gladys and Henrietta had arrived, shaking snow from their boots, arms linked as always, both carrying matching tote bags emblazoned with "So Many Books, So Little Time" in glittering script. Agnes and Pearl settled in with their knitting needles already clicking, unwinding scarves and hanging coats by the door. Even Tabitha Elms had joined them, shaking snow from her hair, notebook in hand, though she'd promised to keep her reporter's instincts in check.

"Just a social visit," she'd assured Agatha upon arrival. "Not everything's a story."

If only you knew, Agatha thought, surveying the cozy gathering.

"Well," she said, once everyone had settled with drinks and treats, "shall we begin? Tonight's selection was *The Silver Key Mystery*. What did we think?"

For twenty minutes, the discussion flowed naturally. Henrietta declared the protagonist "too flighty," while Agnes defended the romance subplot as "perfectly reasonable for a woman of a certain age." Martha Peck criticized the author's descriptions of baked goods as "clearly written by someone who's never made a proper sponge cake."

Agatha watched and waited, letting the conversation meander until Gladys inevitably mentioned the climactic scene in the bank vault. "I thought it was terribly unrealistic," Gladys said, waving a cookie for emphasis. "The way she just waltzed into that bank in Beverly Hills and opened that safety deposit box. As if it would be that easy!"

Agatha exchanged a quick glance with Emma. *Now.*

"Actually," Agatha said casually, "it's not that difficult if you have the right key and identification." She reached into her pocket, letting the edge of the key flash briefly in the light before tucking it away again. "Though I suppose I'll find out for myself soon enough."

The room went suddenly, gloriously silent.

Gladys's cookie stopped midway to her mouth. "I beg your pardon?"

Lorraine, right on cue, gasped dramatically. "Agatha! You weren't going to tell them about your trip?"

"What trip?" Martha Peck demanded, leaning forward so eagerly she nearly upset her teacup.

Agatha feigned reluctance. "It's nothing, really. Just a

quick visit to Los Angeles to check on a safety deposit box. A family matter."

"Los Angeles?" Tabitha perked up instantly, her notebook appearing as if by magic. "When? Why? Is this connected to the Monroe sisters?"

"It's just a small errand," Agatha demurred, watching the room carefully. "Nothing newsworthy."

"Nonsense!" Lorraine exclaimed, draping herself elegantly across an armchair. "Our Agatha, jetting off to Los Angeles on a mysterious quest! Following a key found in Vivian Monroe's old theater! It's practically a movie plot!"

Emma shot her a look that clearly said *dial it back*, but the damage was done.

"A key?" Gladys echoed, her eyes gleaming with the particular light that only fresh gossip could ignite. "From Vivian Monroe?"

"When are you leaving?" Doris asked.

"Are you going alone?" Henrietta added.

"Will you bring back autographs?" Pearl chimed in.

Only Martha Peck remained suspiciously quiet, her small eyes narrowed as she studied Agatha's face.

"It's really not that exciting," Agatha said, allowing just enough hesitation in her voice to suggest the opposite. "I'm leaving tomorrow morning. Emma and Lorraine are coming with me. Just a quick trip, there and back."

"Hmph," Martha sniffed. "Sounds like a waste of time and money to me."

"Oh, I don't know," Tabitha said thoughtfully. "A safety deposit box key from Vivian Monroe could hold all sorts of interesting things. Old photos. Love letters. Maybe even evidence about that screenwriter's death everyone whispers about."

Mike, who had been circling the room during this exchange, suddenly stopped near the window, his nose working the air. He gave a soft, almost imperceptible growl.

Agatha followed his gaze.

A shadow moved across the snowy sidewalk outside, too quickly to identify, but definitely there. Watching.

"Well," she said, redirecting the conversation smoothly, "enough about my boring errand. What did everyone think about the detective's technique in chapter seven?"

The book discussion resumed, but the seed had been planted. Agatha could practically see the invisible threads of gossip forming, ready to spin outward the moment the meeting ended.

By the time the last member left. Gladys, predictably, who lingered to "help clean up" while pumping Agatha for additional details, pulling on her coat reluctantly, the trap was set.

"Well?" Emma asked, locking the door behind Gladys and flipping the sign to CLOSED. "Think they bought it?"

"Bought it, gift-wrapped it, and scheduled it for next-day delivery," Lorraine declared, collapsing dramatically onto the sofa. "Gladys was practically vibrating with excitement. I give it until sunrise before every soul in Bristol Lake will be speculating about what's in that mysterious safety deposit box."

"And the shadow outside?" Celeste asked, glancing nervously toward the frost-covered window.

"Definitely someone watching," Agatha confirmed. "Mike noticed before I did."

"Do you think they might try to take the key?" Celeste asked, eyes widening behind her glasses.

Emma paused, considering this. "If this key was that important, why would the key be hidden in Vivian's theater in the first place? Maybe she didn't realize its significance when she stored it there."

"Or maybe that's exactly what she wanted," Agatha mused. "To hide the problem somewhere no one would look until she was gone."

She scratched Mike's ears appreciatively as she began gathering the empty mugs. "It worked, though. Now whoever left the roses thinks we're leaving town tomorrow."

"While we're actually staying right here," Emma said with a satisfied smile. She pulled back the curtain, peering into the winter darkness. "Hiding in plain sight."

"I still wish we were really going," Lorraine sighed, folding napkins with uncharacteristic precision. "C'est la vie! Perhaps next time I shall play the role of French tourist. No one suspects a woman with a beret and an exaggerated accent, n'est-ce pas?"

She struck a pose that suggested she'd practiced it extensively, one hand on her hip, the other gesturing dramatically toward an invisible horizon.

"Maybe someday," Agatha promised. "But first, we need to find out who's been threatening us."

"So what now?" Celeste asked.

Agatha pulled out a town map she'd marked earlier. "Now, we set up our surveillance. Emma and I will stay here tonight to watch the bookstore, in case whoever left that rose tries something. Lorraine, you'll make a big show of going home to pack for our 'trip,' but circle back through the alley. Celeste, you'll actually go home as normal."

"But I want to help," Celeste protested.

"You are helping," Agatha assured her. "We need someone going about their normal routine to maintain appearances. You can be our eyes and ears in Petunia

Heights. If whoever's watching us is thorough, they might follow you to make sure you're not part of our plan."

Celeste's eyes widened behind her glasses, a mixture of nervousness and excitement. "So I'd be like... A decoy?"

"Exactly," Agatha nodded. "Just go home as usual, but keep your phone handy. If you notice anyone suspicious in Petunia Heights, or if anyone asks about our 'trip,' text us immediately."

Celeste brightened at this important assignment. "I can do that! I'll be super observant, I promise."

"What about tomorrow morning?" Emma asked. "When we're supposed to be 'leaving'?"

"We'll make a show of loading bags into my car," Agatha explained. "Then drive out of town, circle back on the old logging road, and return through the east entrance where nobody will notice."

"Clandestine!" Lorraine exclaimed with delight. "I feel like a spy in a novel!"

"Let's hope it's a mystery with a happy ending," Emma said.

"It will be," Agatha replied, her hand closing around the safety deposit box key in her pocket. "One way or another, we're going to find out who's behind these threats."

As they finalized their plans, Agatha felt a curious mixture of determination and anticipation. Whatever secrets Vincent Cleary had locked away years ago, someone in Bristol Lake was willing to go to great lengths to keep them buried.

But they'd picked the wrong town, and definitely the wrong bookshop owner to intimidate.

31

THE MAGAZINE

By midnight, the shop was dark except for a single lamp in the back office. Agatha and Emma had converted the reading nook into a makeshift surveillance post, with blankets, thermoses of coffee, and a clear view of both the front door and side alley.

Mike lay alertly at Agatha's feet, occasionally raising his head to sniff the air.

"Anything?" Emma whispered, peering through the blinds.

"Not yet," Agatha replied. "But it's early. If our shadow friend took the bait, they'll want to make sure we're really leaving tomorrow before making a move."

"Do you think they'll try to stop us from going? Or follow us?"

"I don't know," Agatha admitted. "But either way, we'll be ready."

Her phone buzzed with a text from Lorraine: *Position secured. No suspicious activity on Central Avenue. Though Mr. Porter's cat is behaving very suspiciously near the trash bins.*

Emma smiled. “At least Lorraine's enjoying herself.”

“She always does,” Agatha said fondly. “It's one of her best qualities.”

Around two in the morning, Lorraine appeared in the doorway, her scarf askew and her hair looking windblown. She blinked against the dim lamplight.

“I'm bored out of my mind,” she announced, voice scratchy. “Do you mind terribly if I take a couple of those gossip magazines Rosa left you? I need something shallow and sparkly to keep me from slipping into madness.”

Agatha smirked. “Sure. Go ahead. Just don't fall into a scandal spiral and forget we're supposed to be catching a threat.”

“No promises.”

Lorraine wandered over to the boxes in the back room. The vintage magazines Rosa had left to Agatha in her will. Rifling through with the sort of reverence one might reserve for treasure. “Ooh. Tinseltown's Tragic Love Affairs. And... Behind the Velvet Curtain, yes, these'll do nicely.”

She drifted back toward the front and set the two magazines on the small table beside Agatha's purse, already flipping through one. “Did you know people used to fake their deaths all the time in the '60s? Honestly, I'm starting to suspect everyone in Hollywood might be somebody else entirely.”

She settled onto the loveseat with a dramatic sigh, the magazines beside her. “Wake me if the killer shows up. Or if the kettle boils. Whichever comes first.”

As the night deepened around them, Bristol Lake settled into its quiet rhythms. But somewhere out there, Agatha knew, someone was watching. Waiting.

THE NEXT MORNING dawned gray and cold, with no suspicious activity. Their night of surveillance had yielded nothing but stiff necks and excessive caffeine consumption. Fresh snow had fallen overnight, blanketing Central Avenue in pristine white.

"I'm beginning to think we imagined the whole thing," Emma said, stretching her arms above her head.

"The rose with black tissue paper was real," Agatha reminded her, touching her pocket where she'd tucked the warning note. "And that message was clear: 'Return the key to who it belongs. Stop snooping.' Someone doesn't want us looking into that safety deposit box."

"Maybe they got what they wanted," Lorraine suggested, reapplying her lipstick with dramatic precision. "They think we've left town, so they've backed off."

A knock at the front door made them all freeze.

Mike, who had been dozing beneath the register, lifted his head. Not in alarm, but with the familiar tilt that suggested he recognized the visitor.

Agatha peered through the front windows.

Detective Dawson stood on the sidewalk, two coffee cups in hand and a white bakery bag tucked under his arm. His breath formed white clouds in the cold morning air.

"It's just Dawson," she said, relief and disappointment mingling in her voice.

She unlocked the door, allowing him to slip inside with a gust of cold air before quickly relocking it.

"You ladies throw quite a convincing going-away party," he said, setting the coffees and bag on the counter. "Brought sustenance. Eliza's cinnamon rolls. Still warm."

"Bless you," Lorraine declared, diving for the bag.

"Any suspicious activity?" Agatha asked, accepting one of the coffees gratefully.

"Not a whisper," Dawson replied, leaning against the counter. "Which is suspicious in itself."

Agatha pulled out the safety deposit box key, turning it over in her palm. "Maybe we misread the situation. Maybe this isn't as important as we thought."

Dawson's gaze fixed on the key. "May I?"

Agatha handed it over.

He examined it, then pulled out his phone. "Mind if I take a photo? I have a buddy at First National in Los Angeles. He might be able to tell us something without you having to make the trip."

"Be my guest."

Dawson snapped several angles of the key, then sent the images with a brief text. While they waited, they devoured Eliza's cinnamon rolls in comfortable silence.

Fifteen minutes later, Dawson's phone buzzed. He read the message, eyebrows rising.

"Well, that's interesting."

"What?" all three women asked in unison.

"This key style hasn't been used by First National since 1998. They switched to electronic access cards for all their boxes over twenty years ago." He scrolled further. "And the box number on this key was reassigned to a new customer in 2002."

"What does that mean?" Emma asked.

"It means," Dawson said, setting down his phone, "that this key is basically a souvenir. Whatever was in that box has been cleared out years ago."

Agatha turned the key over in her palm, feeling foolish.

All this drama, all this planning, for a key that opened nothing.

"Well," she said finally, "I guess some mysteries are just... Red herrings."

Lorraine sighed dramatically. "And I had my Hollywood outfit all planned."

Despite her disappointment, Agatha couldn't help but laugh. "Next time."

"So what now?" Emma asked. "Do we just... Go back to normal?"

Agatha nodded slowly. "I suppose we do."

Dawson finished his coffee and headed for the door, pulling his coat tight against the cold. "I'll keep an eye out, but my guess is whoever was watching has moved on. Sometimes a cigar is just a cigar."

After he left, the three women looked at each other, a mixture of relief and anticlimax settling over them.

"I still think there was something going on," Lorraine insisted. "That shadow was real."

"Maybe," Agatha agreed. "Or maybe we've all read too many mystery novels."

But as she slipped the useless key back into her pocket, something still nagged at her. Something about the rose. About the way this whole thing felt both too elaborate and too simple.

"Well," she said, standing up and brushing cinnamon sugar from her hands, "time to reopen. The weekend crowd will be here soon."

As Emma and Lorraine helped her restore the shop to its normal appearance, Agatha absently gathered Lorraine's forgotten magazines from the table and stuffed them into her purse without thinking, her mind still turning over the puzzle pieces.

Some mysteries weren't meant to be solved. Some were just meant to distract you from the real story.

LATER THAT EVENING, back at her house, Agatha set her purse down on the entryway table and kicked off her shoes. Mike trotted ahead, tail wagging sleepily as he made a beeline for his favorite blanket near the sofa.

As Agatha reached for her phone, something slipped from her purse and fluttered to the floor.

She bent down, expecting a receipt, but paused when she saw the faded edge of a glossy magazine cover peeking out. The magazines Lorraine had been reading. Agatha had stuffed them in her bag without thinking when they'd cleaned up.

She picked them up and flipped lazily through the first one, not really reading, just skimming vintage photos and garish headlines. The second magazine felt heavier, something was tucked inside.

A clipping slid out and landed at her feet. Agatha picked it up.

It was yellowed and fragile, clearly torn from the pages of one of Rosa's older issues. The headline read: "HOLLYWOOD TRAGEDY: Director's Death Ruled Suspicious. New Witness Vanishes."

Her breath caught.

There was a grainy black-and-white photo of a film set, a blurred crowd in the background. And in the text below, a name she'd only just begun to suspect: Bethany Marks.

A witness who had cleared a rising starlet, Vivian Monroe, was now missing. New evidence suggests the witness may have been more involved than originally believed. Authorities suspect Bethany Marks fled Los Angeles under an alias...

Agatha lowered the clipping slowly, heart pounding. “Bethany Marks,” she whispered.

She sat down on the sofa, curling beneath her hand-knit afghan, the magazines forgotten beside her. Mike dozed contentedly at her feet, twitching in his sleep.

She pulled Rosa's notebook from her bag. The one they'd taken from Rosa's house weeks ago, and opened it to a page she'd marked earlier. Something caught her eye.

The page was faintly smudged, the ink bled slightly where Rosa's teacup had left a pale ring. But beneath some calculations and observations was a name, circled multiple times in Rosa's handwriting: “Bethany Marks.”

Furrowing her brow, she stood and crossed to her cherry wood desk. From the middle drawer, she pulled out the brass-handled magnifying glass Lorraine had gifted her last Christmas.

Back on the sofa, she angled the reading lamp and hovered the lens over another smudged section. There. Shallow grooves beneath an erased note. More of Rosa's handwriting, barely visible.

Her fingers trembled as she reached for her phone and tapped play on Henry Maddox's final audio file. His voice filled the quiet living room.

“She was always just outside the frame... The one no one asked questions about. Not the face of the scandal, but the shadow behind it.”

Agatha spread the evidence across her kitchen table. Rosa's scrapbook pages, the business license with its questionable signature, the magazine clipping. The pieces were all there, but something was still missing. The connection that would make everything fall into place.

She picked up the photograph they'd found weeks ago in Rosa's scrapbook. The one showing a young woman standing behind Vincent Cleary at some industry event in the late 90s. The face had seemed vaguely familiar when they'd first seen it, but Agatha had dismissed it at the time.

Now, she stared at it with new eyes.

Mike whined softly from his spot near the back door, as if sensing her frustration.

"I know, buddy," she murmured. "What am I missing?"

Her gaze drifted to the vintage Acadia program Rosa had left behind during her visit. The touch of the aged paper triggered a memory from just days before Rosa's death. Rosa, standing by the mystery classics shelf, her voice dropping to that conspiratorial tone she used when sharing what she considered valuable information.

"People think small towns don't have secrets," Rosa had said, her eyes narrowing as she glanced out the window toward Central Avenue. "But Bristol Lake has layers, like one of those Russian nesting dolls."

Agatha had smiled politely, accustomed to such pronouncements from longtime residents. "Every place has its history."

"History," Rosa had echoed, her mouth twisting into something between a smile and a grimace. "That's a polite word for it." She'd leaned closer then, the scent of lavender powder surrounding her. "You know what I learned working at the Acadia all those years? People reinvent themselves when they come to small towns. They think no one will look too closely. They think no one will recognize them."

Something in her tone had made Agatha pause. "Are you talking about the Monroe sisters?"

Rosa had tapped the side of her nose knowingly. "That younger one. Bianca. When I saw her standing in the theater lobby... Something clicked." She'd frowned then, frustration flashing across her face. "I just can't place it yet. But I will. It'll come to me in the middle of the night, probably. That's how memory works at my age, inconveniently."

She'd patted her handbag with an almost protective gesture. "I've got photos, newspaper clippings. Things people might pay good money to forget." Her expression had hardened momentarily. "Or to keep buried."

Agatha gasped, the memory colliding with the photograph in her hand. She looked back at the young woman standing behind Vincent Cleary, then at the notes about Bethany Marks from Henry's podcast.

The face. The angle. The scar above the eyebrow barely visible in the grainy photo.

She grabbed her notebook and flipped to the page where she'd written observations about Bianca Monroe. *Quiet. Reserved. Stays in Vivian's shadow. Small scar above right eyebrow.*

"Oh my god," she whispered, the final piece clicking into place. She pressed her pen to the page, circling Bianca's name, her breath caught in her throat. "You didn't just run. You erased yourself completely. Bianca. You're Bethany Marks."

Mike lifted his head, ears perked. He let out a sharp bark toward the window.

Agatha stood, notebook clutched to her chest. "You're right, Mike. We have everything we need."

32

UNMASKING THE KILLER

Snow fell softly against Emma's kitchen windows as Agatha paced nervously, her notebook clutched tightly in one hand. The afternoon light was already fading to winter dusk.

"I know who killed Henry and Rosa," she announced without preamble.

Emma looked up sharply from the tea she'd been pouring. "What?"

Lorraine nearly dropped the basket of fresh muffins she'd just set on the table. "Who?"

"Bianca Monroe." Agatha sat down heavily, spreading her notebook open. "Or rather, Bethany Marks."

"The witness who disappeared?" Emma's eyes widened. "Are you certain?"

"Last night, I found a magazine clipping Rosa had tucked into one of those old Hollywood magazines she left me. It mentioned Bethany Marks fleeing Los Angeles under an alias after Cleary's death." Agatha pulled out the photograph they'd found weeks ago in Rosa's scrapbook. "And then I remembered this. The young woman standing behind Cleary at that industry event. The scar above her right eyebrow."

"Bianca has the same scar," Lorraine breathed. "The one thing plastic surgery couldn't remove. She must have changed everything else, her entire face, but that scar gave her away."

"Exactly. Rosa recognized her. That's why Rosa was blackmailing her, and that's why Rosa had to die."

Mike circled the table before settling at Agatha's feet with a soft whine, as if sensing the gravity of what they were discussing.

"So what do we do?" Emma asked, adjusting her reading glasses. "Call Detective Dawson?"

Agatha shook her head. "Not yet. We need more than just suspicions and a scar. If we go to Dawson with just theories, Bianca will deny everything and we'll never get the truth."

"You're not suggesting we confront her alone, are you?" Emma's voice rose with concern.

"Not alone," Agatha smiled, looking between her two closest friends. "Together. The three of us."

"The Bristol Lake Mystery Club in action," Lorraine said, straightening her shoulders despite her obvious nervousness. She twisted her pearl necklace anxiously.

Emma reached across the table, taking Agatha's hand in hers. "How do we do this?"

"We invite Bianca to the bookshop this evening," Agatha explained. "I'll call her, say I have information about Henry's research that might interest her. She's too curious not to come."

"And if things go wrong?" Lorraine prompted, her voice quavering.

Agatha patted her purse. "I have Detective Dawson on

speed dial. And the bookshop has plenty of witnesses if we need them."

"This is either brilliantly brave or completely foolish," Emma said with a sigh.

"Either way," Agatha said with determination, "we're finally going to get to the truth about what happened to Henry and Rosa."

An hour later, Agatha made the call from her bookshop office, her voice casual as she invited Bianca to discuss "some interesting information about Henry's research." Bianca agreed immediately, her curiosity, or perhaps her concern, overriding any suspicion. Emma and Lorraine helped arrange the reading nook, positioning chairs strategically while Agatha texted Detective Dawson. By the time everything was ready, the winter darkness had settled over Central Avenue, snow still falling softly past the windows.

The bell above the door jingled softly as Bianca entered precisely at seven. The bookshop had been closed to customers, the CLOSED sign prominently displayed despite the warm lights glowing inside. Outside, darkness had fallen early, snow still drifting down past the frost-covered windows.

"Agatha?" Bianca called, brushing snow from her coat, her elegant form casting a long shadow across the wooden floorboards. "You said you had some information for me?"

"Yes, please come in," Agatha said, stepping out from behind a bookshelf. "Thank you for coming on such short notice."

Bianca's smile faltered when she spotted Emma and Lorraine. "I didn't realize this was a group meeting."

"Please, join us for tea," Emma said, emerging from the reading nook with a stack of old Hollywood magazines in her arms.

"Freshly baked lemon cookies," Lorraine added, appearing from the back room with a teapot and cups on a tray.

Mike sat alertly beside Agatha, his ears perked forward as Bianca hesitated, snow melting on her shoulders.

"I suppose a few minutes wouldn't hurt," Bianca said, her eyes darting to the door before she took the armchair they'd positioned facing the three other seats.

Lorraine poured tea for everyone, her steady hands betraying none of the nervousness Agatha knew she felt.

"Fascinating reading material," Agatha said casually, nodding toward the magazines Emma had set on the coffee table. "We've been researching the Vincent Cleary murder case. Such a Hollywood scandal in its day."

Bianca's teacup paused halfway to her lips. "An odd choice for a book club."

"Henry was interested in it," Emma said, watching Bianca. "Before he died."

"I can't imagine why," Bianca said, setting her cup down with a sharp click.

"I think I can," Agatha said, opening her notebook. "He found information about a missing person. Bethany Marks, the key witness who disappeared after the murder."

Bianca's expression remained neutral. "Ancient history."

"Is it?" Agatha asked, pulling out the photograph. "We found this in Rosa's possessions weeks ago. A young woman at an industry event, standing behind Vincent Cleary in the late nineties."

She passed it to Emma, who studied it before handing it to Lorraine.

"Rosa was quite the collector of Hollywood memorabilia," Emma added.

Bianca glanced at the photo with apparent disinterest. "I don't see what this has to do with anything."

Agatha stood, reached into the side table drawer, and pulled out a magnifying glass. She held it over the photograph, then looked directly at Bianca.

"This scar," Agatha said, pointing to a mark above the right eyebrow in the photo, then gesturing to the same spot on Bianca's face. "It's identical. You've changed, aged, but this is definitely you."

"Makeup techniques have advanced considerably since those days," Bianca said coldly. "Any resemblance is coincidental."

"Professional makeup can't explain everything," Lorraine added, her voice stronger now. "The bone structure, the eyes, the scar, you were there."

"Rosa recognized you," Agatha said quietly. "Not as Bianca Monroe, but as Bethany Marks. Didn't she?"

The room fell silent. Outside, a car drove past, its headlights briefly illuminating Bianca's face as it tightened almost imperceptibly.

"That's absurd," she said, but her voice had lost its melodic quality.

"Is it?" Agatha pressed. "Henry pieced it together. The mysterious woman who arrived in town with Vivian, the strange connection between you two, your reaction whenever the Cleary case was mentioned. And then there were the financial irregularities he discovered."

"Gordon's embezzlement," Emma added. "Which you knew about."

Bianca stood abruptly. "I think I should leave. I don't appreciate being ambushed with these ridiculous theories."

"We're not finished," Agatha said, also rising. "You've been manipulating Vivian for decades, haven't you? Making her believe she owed you her freedom when in fact, you were the one who killed Vincent Cleary."

Bianca's eyes widened. "You have no idea what you're talking about."

"I think we do," Agatha said, stepping closer. "Henry pieced it together, that's why he had to die. And when Rosa recognized you from her old Hollywood magazines and started blackmailing you, she became a liability too."

For a long moment, silence filled the bookshop. Bianca's eyes darted between the three friends, calculating. Mike growled low in his throat.

"You have no proof," Bianca finally said. "Just wild theories from amateur detectives playing make-believe."

"Actually," Agatha said calmly, "we have Rosa's notes. Her blackmail attempts. The magazine clipping about Bethany Marks fleeing Los Angeles. The photograph with your distinctive scar. And Henry's research connecting all the pieces." She paused, letting that settle. "And with this much evidence, the DA can order DNA testing. Once that gets started, the truth has a way of speaking for itself. I imagine it's only a matter of time before everything comes out."

Bianca sank back into the chair, her composure beginning to crack. "You have no idea what it was like," she finally said. "Cleary was a monster. He would have destroyed me."

"So you killed him," Agatha said softly.

"He attacked me," Bianca said, the words spilling out now. "I pushed him away. He hit his head on the corner of his desk. He didn't get up."

"So you called Vivian," Agatha prompted, the pieces finally falling into place.

"She came right away," Bianca continued, staring at her hands. "When she arrived, I was hysterical. I told her Cleary had regained consciousness briefly before dying. I said he'd accused her of pushing him during their argument earlier that day."

"But there was no argument that day," Emma said.

"Yes, there was. Vivian and Cleary had fought violently that afternoon, the whole studio knew about it. So when I described finding him with a head wound, suggesting he'd been pushed..." Bianca's smile was chilling. "I could see the doubt creeping into her eyes."

"You made her think she'd blacked out and hurt him," Lorraine whispered, horrified.

"She'd been drinking heavily that week, taking sleeping pills. It was easy to play on her insecurities. I helped her clean up what I claimed were her fingerprints, her traces. All the while saying I believed in her innocence, that I'd be her alibi."

Bianca laughed hollowly. "I told her that for her own protection, I needed to disappear after giving my statement. What she didn't know was that I'd already planted evidence pointing to her. Her scarf under his body, her lipstick on a glass. Just enough to keep suspicion on her, but with my alibi testimony, not enough to convict."

"So she spent decades believing she might have killed him during a blackout," Emma pressed a hand to her chest. "That poor woman."

"And paying you handsomely to maintain your silence," Agatha added.

"Guilt is a powerful tool," Bianca replied simply. "For over twenty years, she's been funding my new life, believing she owed me her freedom. When she decided to return to Bristol Lake and open the theater, I came with her. To keep her close. To keep her paying."

"What about Henry?" Agatha asked.

"Too clever for his own good," Bianca sighed. "He found that old photograph. Started asking questions about Bethany Marks. Then he discovered what Gordon had been doing with the theater's money. Gordon was my insurance policy, you see. I'd helped him set up the embezzlement scheme. If anything ever went wrong, he'd take the fall for the financial crimes while I stayed clean."

"But Henry was going to expose everything," Emma said.

"Yes. So I invited him to the theater that night, told him I had information about Gordon's embezzlement. I gave him cookies I'd baked, laced with digitalis." Bianca's voice was eerily calm. "He ate three of them while we talked. I told him to wait in the projection booth, that Gordon would meet him there to confess everything."

"But Gordon never came," Agatha said.

"No. By the time Henry realized he'd been poisoned, he was too weak to call for help. I paid Rosa to go up there after he died and stage the electrocution. Make it look like an accident with the old equipment."

"Mon Dieu," Lorraine breathed. "Rosa helped you?"

"She was already blackmailing me about my identity. I paid her well to set up the scene. She was surprisingly good at it, no hesitation at all."

"But Rosa got greedy," Agatha prompted.

"She wanted more money. Threatened to go to the police and tell them everything." Bianca shook her head. "I couldn't allow that. So I baked her another batch of cookies, her favorite recipe. A much stronger dose this time. No need for the electrical complications."

"And you tried to frame Martha Peck," Emma said bitterly.

"The poison vial in her things, the bank deposits, it was meant to point away from me. Simple misdirection." Bianca looked up, her eyes cold. "It would have worked if you hadn't kept digging."

"And then you framed Vivian," Agatha said. "That email, your testimony to the police, all lies."

"She believed she deserved punishment anyway," Bianca said dismissively. "She's spent decades thinking she might be a murderer. When I told the police she'd confessed to me, she didn't even deny it. She thought she was protecting me. Her loyal friend who'd given her an alibi all those years ago."

The manipulation was breathtaking in its cruelty.

"And now?" Bianca asked after a moment. "What do you plan to do with all this... Information?"

"Justice," Agatha said simply, reaching for her purse and the phone inside.

Bianca laughed coldly. "It's your word against mine. Three amateur sleuths with wild theories and no real evidence."

Her hand moved to her own purse, the motion deliberate and slow.

"I wouldn't do that if I were you," came a firm voice from the back room.

All four women turned as Detective Dawson stepped through the doorway, his expression grim.

"Detective?" Bianca's voice faltered. "What are you doing here?"

"Following a hunch," he said, nodding to Agatha. "Got a text from our local bookshop owner about thirty minutes ago. Thought I'd better check it out."

Agatha gave a small smile. Speed dial had seemed like a safer option once they'd started down this path.

"You heard?" she asked.

"Everything," Dawson confirmed. "We've been recording. Bianca Monroe, or should I say Bethany Marks. You're under arrest for the murders of Vincent Cleary, Henry Maddox, and Rosa Fielding."

Bianca's face drained of color. "You can't... "

"We also have a warrant to search your home and office," Dawson continued, nodding to two uniformed officers who had quietly entered through the shop's back door, letting in a gust of cold air. "Based on some financial records we found in Henry's belongings and information Agatha provided."

As the officers read Bianca her rights, the front door opened, bringing another swirl of cold and snow. Gordon Lane stood frozen in the doorway, his face ashen when he saw the police.

"Gordon?" Agatha gasped. "But you're supposed to be... "

"In Vietnam," Emma finished, her eyes widening in shock.

Lorraine grabbed her pearls so quickly one snapped off and clattered to the floor. "Mon Dieu! Sacrebleu!" she exclaimed, then fell momentarily speechless.

Even Dawson looked stunned. "Well, well," he recovered quickly, his professional demeanor returning. "Perfect timing. Gordon Lane, you're also under arrest as an accessory to murder and for embezzlement."

Lorraine's eyes went wide. "The man in the alley," she breathed. "That was Gordon."

"Not the Petunia Heights strangler after all," Emma said dryly. "Just a financial criminal hiding behind his business partner."

Lorraine pressed a hand to her heart. "Mon Dieu. Patricia Howe screamed loud enough to wake the entire street over a man hiding from a fraud investigation who was supposedly in Vietnam."

As they led Bianca toward the door in handcuffs, she turned with a final, scornful laugh and locked eyes with the room. "He was never in Vietnam. He's been hiding in my guest house the entire time."

"Get her out of here," Dawson said firmly, and the officers guided Bianca outside into the snowy night as Gordon followed in handcuffs, his shoulders slumped in defeat.

As the police cars pulled away, their lights flashing red and blue against the snow, the three friends sat in stunned silence.

"We did it," Lorraine finally whispered. "We solved it."

"I still can't believe Bianca was Bethany Marks all along," Emma said, shaking her head. "Hiding in plain sight for over twenty years."

"The perfect disguise," Agatha agreed. "And the perfect manipulation. Making Vivian believe she was a murderer, then swooping in as her savior."

"What about Vivian?" Lorraine asked. "Will she face charges too?"

Dawson, who had stayed behind to take their statements, shook his head. "I don't believe so. If what Bianca said checks out, Vivian was manipulated for over twenty years. Made to believe she'd killed Cleary, then manipulated again into confessing to crimes she didn't commit. As far as I can tell, she's another victim here."

He took the seat Bianca had vacated. "I have to say, ladies, that was either the bravest or the most foolish thing I've ever seen."

"Sometimes the truth needs a little push," Emma said with a small smile.

"Next time, maybe give the police a bit more notice," Dawson suggested, though a hint of admiration softened his reproach.

"Where would be the fun in that?" Lorraine asked innocently, finding her voice again.

They all laughed, the sound chasing away the last shadows of tension from the cozy bookshop.

Later that evening, after Dawson had gone and the official statements had been given, the three friends sat among the bookshelves with fresh cups of tea and the remaining lemon cookies. Untouched, as none of them could quite bring themselves to eat them after Bianca's confession.

"Another mystery solved," Emma said, raising her teacup in a toast.

"To Henry and Rosa," Agatha added softly. "May they both rest in peace."

"Even though Rosa turned out to be an accomplice..." Lorraine shook her head in disbelief. "I still can't believe it. The woman who made the best snickerdoodles at the bake sale."

"People are complicated," Emma said gently. "Greed can make people do terrible things."

"And to us," Lorraine finished, raising her cup higher. "May we never have another adventure quite so dangerous."

"I wouldn't count on that," Agatha smiled, as Mike rested

his head contentedly on her foot, finally relaxed now that the danger had passed.

The mystery was solved. Justice would be served. Vivian would finally be free of the guilt that had haunted her for over two decades.

And Bristol Lake would carry on. Small, dramatic, and bound by the friendship of three women who refused to let injustice stand.

Exactly the way they liked it.

33

THE PERFORMANCE ENDS

The bell above the door jingled softly, and Agatha looked up from the register.

The woman who stepped in looked familiar in the way that took a moment to place. Dark hair, charcoal coat, the unhurried ease of someone on holiday rather than passing through.

"I remember you," Agatha said. "You came in a few weeks ago. Looking for Old Hollywood mysteries."

The woman smiled, genuinely pleased. "Brittany Adams. I ended up buying three of them. Couldn't put them down." She glanced around the shop with undisguised warmth. "I kept thinking about this place. Bristol Lake too. So I came back. I'm staying at the cabins by the lake for the week."

Lorraine materialized from behind a bookshelf like a woman who had been listening the entire time, which she almost certainly had. "The lake cabins in February? You are either very brave or very romantic, ma chérie."

Brittany laughed. "A little of both, maybe."

She browsed for a few minutes, selected two more titles,

and left with a cheerful wave and a promise to return before the week was out.

Agatha watched her go, then let out a small breath that was almost a laugh.

"What?" Emma asked, looking up from her notes.

"That woman — back in January, when everything was unraveling — she stumbled over her own name. Said Beth, then corrected herself to Brittany." Agatha shook her head. "At one point, I genuinely wondered if she could be Bethany Marks."

Lorraine stared at her. "The woman who just bought two cozy mysteries and is staying at the lake cabins."

"I know."

"Ma chérie." Lorraine pressed a hand to her heart. "This investigation has done things to your mind."

Emma bit her lip, clearly trying not to smile. "To be fair, it wasn't the worst theory you had."

Agatha laughed — a real one, the kind that had been in short supply for weeks. "No," she agreed. "But it might have been the most embarrassing."

A COOL FEBRUARY evening had settled over Bristol Lake by the time Agatha finished tallying the day's receipts. The shop was quiet, just the occasional creak of old floorboards and the soft ticking of the wall clock keeping her company. Mike dozed beneath the counter, his gentle snores providing a comforting rhythm to her work.

A knock at the door made Agatha look up in surprise. She'd flipped the sign to CLOSED nearly an hour ago.

Vivian Monroe stood in the doorway, elegant as always in

a charcoal gray coat, though somehow softer around the edges than Agatha remembered. The harsh lines of her face seemed to have gentled, as if a great weight had been lifted from her shoulders.

"I'm sorry to disturb you," Vivian said. "I saw the light was still on."

Agatha set down her pen. "It's alright. Come in."

Mike lifted his head, ears perked with interest rather than suspicion. He watched Vivian as she stepped inside, closing the door gently behind her.

"I'm leaving tomorrow," Vivian said without preamble, moving toward the counter with measured steps. "I thought I should... Say goodbye."

"Leaving Bristol Lake?" Agatha asked, though she wasn't particularly surprised. After everything that had happened, it seemed inevitable.

Vivian nodded. "There's not much left for me here now." She glanced around the bookshop, her gaze lingering on the cozy reading nook by the window. "I've sold the theater to the historical society. They'll run it as a community venue."

"That's generous of you."

A hint of a smile touched Vivian's lips. "Consider it my apology to the town. For all the disruption."

An awkward silence settled between them, filled with unspoken questions and the echo of recent trauma.

"Would you like some coffee?" Agatha offered finally. "I was just about to make myself a cup."

"That would be nice," Vivian said, surprising them both.

As Agatha busied herself with the electric kettle behind the counter, Vivian drifted toward the mystery section, her fingers trailing lightly over the spines of well-loved books.

"I never thanked you," she said quietly, her back to Agatha. "For uncovering the truth."

Agatha placed two mugs on the counter. "I'm sorry about how it all turned out. Bianca's betrayal must have been devastating."

Vivian turned, her face composed but her eyes revealing a depth of pain that made Agatha's heart twist unexpectedly. "Twenty-five years," she said softly. "Twenty-five years, I believed I might have killed Vincent during a blackout. That I was capable of such violence."

"And Bianca encouraged that belief."

"She crafted it perfectly." Vivian accepted the steaming mug Agatha offered. "I'd been drinking heavily that week, taking sleeping pills. When she told me she'd found Vincent dead and that there were signs I'd been there earlier... I couldn't remember clearly. I panicked."

"And she offered to be your alibi," Agatha said, understanding dawning. "To protect you."

"While making sure I remained terrified that the truth might come out." Vivian's laugh was hollow. "A masterful performance, really. Worthy of an Academy Award."

They moved to the reading nook, settling into the comfortable chairs that had hosted countless book club discussions and friendly gossip sessions. Mike followed, curling up at Agatha's feet but keeping a watchful eye on their visitor.

"There's one thing I still don't understand," Agatha said, her eyes on Vivian. "Detective Dawson mentioned you've been sending money to Arizona every month for nearly thirty years. If you weren't being blackmailed, what was that about?"

A flicker of surprise crossed Vivian's face, followed by

something softer, almost vulnerable. For a moment, she seemed to debate whether to answer, then her shoulders relaxed.

"My Aunt Loretta," she said. "She lives in a retirement community outside Scottsdale."

"Your aunt?" Agatha echoed, not bothering to hide her surprise.

Vivian nodded, her perfectly manicured fingers tracing the edge of her teacup. "She raised me after my parents died. Worked two jobs, waitressing during the day, cleaning offices at night. Never made much, but she made sure I had dance lessons, acting classes." A small, genuine smile touched her lips. "She's the reason I made it in Hollywood."

"So you've been supporting her all these years," Agatha said, the pieces clicking into place.

"She refused to move to California. Said the sunshine was too showy." Vivian's laugh was unexpectedly warm. "Arizona suited her better. Independent, a bit rough around the edges. When she retired, her Social Security wasn't enough, so..." She shrugged. "It's the least I could do."

The shop door opened again, the bell jingling cheerfully as Emma and Lorraine bustled in, arms laden with takeout bags from Mabel's Diner.

"We thought you might be hungry after... " Emma began, then stopped short when she spotted Vivian. "Oh! We didn't realize you had company."

"Please, join us," Vivian said, gesturing to the empty chairs. "I was just explaining about my Aunt Loretta in Arizona."

Lorraine set down the bags and slipped into a chair, curiosity overriding any awkwardness. "Aunt Loretta?"

Agatha quickly filled them in on what Vivian had shared.

Lorraine pressed a hand to her heart. “Mon Dieu, that's actually quite sweet.”

“Don't sound so surprised,” Vivian said, the familiar edge returning to her voice, though not as sharp as before. “Even Hollywood villains have their soft spots.”

Agatha caught her eye. “Why keep it a secret?”

Vivian considered this for a moment. “Aunt Loretta always hated charity. Wouldn't want anyone knowing she needed help. And I...” She paused. “I suppose I've spent so long maintaining my image that letting people see the real me just feels... Uncomfortable.”

“The ice queen has a heart after all,” Lorraine murmured.

“A heart, yes,” Vivian replied with a flash of her old spirit. “Just not an open book.”

Emma opened the takeout bags, the savory aroma of Mabel's chicken pot pie filling the shop. She hesitated, then offered a container to Vivian. “Would you like to join us? There's plenty.”

For a moment, Vivian looked genuinely taken aback by the simple kindness. Then she shook her head gently. “Thank you, but I should be going. I have a long drive ahead of me tomorrow.”

“Where will you go?” Agatha asked.

“Europe, I think. Somewhere with history but without memories. Somewhere I can be neither Vivian Monroe nor the woman I was before.” She set down her mug and stood, straightening her coat with that familiar grace. “A fresh start.”

“You deserve that,” Agatha said, rising as well.

Vivian moved toward the door, then paused, turning back. “I want you to know. I never wished harm on Henry. Or Rosa. If I'd known what Bianca was planning...” Her voice trailed off.

"I believe you," Agatha said simply.

Lorraine caught Vivian's arm just before she reached the door. "One more thing, chérie. Vera Martin. Whatever happened to her?"

Vivian's expression softened unexpectedly. "Vera's fine. More than fine, actually." She paused, as if deciding how much to share. "She invested in the Acadia early on. But she made me promise not to display her name anywhere. She left Hollywood a long time ago and wanted nothing connecting her to it." A small smile touched her lips. "She became a monk. In Tibet."

The room went very quiet.

"A monk," Lorraine repeated.

"She says she's never been happier." Vivian straightened her coat. "I'm actually flying out to visit her in a few months."

A look of genuine gratitude crossed Vivian's face. "Goodbye, Ms. Royale. Take care of your charming little town. It's special." Her gaze swept across the three women, then down to Mike, who had risen to his feet. "More special than I understood when I arrived."

With that, she slipped out into the night, the bell chiming softly behind her.

Lorraine stood perfectly still for a moment, processing this. Then she pressed both hands to her chest. "Vera Martin. A monk in Tibet." She turned to Agatha. "I have been chasing that woman's mystery for thirty years and the answer was peace and enlightenment." She shook her head slowly. "I need a lemon bar."

Emma smiled. "Well! That was unexpectedly moving." She reached for her container of pot pie. "Do you think we'll ever see her again?"

Agatha moved to the window, watching Vivian's elegant

figure disappear down the darkened street. “I don't know,” she said thoughtfully. “But I hope she finds what she's looking for.”

Emma raised her water glass in a small toast. “To fresh starts.”

“And to Bristol Lake,” Agatha added, returning to her friends. “Home of second chances and surprisingly good mysteries.”

Mike barked once, as if in agreement, making them all laugh as they settled in to share their meal and the comfortable certainty that, for now at least, all was well in their corner of the world.

EPILOGUE

Six weeks later, Bristol Lake was beginning to shake off winter's grip. The early February sun hung a bit longer in the sky each day, and while patches of snow still clung stubbornly to the shadowed corners of Central Avenue, the worst of the cold had passed. Icicles dripped from storefronts, creating small puddles that reflected the brightening blue sky.

Inside One Deadly Chapter Books & Brew, Thursday evening book club was in full swing.

"I still say the butler did it," Gladys insisted, waving her copy of *Murder at Midnight Manor* with enough enthusiasm to nearly knock over Emma's teacup.

"The butler is *always* too obvious," Henrietta countered, selecting another cookie from the plate Lorraine had brought. "It's clearly the niece with the inheritance motive."

"Ladies, ladies," Lorraine interjected, adjusting the emerald scarf draped artfully around her shoulders. "Why not both? A conspiracy of greed and opportunity! Very French noir, très dramatique."

Agatha smiled from her armchair, watching the friendly debate unfold. Mike dozed contentedly at her feet, occasionally twitching his paws as he chased dream squirrels through imaginary snow. The bookshop felt exactly as it should, warm, welcoming, and wonderfully ordinary.

Martha Peck sat in her usual spot by the window, knitting needles clicking with precise rhythm. She'd returned to book club two weeks ago, shoulders a bit less rigid, lips a fraction less pursed. Being publicly exonerated had done wonders for her disposition, though she'd never quite apologized for her initial frostiness toward Agatha.

"The scones are excellent tonight, Agatha," Martha said, which was as close to an olive branch as anyone was likely to get.

"Thank you, Martha. It's from Eliza's bakery."

"Hmph. Well, she does know her way around a proper scone." Martha paused in her knitting. "I heard the Acadia had a sold-out showing last weekend. That murder mystery film festival."

"Completely sold out," Emma confirmed, flipping through her worn paperback. "The historical society is doing wonderful things with the theater. Very community-focused."

Celeste, who'd been quietly scrolling through her phone, looked up with a grin. "They're planning a classic film series for summer. And they want to partner with the bookshop, maybe do themed book and movie pairings?"

"Oh, that sounds delightful!" Lorraine clapped her hands, bracelets jingling. "Film noir night with hardboiled detective novels! Hitchcock with psychological thrillers! The possibilities are endless!"

"We could do signing events with local mystery authors

too," Agatha mused, her mind already spinning with ideas. "Maybe a monthly author talk before the screening."

The conversation flowed easily from there. Book recommendations, town gossip (Mabel's Diner was adding French toast to the menu, much to Lorraine's delight), and speculation about whether spring would arrive early this year.

As the group began gathering their things around nine o'clock, Emma lingered by the counter while Agatha tallied up the evening's sales from the small display of bookmarks and tote bags she'd set out.

"Feels good to be boring again, doesn't it?" Emma said with a wry smile.

"Wonderfully boring," Agatha agreed. "Though I got a postcard from Vivian yesterday. She's in Florence. Says the art is extraordinary and the pasta even better."

"Good for her." Emma zipped up her coat. "She deserves some peace."

"We all do."

Detective Dawson appeared in the doorway, already unbuttoning his coat like he planned to stay awhile. "Evening, ladies. Am I too late for book club?"

"Just wrapping up," Agatha said. "But there are leftover cookies if you're interested."

"Always." He moved to the counter, accepting the plate Agatha offered. "Actually, I wanted to give you an update. Bianca's trial date is set for late May. The DA says it's an airtight case, her confession, the evidence, everything."

"And Gordon?"

"Cooperating fully. He'll likely get a reduced sentence for testifying." Dawson took a cookie, then added more quietly, "You did good work, Agatha. All of you did."

A faint flush crept up Agatha's cheeks. “We just asked the right questions.”

“You did more than that.” His expression softened. “Bristol Lake's lucky to have you looking out for it.”

After Dawson left, promising to stop by the following week for coffee, Lorraine emerged from the back room where she'd been “organizing” (which mostly meant admiring the vintage magazines Rosa had left behind).

“He likes you, you know,” she said without preamble.

“Lorraine... “

“I'm just saying, a handsome detective who appreciates amateur sleuthing and brings you information? That's rom-com material, ma chérie.” She winked. “But I'll say no more. For now.”

Emma laughed. “Come on, Lorraine. Let's leave Agatha to close up in peace.”

After her friends departed with final hugs and promises to meet for brunch on Sunday, Agatha moved through the familiar routine of closing the shop. She straightened shelves, wiped down the coffee counter, and double-checked that the register was properly locked.

Mike followed her from room to room, his nails clicking softly on the hardwood.

“Just you and me, buddy,” she murmured, scratching behind his ears. “Another day, another mystery solved. Well, no new mysteries today. Just books and friends and normalcy.”

Mike wagged his tail in approval.

As Agatha reached for her coat, she paused, taking in the quiet shop around her. The familiar scent of books and coffee, the soft glow of the reading lamps, Mike already waiting patiently by the door. After everything that had happened, the stillness felt like a gift.

She flipped off the lights and locked the door behind her. Central Avenue was quiet under the streetlamps, the last patches of snow glittering in the pools of light. Somewhere in the distance, a dog barked. A car drove past, its headlights washing over the familiar storefronts.

Bristol Lake was her home. Its people were her people. And for the first time in weeks, all felt right with the world.

"Just you and me, boy," she murmured to Mike. "No mysteries tonight."

Mike trotted contentedly beside her, his breath forming small clouds in the cold evening air.

For now, that was more than enough.

LORRAINE'S "SECOND CHANCE" LEMON BARS

Recipes from the Bookshop & Beyond

At *One Deadly Chapter Books & Brew*, stories aren't the only thing baking, so are memories.

Whether it's a tray of fresh lemon bars shared after solving a mystery, or a batch of cinnamon apple muffins fueling a cozy gossip session, the heart of Bristol Lake is found in simple, shared moments.

Here are two favorite recipes straight from the ovens and adventures of One Deadly Premiere. Best enjoyed with friends, laughter, and a good story to tell.

Inspired by the town's love of fresh starts, second chances, and of course, sweet endings.

Ingredients:

- 1 cup unsalted butter, softened
- 2 cups all-purpose flour
- 1/2 cup powdered sugar (plus extra for dusting)

- 1/4 teaspoon salt
- 4 large eggs
- 1 1/2 cups granulated sugar
- 1/4 cup all-purpose flour
- 2/3 cup freshly squeezed lemon juice (about 3-4 lemons)
- 1 tablespoon lemon zest

Instructions:

1. Preheat the oven to 350°F (175°C). Grease a 9x13-inch baking dish and line with parchment paper.
2. In a medium bowl, beat together the butter, 2 cups flour, powdered sugar, and salt until crumbly.
3. Press the mixture evenly into the bottom of the prepared baking dish to form the crust.
4. Bake the crust for 18-20 minutes, until lightly golden.
5. Meanwhile, whisk together the eggs, granulated sugar, 1/4 cup flour, lemon juice, and lemon zest until smooth.
6. Pour the lemon mixture over the hot crust.
7. Return to the oven and bake for an additional 20-25 minutes, or until the center is set.
8. Let cool completely before dusting generously with powdered sugar.
9. Cut into squares and enjoy, preferably while plotting your next cozy mystery!

Lorraine's tip: For *extra drama,* garnish with a few fresh raspberries or candied lemon slices!

ELIZA'S COZY "MYSTERY MUFFINS" (APPLE CINNAMON)

Perfect for book club meetings, sleuthing sessions, or just curling up with a cup of tea.

Ingredients:

- 2 cups all-purpose flour
- 1/2 cup granulated sugar
- 1/4 cup packed brown sugar
- 2 teaspoons baking powder
- 1/2 teaspoon baking soda
- 1/2 teaspoon salt
- 1 teaspoon cinnamon
- 1/2 teaspoon nutmeg
- 1 1/2 cups peeled and diced apples (about 2 medium apples)
- 2 large eggs
- 1/2 cup vegetable oil (or melted butter)
- 3/4 cup buttermilk (or substitute with regular milk + 1 tsp lemon juice)
- 1 teaspoon vanilla extract

Optional Cinnamon-Sugar Topping:

- 2 tablespoons granulated sugar
- 1/2 teaspoon cinnamon

Instructions:

1. Preheat the oven to 375°F (190°C). Line a 12-cup muffin tin with paper liners or grease it lightly.
2. In a large bowl, whisk together the flour, sugars, baking powder, baking soda, salt, cinnamon, and nutmeg.
3. Stir in the diced apples until coated.
4. In another bowl, whisk together the eggs, oil, buttermilk, and vanilla.
5. Pour the wet ingredients into the dry ingredients and stir gently until just combined (do not overmix).
6. Scoop the batter evenly into the muffin cups.
7. If using, sprinkle the tops with cinnamon-sugar mixture.
8. Bake for 18-22 minutes, until golden and a toothpick inserted into the center comes out clean.
9. Serve warm, with a mystery novel in one hand and a cozy blanket in the other.

Eliza's advice: "These muffins keep secrets, and flavor, for days. Just like a good mystery.

ALSO BY ELLA ANDREW

The Agatha Royale Mystery Series

• One Deadly Chapter

• One Deadly Batch

• One Deadly Needle

• One Deadly Safari

• One Deadly Christmas Tree

The Ashford Creek Mysteries

Quick reads perfect for your lunch break or evening escape

• Death at the Teacup Inn

• Death at the Sweet Festival

• Death by Recipe

• Death at the Halloween Vigil

• Death at Rosemary Cottage

• Death at the Friendsgiving Table

Each Ashford Creek Mystery is a complete story you can enjoy in about 2 hours.

All books available on Amazon